TRIMMED TO DEATH

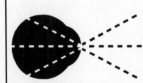

This Large Print Book carries the
Seal of Approval of N.A.V.H.

TRIMMED TO DEATH

NANCY J. COHEN

WHEELER PUBLISHING
A part of Gale, a Cengage Company

Farmington Hills, Mich • San Francisco • New York • Waterville, Maine
Meriden, Conn • Mason, Ohio • Chicago

Wheeler Publishing Large Print Cozy Mystery.
The text of this Large Print edition is unabridged.
Other aspects of the book may vary from the original edition.
Set in 16 pt. Plantin.

LIBRARY OF CONGRESS CIP DATA ON FILE.
CATALOGUING IN PUBLICATION FOR THIS BOOK
IS AVAILABLE FROM THE LIBRARY OF CONGRESS

ISBN-13: 978-1-4328-6686-0 (hardcover alk. paper)

Published in 2019 by arrangement with The Evan Marshall Agency

Printed in Mexico
1 2 3 4 5 6 7 23 22 21 20 19

TRIMMED TO DEATH

CHAPTER ONE

"Here they come. Look sharp," Marla Vail said to her friend, Tally Riggs. The judges headed down the line in their direction. Marla's heart rate accelerated as they got closer. Being the last two contestants might be a good thing. Tally and Marla's entries would linger in the judges' minds more so than the other ten, even if those included chocolate Kahlua cake, blueberry crumble, and plum almond tarts.

"The money raised by the bake-off goes to a good cause," Tally reminded her. "It doesn't matter if we win or not." She stood next to Marla behind a table displaying her lemon bread pudding. Tally brushed a stray blond hair off her model-perfect face. Her tall frame made Marla's five-foot six-inch height feel short.

"I know, but a ten-thousand-dollar business grant is hard to let go." Marla wanted to add a bistro to her hair salon and day spa. Winning the prize would allow her to move forward with her plans. But she'd be happier if Tally won. Her widowed friend had yet to reopen her dress shop after the horrific car crash that had killed her husband and put her in the hospital. Despite having generous benefits from Ken's life insurance policy, Tally could use the money to raise her son and rebuild her business.

"Look at the crowd," Tally pointed out. "Ticket sales must be good."

People gathered by the cluster of tables under white tent awnings. From the paper plates and plastic forks in their hands, they couldn't wait for the judging to end so they could sample the goods. As instructed, both Marla and Tally had brought extra portions.

A strong breeze swept by, lifting the corners of their tablecloths. An early October cold front in South Florida made Marla glad she'd worn a sweater along with jeans and ankle boots. Dry grass crunched underfoot as she shifted her feet. The day had turned out sunny with clear skies for the fall harvest festival at Kinsdale Farms. Located at the western edge of Broward County, the produce farm hosted this event each year. Various businesses sponsored the competitions that entrants applied for months in advance.

One of the judges lingered at table number eight to speak to the caramel-skinned woman there. He must have said something that displeased her, because her mouth thinned and her eyes narrowed. Marla recognized the judge as Carlton Paige, food critic. His pudgy face and rotund figure were hard to miss. Rumor said restaurateurs cringed when he entered their premises. The lady's response made his lips curl in a sneer before he moved on.

Now only two entrants separated the judges from Marla. She glanced at the women but they were strangers to her. She'd been busy setting up earlier and hadn't met the other contenders, although Teri DuMond was a familiar face. The chocolatier ran tours at the factory where she sold artisan chocolates. Teri had waved a greeting to Marla before the judging began.

Marla's breath came short as the judges neared. It was silly to feel so nervous. Nonetheless, she scanned the throng looking for her husband Dalton's reassuring figure but spied him nowhere. He had entered his own competition for best home-grown tomatoes. That contest awarded a hundred-dollar gift certificate to a plant nursery.

"Number eleven, what is it you have for us?" said the sole female judge in a Southern accent. Marla's attention whipped forward. The judge wore her bleached hair piled high atop her head like cotton candy. Her rosy lips formed a pout as she regarded Marla with an assessing glance. Huge gold hoop earrings matched the heavy chains around her neck.

"My entry is a coconut fudge pie. You must be Raquel Hayes. I watch your cooking show on TV. It's an honor to meet you. All of you," Marla amended hastily.

Tristan Marsh looked down his nose at her. The pastry chef from The Royal Palate made up the last of their trio. He had a thin face with a pasty complexion like the flour he used in his confections. From his slender frame, she surmised he had a fast metabolism, spent a lot of time at the gym, or didn't taste too many of his own creations.

Carlton Paige, the food critic, picked up a plastic fork and a sample slice of her dish. "God, I hope this isn't as awful as the last few entries. They tasted like cardboard," he said in an annoying nasal tone.

Raquel grimaced. "I've had my fill of sweets for the day. This one had better be good."

"None of them can equal my artistry,"

10

Tristan announced. He put a piece in his mouth and rolled it around on his tongue before he chewed and swallowed. His face gave nothing away about his opinion.

"Oh, come on, you can't expect these amateurs to do anything fancy," Carlton replied. His brows lifted as he tasted her dessert. Marla took that as a hopeful sign.

"Marla might not be in the food industry, but she's a great baker," Tally said in Marla's defense. "She used to experiment with rare fruit recipes. You'd love her lychee upside-down cake. I told her she had to enter this contest."

Marla's cheeks warmed. "Tally likes anything with chocolate. She doesn't have to worry about her figure like I do. If I didn't love her, I'd be envious."

Carlton gave Tally a smarmy onceover. "You're not too thin, which is a good thing. A man likes a good handful, if you know what I mean."

"Keep it in your pants, lover boy," Tristan admonished him. He glanced at Raquel, who'd tasted Marla's entry. "Well, how do you like it?" The pastry chef's effeminate gesture matched his manner of speech.

"You know I can't talk in front of the contestants. You'll see after the tallies are done. Tally, you get it?" Raquel flicked a glance at Marla's friend and chuckled at her pun. Her breasts jiggled with her movements.

Dear Lord, this trio of clowns is judging our entries? They seemed less than thrilled to be there. The publicity must be worth it. All of them would benefit from being in the spotlight.

"I don't have a hope in hell of winning," said the lady on Marla's left after the judges departed. All the winners from the various contests would be announced later. "I'm Alyce Greene, by the way."

Marla admired the woman's white bomber jacket with silver trim decorating each sleeve. "I'm Marla Vail, and this is my friend, Tally Riggs. It's our first time doing a bake-off contest."

"I'm glad to see so many guests. Ticket sales must be brisk. That'll be great for the Safety First Alliance."

The non-profit organization educated the public against leaving children and pets in hot cars. Marla had signed up as a volunteer when she'd heard about their cause. "Yes, I understand eighty percent of the proceeds will be donated to the group," she said. "I wish it could be more, but I suppose the sponsoring company has to make back some of their administrative costs."

The contestants handed out dessert samples to the crowd that converged on their booths. The guests had each paid a dollar per ticket, which entitled them to one item. Some gluttons descended on the tables with handfuls of tickets.

"What would you two do with the prize money if you win?" Alyce asked Marla and Tally once the mob dispersed.

Each contestant had paid a fifty-dollar entry fee along with the submission of a business plan that included a food component. City council members had vetted the proposals and selected the entrants. Marla felt lucky to be chosen, although she'd entered more due to Tally's urging than a desire to win.

"I own a salon and day spa," she replied. "If I had the extra cash, I'd add a bistro menu to my services."

"And I plan to open a boutique café," Tally commented. "It's a hot concept, combining a clothing store with food services. How about you?"

Alyce gave them a wry glance. "I don't need the funds for myself. I write a popular food blog, and it's monetized through affiliate ads. My husband owns a food truck operation. I'd pay off his starter loan so he could expand the business."

"What's this I heard about funds?" The contestant on Alyce's other side wandered in their direction.

Alyce frowned at her. "I was just telling them about my food blog. Ladies, have you met Francine Dodger?"

Marla and Tally introduced themselves, while Marla noted similarities between the other two women. Both had brown hair and similar statures. Alyce's eyes matched her brunette hair color, while Francine had green eyes, but otherwise they shared the same even features.

"I love your hairstyles," Marla said. "Those pixie cuts look cute on both of you. Where do you get your hair done?"

"We go to the same stylist. It's Karen at Salon Style," Alyce replied.

"Are you related to each other?"

Francine darted a glance at Alyce before responding. "If we were, I'd convince Alyce to blog for my publication. I'm the publisher of *Eat Well Now* magazine." She shivered in the cool air and wrapped her arms around her chest.

Without a sweater, Francine must be cold in her short-sleeved top. Its purple color along with her green eyes reminded Marla of Mardi Gras in New Orleans.

"I'm a subscriber," Tally said in an eager

tone. "I love the Vintage Finds column. That's my favorite section."

Marla had heard of the periodical but hadn't read it. "I like to cook, but my passion is doing hair. My reading tastes lean toward trade journals and hair fashion magazines."

"What's the name of your salon?" Alyce asked.

"It's the Cut 'N Dye. May I give you my card?"

The other women reached into their purses, and they all exchanged business cards.

"You must be freezing in that skimpy top," Alyce said to Francine. She took off her white bomber jacket. "Here, wear this. You'll need it to stay warm during the game, but don't get it dirty or you'll pay for the cleaning bill."

"Thanks, it's colder than I'd expected today." Francine accepted the jacket and threw it on. "Are you ladies joining the live scavenger hunt?"

Tally gaped at her. "Don't tell me you're Find Franny?"

Francine's mouth split into a grin. "Yep, that's me. The game is so much fun each year, and Kinsdale Farms has so many places to hide."

15

Marla glanced at her watch. They had to load their supplies into the car before participating in other activities.

"We'd better get this stuff cleaned up," she said. "The kids' craft corner starts in twenty minutes, and I see the organizers eyeing our tables."

Alyce and Francine left to clear their spots, while Marla retrieved a large trash bag from her stash of supplies.

"Let's meet back at the ticket booth," Tally suggested, stacking the empty paper plates on her table. "We have some free time before the Find Franny game starts."

"Okay, but I'd like to meet the other contestants before we leave."

"Let me introduce you to Becky Forest. She's the person who told me about this competition." Tally directed Marla over to the woman who had exchanged words with Carlton Paige earlier. She'd just finished loading her plastic containers onto a foldable dolly. "Becky, this is my friend, Marla Vail. Becky is curator of the city's history museum. She's in charge of the exhibit detailing early Florida food practices."

Marla raised an eyebrow. "I haven't been over there, I'm sorry to say. Tally must love it, though. She's into vintage cookbooks and the historical details that accompany the

16

recipes."

The woman's cocoa eyes sparkled. "I know. Tally is one of my avid fans. I've had several cookbooks published, and she's bought them all. Did you taste my blueberry crumble? It's one of our original Florida recipes."

"I'm afraid I didn't have the chance."

"Too bad. You should visit the museum. Ask for me, and I'll give you a personal tour." Becky handed her a brochure. Silver highlights glinted in her ebony hair as she angled toward the sun.

Marla scanned the information before stuffing the brochure into her cross-body purse. "My husband would enjoy your museum. He watches the History Channel all the time. I'm surprised he hasn't mentioned it to me before."

A frown creased Becky's forehead. "Our publicity budget is so small that many residents haven't heard about us. If I win today, I'd use some of the prize money for advertising. Oh, there's Raquel. I have to speak to her before she gets stuck at the judging stand. Please excuse me." After giving them a nod, Becky hurried off with her wheeled bundle in tow.

"Hey, guys, it's good to see you again." Teri the chocolatier meandered over. The blonde looked as perky as when Marla had first met her. She'd entered her chocolate Kahlua cake in the contest.

"What would you do with the prize money?" Tally asked her after they'd exchanged pleasantries. "You already own an artisan chocolate factory with a dessert café."

"I'd like to start a line of beauty products with cacao as an ingredient. After all, every day is Valentine's Day when it comes to chocolate." Teri chuckled at her tag line.

"Good luck with that." Tally signaled to another contestant. "Marla, you have to meet Gabrielle. She runs a home-based catering service and hopes to expand her business. I'd rather convince her to run the café in my new shop instead. She made the fabulous pineapple torte in today's entries." They went through another round of introductions.

Marla greeted the woman whose copper highlights blended in well with her medium brown hair. "I didn't realize you knew so many people here," she said in an aside to Tally.

Gabrielle heard her remark. "Tally and I met at a museum talk given by Becky," she explained in a voice as smooth and sexy as aged whisky. "The curator's research is so

18

interesting."

"So I gather." Marla had been missing out on this gem. She'd have to visit the museum after all these recommendations. A flash of purple caught her attention, and she recognized Francine's colorful top. "Hey, who's that hunky guy over there talking to Francine?"

Teri pointed in the man's direction. "Zach Kinsdale. He's the eldest brother of the clan that owns the farm. They sell my signature chocolates in their farmers' marketplace."

"It's generous of them to host the festival." Marla scanned the crowd, searching for her husband. She didn't spy his tall figure anywhere.

Tally nudged her with an elbow. "Are you kidding? This event is a gold mine for them. Thousands of residents come out every year. It must bring in tons of new customers."

"That's true. Look, I'd better find Dalton to tell him we're entering the Find Franny contest. I'll connect back with you at the ticket booth. Bye, ladies," she told the others.

After she'd loaded her supplies into the car, Marla sought her husband. The judging at his homegrown tomato competition had ended, and he'd donated his specimens to onlookers. He stood by his designated table, peering at the crowd through dark sunglasses. A grin lit his face as he noticed her approach.

"How'd it go?" he asked. He cut a handsome figure in his belted blue jeans and tucked-in sport shirt.

Marla's nerves fired at his proximity as her body responded. "Fine. We met the judges and the other contestants. Tally and I want to join the Find Franny hunt."

"You go ahead. I'm starving. The barbecue wagon is calling to me."

"I thought you wanted to pick strawberries when we finished here."

"It might be better to come back another time when there's less of a crowd."

Marla surveyed the fields stretching into the distance. "Not too many folks are out there today. Guess they're more interested in the fun goings-on."

"Let's meet inside the market at four o'clock," Dalton said in his commanding tone. "Where's Tally?"

"She's talking to some people she knows."

"Too bad she didn't bring Luke. He might have enjoyed this place."

The mention of Tally's baby brought a twinge of longing to Marla's heart. She'd cared for the infant while Tally was in the hospital and missed him dearly.

"It's good for Tally to get out on her own and meet new people. It'll help her heal and accept her loss. When she reopens her dress store, she'll have even less free time. Besides, she spends hours with Luke already." Her friend still had to recover psychologically, if not physically, from her hidden wounds.

"She's checked in with the sitter, hasn't she?" Dalton asked, a crease between his brows. As a homicide detective, he tended to be suspicious of everyone, especially after the last case that had hit close to home.

"Of course she's called. Don't be such a worrywart. With her video monitoring system, Tally can see Luke on her cell phone." When Dalton opened his mouth to speak, Marla put a finger to his lips. "Don't say it. If we ever have children, we'll have to learn to trust someone as well. I'm not going to be glued to the house with a baby."

His gaze sparked, and he rubbed her belly. "I can't wait for you to have that choice."

Marla stepped back. "We have Brianna in the meantime, and she keeps us busy enough." Her stepdaughter would be a senior in high school next year, and then she'd go away to college. They'd be empty nesters unless Marla got pregnant.

"I'd better see what Brianna is doing, now

21

that you've reminded me," Dalton said.

"Leave her alone, Dalton. She might be driving, and you don't want to distract her."

His frown deepened. "Why does that thought upset me?"

"She'll be fine. You have to let the baby bird learn how to fly."

As Marla turned away, she realized she had her own issues with letting go. An ache in her chest for Tally's son hit her hard. She missed his sweet innocence and powdery baby smell. Her gaze fell upon all the couples with strollers at the fair, and she heaved a sigh. It had taken her a long time to consider having children of her own. Now she had to live with her decisions.

The Find Franny game would be a fun diversion. She paid the five-dollar registration fee and received a printed set of rules along with a card divided into eight sections. Gamers had to get each square stamped before finding Francine.

"We have to split up," Marla said to Tally with a note of disappointment. They'd met up again at the registration table. "This says no teams are allowed. That sucks."

Tally chuckled. "You should love this game. It will test your sleuthing skills, Marla. You might be the expert in solving murder cases along with Dalton, but I'm good at finding things. I bet I win first place."

Marla's heart warmed. Seeing Tally happy was a prize in itself. "Hey, I've got this. It'll be easy. All we have to do is follow the clues. May the best woman win!"

As Tally loped off in another direction, Marla grinned at the challenge ahead. After all, what could be so difficult about a live scavenger hunt?

CHAPTER TWO

Marla scrutinized the squares on her card, reading the instructions on how to identify the individuals involved. Each person wore an item of clothing depicting a particular character. Patty Pepper, Eddie Eggplant, Tommy Tomato, Betty Blueberry, Carl Carrot, Mabel Mushroom, Laura Lettuce, and Kenny Kale made up the eight squares.

To earn a stamp, participants had to correctly answer a question. Franny the Queen Bee would present each gamer with a token when they found her last and had all eight squares stamped. The first person to turn in the stamped card and token won the grand prize.

Marla discovered Patty Pepper weaving through the crowd. The middle-aged woman had on a sweater with red and green peppers woven into the design.

"Here's your question, dear," Patty said when Marla stopped her. "Which foods are better for you — red or white?"

Marla didn't even have to think about it. She'd been told often enough by Tally to avoid white foods like pastries, breads, and pasta. "Beta-carotene is a pigment found in many fruits and vegetables. It gives them their color and has healthful properties, so the answer is red."

"That's correct. The human body converts beta-carotene into vitamin A. We need this substance for healthy skin and good eye health." The woman stamped her card and gave her a spiel about colorful foods like carrots, cantaloupe, sweet potatoes and peppers.

As Marla moved on, she decided the game wasn't as easy to play as she'd thought. An hour or more passed before she tracked down the other individuals. They kept moving and could be anywhere on the property.

Finally, she had one more to go. Eddie Eggplant was the most elusive, but she finally discovered him in the thatched-roof hut chowing down on barbecued chicken.

"Should you eat the skins of certain produce, like eggplant, apples, or potatoes?" he asked her between mouthfuls.

Marla's stomach growled. The aroma of grilled food was hard to ignore. "Skins can contain a lot of nutrients, so the answer is yes. I've been peeling my eggplants, though. Is that wrong?"

He stamped her card. "Eggplant is a vegetable belonging to the nightshade family, which includes potatoes, tomatoes, and bell peppers. Its skin contains an antioxidant that protects your cell membranes from damage. You can eat the skin, although you'd probably want to peel it on larger eggplants."

Marla nodded her agreement. Eggplant skin could be tough to chew when too thick. "Is eggplant flesh beneficial at all?" She liked eggplant parmigiana but wasn't clear on its nutritive value aside from the tomato sauce.

He stuffed a forkful of cole slaw into his mouth. "Eggplants contain chlorogenic acid, which has anti-cancer properties among other benefits." The man didn't seem inclined to elaborate. His meal clearly interested him more than their conversation.

"Thanks; I'll try to pick one up at the fresh market. Enjoy your dinner."

Aware that it was almost time for her to meet Dalton, Marla scanned the crowd, looking for Francine. Was she still wearing Alyce's white jacket over her purple top? Francine was listed as the queen bee. Marla

26

presumed this was because of the worker bee's role in pollination. Would Francine be wearing a fake crown? Or perhaps a hat with a bee stinger?

The sun beat down on her head as she traipsed from one site to another without spotting her quarry. Francine didn't seem to be anywhere around the main buildings or vendors' alley. Marla had even sped through the petting zoo and kiddie area, peeking inside the bounce house.

Maybe Francine had taken refuge in the sparsely populated fields. The crowd tended to congregate near the festival tents. Soon the judges would gather on the makeshift stage to announce the winners from the day's competitions. Country music from the band was still going strong, but the musicians should be winding down soon.

Wait, what about the open shacks behind the marketplace building? Marla had passed various sheds on her way in from the parking lot. They held empty crates, farm equipment, and a variety of tractors. Francine could be hiding in their vicinity. But when Marla tromped over, she didn't see any sign of her target.

Had anyone else finished the game? Marla meandered over to the registration desk and asked the lady in charge. Nobody had turned in a finished card, the woman told her with a puzzled frown. Usually they had a winner by now.

A pit of worry gnawed at Marla's stomach. Where could Francine have gone? She didn't spy a bee-themed hat or a glittering tiara anywhere.

That left the fields. She wasn't keen on trudging down rows of strawberry plants. A text message to Tally confirmed that her friend hadn't finished the game yet either. Marla called Dalton next. If he was free, maybe he could help. Otherwise, she'd have to give up for lack of time.

"We have twenty minutes before they announce the winners at the judging stand. I'll help you find her," Dalton said in his deep voice that never failed to thrill her. "You take the left side facing the fields. I'll go to the right when I get over there. I'm at the olive tent. I bought a couple of jars of their tapenade mixture."

"Okay, but Francine could be pretty far back if no one else has found her." The rows of plants stretched endlessly into the distance. Tall stands of sugar cane placed at periodic intervals acted as a wind breaker to protect the crops. Could Francine be hiding behind the nearest clump?

Concerned about the woman's absence,

Marla headed down the dirt path. The scent of sun-warmed fruit entered her nose. Too bad they didn't have time to go picking this visit.

Why would Francine make it so hard for people to find her? The game was due to end shortly.

Nobody else was around when Marla crossed the second set of sugar cane barriers. The tall grasses exceeded her height and blocked the view ahead.

On the far side, a water-filled ditch bordered the tall plants before the U-pick rows started up again. A sparkle in the sunlight caught her glance.

She veered left, stopping short when she saw a tiara on the ground. Bile rose in her throat, and she stifled a scream. Lying beside the fallen crown was a woman sprawled facedown, her white jacket marred with blotches of red. She lay as still as the over-picked plants.

Marla clapped a hand to her mouth. Oh. My. God. This couldn't be happening.

Her gaze swung to the matted blood at the back of the woman's head. What did that signify? Then again, did it matter right now?

Marla knelt to feel for a pulse. She retracted her hand quickly from the clammy

29

flesh. There wasn't anything further she could do to help Francine.

Her identity was obvious. She still wore the jacket Alyce had given her. Marla recognized the woman's pixie haircut and the purple top peeking out from her borrowed outerwear.

No wonder the gamers couldn't find Francine. The sugar cane hid her body from view.

What now? Should she call for help, or go to get someone in person? Her heart raced as she made a decision. She'd call Dalton. He would know what to do.

Marla grabbed her cell phone and punched in his number, reassured by his quick response.

"I found Francine," she said in a squeaky tone. "Come quick. I'm beyond the second set of sugar cane plants."

Dalton couldn't have been far because he made it there in minutes. He halted beside her and peered at the woman's body in disbelief.

"Good God, Marla. Not another one." This wasn't the first time she'd summoned him for similar reasons. He stooped to palpate Francine's neck. "She's gone. Did you see anyone else around?" he asked as he straightened and surveyed the field.

"No, but this could have happened a while

30

ago. The game has been going on for a couple of hours."

"You're certain it's Francine? When was the last time you saw her?"

"We'd split up after the bake-off contest. I registered for the scavenger hunt, and then I had to get my card stamped by the other characters. Francine may have come out here to hide before the game even started."

"So that would have given someone plenty of time to whack her on the head and get away."

"Do you think the blow is what killed her?" Marla's glance darted to the rows of strawberry plants, the water-lined canal, and the tall sugar cane. Was the culprit watching them from some hidden viewpoint? Should they be worried he might return?

"That's not for me to say. The medical examiner will determine the exact cause of death. Hey, you're trembling. Sorry, you don't deserve this." Dalton pulled her into his arms, where she nestled to absorb his strength.

"Why is it always me?"

He chuckled against her hair. "The universe must know you're a seeker of justice. You can stay out of it this time. We're still in Palm Haven, meaning it's my jurisdiction. Has Tally left? She could give you a ride home. I'll be here for a while."

Marla stepped back, her pragmatism restored. "Can't I help? We're better as a team. You've even called me your sidekick before."

"You'll be in the way when my men arrive. It's smarter for you to go home. We can review things later."

He still needs me as a sounding board, Marla thought with an ounce of gratification.

While he used his cell phone to call for backup and then to take photos, Marla contacted Tally. "Where are you? I may need a ride home."

"I'm at the judging stand. Where are you? They're about to announce the winners."

"Do you see Alyce anywhere?" Marla asked.

"She's over here. What happened to Francine? I got my card stamped but couldn't find her for the final token."

"I've discovered her hiding place. Stay there. I'll join you in a bit." She turned to Dalton. "Tally says Alyce Greene is at the judging stand. She and Francine knew each other. They're similar in appearance. Alyce loaned Francine her jacket because she was cold."

"Both women participated in the bake-off

contest?" Dalton asked for clarification. "Did Francine come with anyone else, or was she alone?"

"I have no idea, but I can ask around. Meanwhile, you should get a list of names and addresses from the bake-off organizer. That would include three judges and ten other contestants besides me and Tally."

"Good idea." He pulled out his notebook from a pocket and scribbled in it. "Has anyone noticed Francine's absence from the scavenger hunt?"

"None of the contestants would have finished the game. If someone did, they might have been the last person to see her alive."

"And the winners are being announced now? Why don't you go over there and see what's going on."

"Can I tell Tally anything?"

"Yes, but don't let anyone overhear you." He bent to examine an imprint in the dirt.

Aware his attention had diverted, Marla trudged down the central aisle back toward the raucous crowd. A loudspeaker blared with the announcer's voice from the make-shift stage.

"And the homegrown tomato award goes to Dalton Vail," Marla heard as she approached. The emcee scanned the crowd for the winner.

Marla jumped up and waved her hand. "Hey, that's us!" She rushed over to accept the hundred-dollar gift certificate to a local nursery on behalf of her husband. "Have you done the bake-off competition yet?"

"No, ma'am. That comes after the Apron Artistry award."

Marla searched the crowd for Tally's tall form and found her standing off to the side. On her way over, she passed Carlton Paige ambling toward the assemblage. They bumped arms. Marla meant to excuse herself, but Carlton's eyes nearly popped out of his head as he spied Alyce. The slim woman stood by the judging stand with an impatient expression.

"What are *you* doing here?" he demanded, his face reddening.

"What do you think?" Alyce retorted, turning up her short nose. "I have as much chance of winning as anyone. I'm sure you voted against me, though."

Raquel sidled up to them. "We'll see. I'm sure it won't be Francine, despite her threats," she remarked with her Southern accent. "Hey, Tristan is still here. I thought he was leaving early to return to his restaurant."

"What do you mean about Francine?"

34

Marla asked, but just then the third judge hobbled into view.

"Isn't it almost time?" Tristan said. "I have to leave, but I wanted to stay for the photos."

"You're limping." Raquel pointed to his dirt-encrusted boots.

"The soil here is uneven. I twisted my ankle at a dip in the grass."

Marla's eyes narrowed. None of them had remarked upon Francine's absence. Francine had been wearing Alyce's jacket. Carlton had been more surprised than the others at seeing the food blogger. Was that significant?

Come to think of it, Tristan had a limp she hadn't noticed before. And Raquel had stated definitively that Francine wouldn't win. Why? Was she aware the woman was out of the picture?

"Who else is still around?" Marla asked upon reaching Tally and telling her she'd spotted their judges.

"I think everyone is here, except for Francine. Whatever happened to her?"

"I'll tell you if you don't breathe a word." Marla leaned inward and whispered into her friend's ear.

Tally's eyes widened. "Omigod, Marla, that's horrible."

"It looked as though she'd been bashed on the head." Marla shuddered at the visual image.

"Why was she out in the fields in the first place?" Tally asked.

"To hide for the Find Franny game, I would presume."

"Is Dalton taking charge of the investigation?"

"Yes, this falls under his jurisdiction in Palm Haven. Can you give me a ride home? He'll be here late. I'll have to transfer the veggies I bought into your car."

"Of course. This place is going to turn into a madhouse."

At that moment, the emcee announced the award for the apron design contest. Marla's ears perked up. Their competition came next.

The announcer gestured for a large man to ascend the stage. He wasn't big so much as muscular, Marla decided, observing his arrogant stride across the raised platform. The man wore a sport coat, which seemed out of place at a farm festival.

"Allow me to introduce the bake-off sponsor, Tony Winters," said the emcee. "Tony is vice president of Amalfi Consolidated. His company supplies the wonderful olive oils and other imported goods you can buy at the marketplace store. His lovely wife, Janet, organized today's events for us."

Tony crossed the stage to loud applause. He held an envelope in his hand. "As you know, the prize for this contest is a small business grant. In addition to paying an entry fee, each entrant had to submit a business plan related to the food industry. The city council selected the twelve competitors. At the festival, members of the public were invited to purchase tickets to sample the entries. Our company donates a portion of the proceeds to the Safety First Alliance. This worthy organization aims to protect our children and elderly from being left in hot cars. I urge you to stop by their booth over there and collect a brochure. Meanwhile, it gives me great pleasure to announce the winner of this year's bake-off competition."

The crowd fell silent as he tore open the envelope. A ten-thousand-dollar award was a significant prize. Local news people up front poised their cameras to snap photos while others took video recordings.

"And the prize goes to Gabrielle Sinclair for her pineapple torte and her plan to go public with her catering business. Gabrielle, I offer my sincere congratulations. You'll do us proud."

The highlighted brunette rushed onstage to accept her award. "Thank you so much. I can't wait to use this money to expand my services. We've been home-based until now, but with these funds I can hire more staff and lease a place in town." She kissed Tony on the cheek and took the check from his hand.

"Darn, now I'll have to find another partner for my boutique café," Tally griped.

"Have you spoken to anyone else about it, or did you have your heart set on Gabrielle?" Marla asked.

"I haven't really been looking, but I can start a new search. I'm eager to get my business up and running, Marla. I think I've found the perfect location. We should make a date so I can show you."

"Most definitely. I'd love to see it." Sirens sounded in the distance, while Marla's attention returned to the emcee, who stood alone on the stage once more.

"Unfortunately, nobody has brought in a token for the Find Franny game this year. Francine must have hidden herself so well that she couldn't be found." He chuckled at his remark. "But we have prizes for those of you who've earned your stamps. Local businesses have generously donated goods and services, so please turn in your cards at the ticket desk. The first twenty people with filled cards will get a prize."

A ripple of excitement passed through the crowd, but it quickly turned into confusion. A bevy of police cars arrived along with a crime scene van and a sedan that Marla recognized as belonging to the medical examiner. A cloud of dust trailed in their path as they skidded to a halt on a patch of grass.

She swallowed hard, anticipating what would follow.

Soon word would get out that a body had been found in the fields, and it was none other than the elusive Find Franny.

CHAPTER THREE

Dalton, taking over as lead investigator on the case, dismissed Marla and Tally. He'd get their formal statements later. Meanwhile, Tally had to get home to her son.

"I hope you'll let me know what you learn about Francine," Tally said during the drive east on I-595. "I can't believe she's dead."

"Tell me about it. Dalton isn't happy I found another body."

"He must be used to it by now. Someone had to be upset with Francine to whack her on the head."

"That would make it a crime of opportunity, especially if this person followed her to the fields. I can't help wondering if it was one of us. From the bake-off, I mean. Francine had words with some of the other contestants."

"Oh, come on. Francine wasn't all that friendly with the judges, either. Or it could have been somebody from the scavenger hunt."

"Not as likely. The people who played characters in the game stuck around the festival area and weren't hard to find." Marla stared at the scenery as they passed an IKEA store on the left and shopping strips on the right.

"Did you notice anyone missing from the bake-off contestants before we met up at the judging stand?" Tally asked.

"I was busy looking for Francine. What about you?"

"I've got nothing. How do we know Francine was the intended target? She wore Alyce's jacket. If she got hit from behind, the bad guy could have mistaken her for Alyce."

"That's always a possibility." Marla recalled Carlton's surprised expression upon spotting Alyce by the bandstand.

"Anyway, let's put aside this unpleasant topic," Tally said, her grip firm on the steering wheel. "Too bad neither of us won the bake-off. At least Dalton got the prize for best homegrown tomato."

"He'll be very proud. I haven't let him know yet. He has enough on his mind right now. As for our competition, I'm glad the Safety First Alliance benefits from the ticket

41

sales and entry fees, although I would have liked for you to win."

Tally shrugged. "I'll use some of Ken's life insurance money to restart the shop. I'd planned to do that anyway. I love the new location I've found. The restaurant on the corner will draw in visitors from Sawgrass Mills Mall, and the rates are reasonable since the center is still new. Plus, this would be a five minute drive to the day care center, so that's a bonus."

"I assume there isn't anywhere in Palm Haven you can go?" Marla said in a wistful tone. She didn't the idea of Tally moving farther away.

"I need a fresh start, Marla. I'll likely sell the house and move closer to my new shop. I've told you all this before. But what about your plans? We're always talking about me. You've been trying to get pregnant for months now."

Marla, startled by the remark, emitted a cough to hide her reaction. "We're not getting anywhere in that regard. Do you think it's too early for me to see a fertility specialist?"

"What does your gynecologist say?"

"He says to be patient. I'm thirty-eight, and it could take me longer to conceive. But what if my chance has come and gone?"

"So make an appointment with another doctor and get a second opinion."

"Dalton says I shouldn't stress over it. We hadn't planned on having children when we got married."

Tally nodded. "And now that you want them, it's more difficult. I wish I'd had the opportunity to have more than one child. Luke is a doll, but he could use a brother or sister."

Marla cast her friend an oblique glance. She'd been hesitant to broach this subject. Tally had been mourning her husband ever since she'd woken from the post car-crash coma. "You might meet someone else," she suggested.

"True, but the thought of dating scares me more than being alone for the rest of my life."

Marla lifted her brows. It sounded as though Tally had been considering the prospect of going out again. Although she was six months younger than Marla, Tally could pass for a woman in her late twenties. Any guy would be lucky to snag her attention.

"You're still young," Marla told her friend. "Ken would want you to be happy. When you're ready, I'll bet there will be some decent guys out there for you."

"I'm not rushing into anything in that regard. It's too soon." Tally's grip tightened on the wheel. "I can't apologize to you enough for keeping secrets between us. When Ken got involved in that insurance fraud case and I found out about it, I should have confided in you. Instead, I shut you out."

"Ken swore you to secrecy. He meant to protect you. We've talked about this."

"But I alienated you and put the cold freeze on our friendship. My silence almost cost Luke his life. I should have told you what I knew."

"And what was that? Someone in Ken's office was filing false claims, but he didn't know which team member was involved? He reported his suspicions and agreed to help track the culprit. You got involved once he told you what was going on."

Tally winced. "You don't have to remind me. I wonder what would have happened if I hadn't been in the car that night."

"You went along because you loved your husband." Marla recalled her friend's explanation of events once she'd regained her wits. Tally had confessed the whole sorry story and begged forgiveness from Marla for not confiding in her. "If Dalton told me about a case and swore me to secrecy, I'd

44

do the same. We're past this, Tally. No matter what gets thrown at us from now on, we'll be here for each other."

Tally nodded, her eyes glistening. "You got that right. Moving on to the present, who can I ask to work with me on my business plan, since Gabrielle will no longer be interested?"

Marla was glad to change the subject. She and Tally had discussed the secrets of the past ad nauseam. It had restored their friendship and made them stronger together.

"You'll find another chef," she offered in a soothing tone. "Look for a talented professional who's starting out and wants a place to display her skills."

Tally's face brightened. "That's an idea. I could approach graduates from the local culinary school. But they'll eventually want to move on to bigger and better things."

"Not necessarily. They might want to keep a foothold in your shop as an advertisement. If people get a taste, they may follow the chef to her newest restaurant."

"True, I can play up that angle. Thanks, Marla."

They fell silent during the rest of the drive home, while Marla pondered on how far Tally had come since she'd opened her eyes

45

in the hospital.

The news that Ken had been killed in the accident and that it had been a deliberate attempt on their lives had hit hard. Marla had stayed by her side while Tally underwent months of rehab to regain her strength. Eventually, she'd rallied for the sake of her infant son. Tally had sold her husband's insurance agency and invested the money. Along with Ken's life insurance proceeds, she had enough for a comfortable life.

"Let me know what you learn from Dalton," Tally told her after they'd pulled into Marla's driveway. "It was such a fun event until you found Francine."

"Sure, we'll talk soon. Give Luke a kiss for me."

Marla entered her house through the front door. Their two dogs leapt to greet her. She bent to give Lucky and Spooks each a friendly pat. The golden retriever and cream-colored poodle trailed her into the kitchen.

Brianna called out a greeting from the family room. The sixteen-year-old slouched on the sofa watching one of her recorded shows. Her straight brown hair hung down her back, and a smidgen of dark liner ringed her eyes. She wore a pair of jean shorts and a patterned top and had kicked off her sandals.

After putting her show on pause, Brianna gazed at her with curiosity. "Where's Dad? Why didn't you come in through the garage?"

"Tally brought me home. There was an incident at the fair. Your dad has been delayed." Marla related what had happened, ending with Francine's death and the subsequent storm of police vehicles on the farm's property.

"You've got to be kidding. A woman was murdered?" Brianna exited the recording and switched off the TV.

"I can't believe it either." Marla threw her purse on a counter, washed her hands at the kitchen sink, and then joined Brianna on the L-shaped sofa. "Why does this always happen to me?"

"The universe must know you can deal with it," Brianna said, echoing Dalton's theory. "Tell me about the dead woman."

Marla found she wanted to talk. Even though Francine was nearly a stranger, nobody should experience a premature death by force. "We met at the bake-off. Francine was publisher of *Eat Well Now* magazine."

"Did you see her arguing with someone

47

she might have ticked off?"

"Not that I recall, but I did sense an undercurrent at the bake-off. Some of those folks knew each other, and I didn't get a friendly vibe."

"Does she have family in the area?"

Marla's brow furrowed. "I don't know anything about her personal life. Your father will have to investigate those things along with the contest judges and other participants."

"Maybe someone at the publication wanted her out of the way. Why did she enter the competition? Didn't entrants have to submit a business proposal?"

"Good point. Maybe Francine's proposal would have disrupted things at the magazine. I'll suggest to Dalton that he take a look at everyone's business plans."

Brianna gave her a sympathetic smile. "I'm sorry you or Tally didn't win."

"Thanks, but I'm happy the Safety First Alliance benefits from the event. Hey, your dad won the best homegrown tomato award. He doesn't even know it yet. I accepted the certificate and prize on his behalf."

"Awesome! He'll be excited. But what about your own plans since you didn't win?"

She heaved a sigh. "I suppose Arnie can

continue to supply bagels for our customers."

Arnie Hartman ran the deli next door to Marla's salon and day spa. They'd been friends for years. She wouldn't want to compete with him, even though it would have been nice to have a bistro in her day spa. She'd consider it a courtesy to clients who didn't care to leave the premises. She had been selling Tally's dress shop stock in her spa's lounge and was thinking ahead to when her friend reopened her boutique. The space would be perfect for a cozy café.

Speaking of food, she needed to prepare dinner. She rose and shot Brianna a regretful glance. "I feel sorry for the guy who owns the farm. The negative publicity might cause him to rethink hosting the event next year. It brings in a lot of money to various causes."

"Not your problem, Marla. But this is." Brianna scampered from the couch to follow her into the kitchen. "I'd like to start prepping for the SATs, and I'll need your help with the math portion. Not the calculations, but the real-life applications. You do the bookkeeping for the salon. Teach me what you know."

On Tuesday morning, Marla entered Bagel

49

Busters to get the salon's customary bagel platter for clients. The deli's proprietor stood behind the cash register, wearing his usual apron over a tee shirt and jeans. His mustache quivered as he grinned at her arrival.

"I hear you've had an exciting weekend," Arnie Hartman said, his voice retaining a slight New York accent. "I saw the news on television. How's the investigation going?"

"Dalton has a few leads. His team found the murder weapon, but it didn't have any prints." They'd discovered the shovel lying in a water-filled ditch bordering the row of sugar cane plants, but she couldn't reveal this fact. "Either the killer had wiped it clean, or the person had been wearing gloves. The most logical culprit would be a farm hand. I assume they wear work gloves to operate their equipment, and they have plenty of tools lying around. Who else would come prepared that way?"

"Is Dalton suspecting someone among the farm staff?" Arnie asked.

Marla spread her hands. "He hasn't discussed a whole lot with me at this stage. It's too early in the investigation, and he has interviews to conduct."

"Can you sit a minute?" At her nod, Arnie signaled to a waitress to stand in for him.

He led Marla to an empty table where they took seats across from each other.

"I can't stay long. My first client comes in at nine." Marla wondered what was on his mind. She'd known Arnie for years, ever since she had opened her salon in the same shopping strip. She had been twenty-six then and he'd been thirty. Four years later, his first wife died in a car accident. He was left with two small children.

When he made romantic overtures toward her, Marla had turned him down. She'd been interested in friendship, nothing more. Fortunately, Arnie had reunited with an old classmate and ended up marrying the woman's friend. That had been an interesting encounter, Marla recalled with an inner smile. She and Jill had become close, double-dating with their spouses on occasion.

Arnie folded his hands on the table. "I have a favor to ask you. I'd appreciate it if you'd talk to the farm owner, Zach Kinsdale, to get his viewpoint on things."

"What? You're usually telling me to keep my nose out of police business."

"I know, and I trust your husband to ferret out the truth and bring the criminal to justice. But you have skills that can help and might clear Zach from any suspicion."

51

"What's this man to you, Arnie?" It was unlike him to ask her to get involved.

He sighed and ruffled a hand through his peppery hair. "I'm friends with his son, Rory. He's afraid they'll lose the place."

"I can understand the negative publicity causing a drop in visitors, but it won't last long. By the next harvest festival, people will have forgotten. Or do you know something about the farm that you're not saying?"

"I didn't always want to own a deli, you know," Arnie replied in a wistful tone. "My father had operated a bagel place when we lived in Manhattan, and I grew up working in the restaurant every weekend. Pop expected me to take it over one day, but I wasn't interested. Then Pop dropped dead suddenly. After we buried him, my mom sold the business, and we moved to Florida to be near my aunt."

Marla wondered where he was going with his tale. This was stuff he'd never told her before. Why now?

"I went to high school here, and that's where I met Rory," Arnie continued. "Like me, his father had wanted him to join the family business after graduation. But we had bigger dreams. With all the tourists coming to Florida, we thought we could succeed in

52

the hospitality industry. I used most of my inheritance money and Rory got a loan from his mother to start a boutique hotel on Fort Lauderdale Beach."

"Omigosh, I never knew that about you."

His head bent, Arnie played with the salt shaker on the table. "We failed. It's not a chapter in my history I care to discuss. I've been much more successful with the deli because I had experience in the food business that I didn't have with hotels. I started the deli with my remaining money. Rory went back to work on the farm. But we kept in touch."

"Okay, so you're buddies with one of the owner's sons. What's the big deal?"

"Rory is afraid the sponsors will decide to hold the festival elsewhere next year. This would mean a tremendous loss of income for the farm, which depends on the spring and fall harvest celebrations to bring in customers. Rory overheard his father talking on the phone, and Zach said something about losing the place. Rory and his brothers have families and depend on their jobs. Will you help prove who killed Francine? It'll take the heat off them, and then Rory can breathe easier."

Marla couldn't help herself. His story had captured her interest. "Why does Kinsdale senior think they might lose the farm?"

"Rory has no idea. That would be something for you to ask Zach if Dalton will let you talk to him."

"He won't want me to get involved."

"You can convince him. Please, Marla. I don't want to see Rory get hurt. He's struggled enough to get where he is, and he's finally taking pride in his part at the farm."

"Maybe his dad wants to sell out to a land developer. That's prime property. Broward County doesn't have a lot of sites left for new housing."

Arnie shoved the salt shaker away and eyed the customers lining up at the cashier. "Tell me you'll think about it at least. I have to get back to work."

Marla glanced at her watch and widened her eyes. "Oh gosh, I'm late. Are my bagels ready?" They both rose, and she reached a decision. "All right, Arnie, you don't have to twist my arm any further. I'll see what I can do."

"Thanks, *shaineh maidel*. It means a lot to me."

Wasn't it time for Arnie to stop calling her a pretty lady? Marla accepted the endearment with a fond smile and carried her order of bagels and cream cheese out of the

54

restaurant.

"I hear you found another body," said her next client, senior vice president of Tylex Industries. Babs Winrow shared confidences with Marla and expected the latest news in return.

Marla, sifting through Babs' wet strands of hair, sighed in resignation. "Tally talked me into entering the bake-off contest at Kinsdale Farms. Have you ever been to one of their harvest festivals? They're fun, and we like to pick strawberries while we're there. Anyway, out in the fields, I stumbled across Francine Dodger. She'd been hit on the head, poor woman." That much had been on the news stations.

"Her magazine did a piece on me once," Babs mentioned. "Women entrepreneurs and all. Francine was a go-getter in her own right, but she stepped on a lot of toes on her way to the top."

"I thought her magazine focused primarily on food-related topics."

Babs regarded her through the mirror at Marla's station. "True, but their reporters can dig deep for research purposes. One of them interviewed me about my eating habits and how I managed to stay so slim, but she also included questions on various aspects of my job. I met Francine in person at a

55

social function honoring the subjects of their profile pieces."

Marla could always count on Babs to know people around town. "Did she seem to have any enemies in particular?"

"Francine wasn't always kind in the articles she wrote. Her staff seemed to love her, though. You might want to pay them a visit to see what they can tell you."

Marla picked up a pair of shears and began trimming her client's hair. "I'm not planning to get involved this time." *Liar,* she told herself. *Arnie just asked you to talk to the farm's owner.*

Babs gave a low chuckle. "Sure, darling. Keep telling yourself that you're going to mind your own business for a change. Do I know you, or not?"

Marla rolled her eyes. "Probably better than I know myself after all these years."

"You'll see. Dalton will ask for your input. He values your contributions."

As though the universe heard Babs' words, Marla's cell phone vibrated. She kept the ring tone turned off during work hours. Dalton had sent her a text to call him in a spare moment.

"What's up?" Marla said on the phone after Babs left and before her next customer plunked into the salon chair.

"I'm looking into the contestants at the bake-off as well as the Find Franny characters, but I thought you might hear some gossip that could be useful. Has anyone mentioned the incident?"

"Dalton, I've only had time to do one appointment this morning. But yes, Babs Winrow knew about it. And so did Arnie." She repeated the gist of their conversations.

"Wait until I conduct my initial interviews before you speak to anyone involved," he advised. "And steer clear of the magazine's offices for now. I want to get there first."

"I imagine your team will be examining Francine's desk, computer files, and so forth?"

"Of course. Her death might have been related to something she'd been working on, rather than her activities at the fair."

"That's a viable thread to follow. So you have no objections if I talk to people about Francine as long as I don't directly approach your interview subjects?"

"Go for it. I'll be home late tonight. Don't wait on me for dinner."

"I figured as much. See you later. Love you."

As soon as she rang off, the phone pinged again. Tally was on the other line.

"Marla, are you busy on Thursday morning before you go into the salon? There's something I'd like you to do with me. You'll be helping Dalton with his case at the same time."

CHAPTER FOUR

"Why am I going to the city history museum with you?" Marla asked Tally on Thursday morning. Her friend had picked her up at home after dropping her son Luke off at day care.

"Becky Forest, the woman you briefly met at the bake-off, is giving a talk. I always try to go when the curator speaks. She has such interesting things to say, and this gives you the opportunity to question her about the festival."

"Dalton is already checking into everyone's backgrounds. He hasn't shared his findings with me, and I'm not sure if he's interviewed Becky yet. But you and I are just attending a museum lecture. If we happen to speak to Becky about the festival, it's not as though I'm interfering with his case. Do you have any idea why Becky wanted the prize money?"

Tally cast her a shrewd glance. "The city

59

funds the museum for the most part. Maybe Becky needed the money for her private research."

"What's her specialty again? The proposals had to relate to food in some way."

"She's a paleoethnobotanist. She studies plant remains to determine the food practices of early inhabitants. You know, whether they were farmers or hunters or fishermen."

"I'll admit history was never a favorite subject of mine." That was putting it mildly. The topic had bored her out of her mind until recently. Dalton watched the History Channel, and his interest had sparked hers. When a couple of his recent cases included a historical angle, she became intrigued. Now she actually looked forward to learning more.

They parked in a lot behind the one-story brick building surrounded by stately live oak trees mixed with mahogany and palms. A number of other cars already held spaces there. Marla hoped they'd be able to catch Becky Forest during a free moment for a private chat.

They entered a foyer with a ticket desk and a rack of brochures touting local events. In the center stood a stone statue of an Indian woman holding an infant. Signs pointed to various exhibits in three different directions. She and Tally paid for admission and headed to the auditorium for the lecture.

"The museum has a cool film with lighting and sound effects about the early settlers," Tally told her as they took seats. "We won't have time today to see everything. We'll have to come back another day. You should bring Dalton and Brianna."

Marla paid attention as Becky introduced herself and spoke briefly about their museum programs. The caramel-skinned woman spoke in a confident tone as she segued into her lecture. She looked smart in a navy skirt with a shell top and blazer.

"Southeast Florida has more than one type of ecological environment. You'll be familiar with the Everglades and its rivers of sawgrass along with its hammocks of higher ground. The trees there have a specific orientation based on water flow. Every island has evidence that shows how people used to inhabit the land. For example, animals provided food. People ate alligator meat, fish, and birds. Plants and trees provided wood and other resources, including a type of flour. Another ecosystem included the ocean, not only the tide waters but also our mangrove swamps. Those people ate conch, dolphin, seaweed, sea-grapes, and cocoplums. As you see, our early settlers used hunting, gathering, and fishing methods to acquire food. Agriculture didn't play a role until later."

A gray-haired fellow raised his hand. "What about fresh water lakes and rivers?"

Becky nodded her approval of his question. "We have the New River in Broward County. Turtles, fish, muscadine grapes, and even prickly pear cactus can be found near these fresh water sources. Lake Okeechobee to the north feeds the Everglades. Catfish used to thrive there, and now it's bass. Elderberries and other edible plants grow nearby. Never forget that as our cities expanded west, we've encroached on these lands. Now we have problems in the Everglades such as Burmese pythons, giant African land snails, and green iguanas."

"We've plenty of iguanas in town," another resident complained.

Becky went on to talk more about the earliest natives and their food sources while Marla's mind wandered. The museum appeared to be in good repair. Why did the curator need the ten-thousand-dollar prize money from the bake-off contest?

"I'm interested in purchasing the Morant Collection for the museum," Becky told them after the crowd dispersed. "As an archeologist, David Morant explored over one hundred and sixty sites in Florida and gathered one of the largest private collections of First People artifacts in the state. I've had the privilege of studying his work as part of my research. His grandchildren are seeking a home for the items."

"You would donate your prize to the museum rather than use it to fund your own research projects?" Marla asked. They sat in the curator's office where she'd led them after her lecture concluded.

"That's right. The city gives us only so much money. This collection would bring in publicity, which would lead to an increase in donations. We wouldn't need it so much if Carlton would mention our rotating exhibits in his newspaper column."

"Do you mean Carlton Paige, the food critic who judged the bake-off competition?"

Becky's expression soured. "He'll only do favors if he gets one in return. Go talk to him yourself and see what response you get. Carlton only aims to please himself."

"Maybe you need to reach out to a different editor at the news desk," Tally suggested. "Or are you also interested in coverage for your cookbooks each time you have a new release?"

Becky picked up a pen and clicked it on and off. "Carlton told me to send him my last two books, but he never reviewed them."

"Sorry I missed your latest book launch party. Do you have any copies in the gift shop that you could sign for me?" Tally asked with a hopeful grin.

"Sure, I'd be delighted. I like to recreate our early native recipes using modern ingredients and simpler preparation methods, so they're easy for today's cooks," she explained to Marla. "That was my food tie-in element for the bake-off contest application. The Morant Collection would inspire a new cookbook based on findings from his excavations."

"Did Francine ever profile you in her magazine?" Marla said.

"Not actually, no. My books never got reviewed there, either. Raquel is more supportive in that regard."

"I've seen you on her TV show," Tally added. "It's thoughtful of her to have you as a guest whenever you have a new release."

Becky smiled, her face softening. "I should say so. Raquel is a peach. The others should take lessons from her."

Marla crossed her legs to get more comfortable. She glanced at the knickknacks and books on display in the cozy office. Photos of dig sites and dusty manuscripts covered a counter lining one wall where a lone window let in daylight. She liked the vibe that reflected Becky's love of scientific research.

"I overheard a comment Raquel made at the festival," Marla mentioned in an idle tone. "She said Francine wouldn't win despite her threats. Do you have any idea what Raquel meant?"

Becky's gaze chilled. "No, and if you're implying Raquel had anything to do with that woman's death, you're wrong. Raquel has been kind to me, and I won't see her good name maligned. You should contact her directly for an explanation."

"Somebody had a grudge against Francine. What about the others present?" Marla asked to steer the conversation in another direction.

"You'll have to talk to people yourself, although I don't understand why you'd bother."

Tally stood and gathered her purse. "Marla can't help herself from getting involved when a murder occurs. Her husband is the homicide detective on the case."

Becky's jaw dropped. "You're Detective Vail's wife? I should have figured it out

65

sooner. Did he send you here to question me?"

"Not at all. I thought I'd get your viewpoint as long as we were here. He needs all the leads he can get. Can you name anyone who might have wanted to harm Francine?"

The other woman's face shuttered. She rose, and Marla followed suit. "As I mentioned, go talk to Carlton. That weasel seemed to have a beef with everyone. Otherwise, this conversation is over. Tally, if you'll follow me into the gift shop, I'll be happy to sign my latest cookbook for you."

Ten minutes later, Marla and Tally headed out the door. The humidity had returned along with a warm front. An earthy scent pervaded the air.

"She's touchy about Raquel," Marla said, striding alongside her friend who clutched Becky's recipe book in her hand.

"That's understandable. Raquel is very supportive of her writing efforts. It's a coup to get an appearance on a TV show to hype your new book."

"Still, I sense there's more to it than she's letting on. Becky didn't say much about the other contestants."

"So what? She's right not to spread gossip, although she does seem to have it in for Carlton Paige. Maybe she's resentful because he won't review her books."

"Or she could know something about him that we don't."

Marla dropped Tally off at her house before returning home to get ready for work and to let the dogs out for one last time. She wanted to tell Dalton about her latest conversation but didn't care to disturb him at the station. They'd share news over the weekend. In the meantime, she had to get to the salon before her first client arrived.

Work kept her busy until Sunday, when she finally had the chance to sit down with Dalton at breakfast and discuss the case. She couldn't believe a week had passed since events at the farm.

"I've vetted the list of contestants for the bake-off competition and the characters for the Find Franny scavenger hunt," he told her between mouthfuls of pancakes with fresh sliced bananas. "You're right about Becky Forest. She's the only one who didn't seem interested in personal gain if she won the prize. Her proposed business plan would have benefited the museum."

"Did you see the exhibits when you went to talk to her? You'd love that museum. I'm surprised you haven't taken us there before."

"Truthfully, I'd forgotten about it. And

the traveling exhibits change only once a year."

"Becky seemed defensive of Raquel. Did you find out anything more about their relationship?"

"Raquel invites the curator as a TV show guest to tout her new cookbooks. Nothing odd about it. However, I couldn't find much about the celebrity chef's background. That puzzles me. No one's past is a blank. The other judges didn't shed much light on Raquel, either."

"Is that right? I've watched her show, and she's good at what she does. Her production is educational as well as entertaining. Surely you can verify her professional credentials."

He tilted his head to regard her. "That's the easy part. Here's an idea. You're looking to open a spa café. You could approach these judges and mention that since you didn't win the award money, you need an investor. Then you can skillfully steer the conversation toward their involvement in the contest and their personal history."

"Oh, so now you want my help?" Warmth coiled through her at his subtle praise. "Have you interviewed everyone from the festival already then? Do you have any strong leads on who killed Francine? I suppose you've interviewed her work colleagues as well. What about relatives?"

He shook his head. "She has none in the area. I spoke to an aunt. Her parents are no longer living, and a younger sister died years ago. Francine moved here when she got a position at the magazine."

Marla felt a surge of sympathy for the woman. "How did she get along with people?"

"Despite the lack of family, her life was full. Francine had friends, and she'd hang out on occasion with folks from work. She went to the gym several times a week and volunteered at Bisby Park, taking charge of the herb garden. The other volunteers praised her dedication."

Marla poured herself another glass of orange juice from a pitcher on the table. Brianna sat quietly, scowling at her math textbook. "I promised Arnie that I'd talk to the farm's owner. Since we don't have any particular plans for today, how about if we all take a drive out there? Brie would enjoy picking strawberries."

The teen glanced up with a bright expression. "Great idea. I don't want to sit here doing homework all day. Let's get ready." She wore her hair in a ponytail and a loose top over a pair of distressed jeans. The weather had stayed warm, so they wouldn't need sweaters.

They could take their customary Sunday nature walk at the farm, Marla thought, although she shuddered at the memory of finding Francine's body there. Apparently, the farm had reopened since that fateful day. Maybe she'd shop in the marketplace while Brianna and her dad walked the fields. It would give her an opportunity to chat with the saleslady and to avoid the unpleasant mental images from the rows of crops.

Her stomach churned as they pulled into the farm's parking lot a couple of hours later. "It's a shame this place is tainted by a murder," she told her companions as they walked toward the main buildings. The soil under her New Balance shoes was uneven, and she watched her footing carefully. An occasional squashed strawberry lay amongst clumps of dry grass as a remnant of someone's pickings.

"The memories will fade," Dalton stated, his jaw firm as he strode ahead with a brisk pace. "Newcomers to the area won't know anything about it, and the rest of us will resume coming here because we like the produce. Let's hope the owner's son is wrong about the farm being in jeopardy. Zach Kinsdale didn't say anything to that

70

effect when I interviewed him."

Brianna pointed to the outdoor ticket stand. "How many buckets should we get?"

"I'm going into the market," Marla replied. "You two can go picking without me. I'd rather not return to the fields so soon."

Dalton gave her a perceptive glance. "Are you okay with coming here?"

"Yes, of course. I made a promise to Arnie."

"Don't talk to Zach until we're there. Come on, Brie. I'd like to get some peppers, too, so I'll need two buckets for myself."

They split up. Marla headed inside the market while her family went to the U-Pick side. A blast of air-conditioning hit her as she entered. Several customers were already checking out at the cash register. People came early on the weekends. The parking lot had held a number of other cars. In an hour, the barbecue wagon would open. That drew even more visitors.

She got a cart and proceeded down the aisles, plucking a fat onion here and a bulbous cucumber there. The gourmet food products tempted her, but she didn't really need anything except perhaps more olive tapenade. She paused by the display case holding artisan chocolate pieces. Those must be Teri's confections with their artistic designs.

Didn't the sponsor of the bake-off contest also sell items in the store? Oh yes, the olive oils and other imported goods. So at least a couple of the people from the baking competition had a connection here. Were the farm's owners responsible for vendor contracts, or did they employ a manager for that purpose? She should find out in case Dalton needed to speak to this person.

Marla approached the saleslady. "Is Mr. Kinsdale, Senior around?" she asked after paying for her items. "My husband and I were hoping to speak to him. Dalton is out in the field picking strawberries, but he'll be back any minute."

The plump woman gave her a kindly smile. "I'm sorry, miss, but Sundays are the one day the Kinsdale boys take off. They won't do any work on the Sabbath."

"You mean, none of the family is here?" Her spirits plunged. How would she keep her promise to Arnie now?

"You got it. The sales staff runs the U-Pick and marketplace anyway. The barbecue wagon is a separate franchise. So are the vendor carts outside."

"I see. Who's responsible for ordering items to stock in the store?"

"That would be our sales manager, although Zach may recommend products to him. Sometimes the boss will come across a vendor or an item he likes, and he'll tell the manager to make an offer on it." Her eyes narrowed. "Why, do you have something you think would be a good addition to our inventory?"

"I really wanted to talk to the senior Kinsdale about it. Does he go to church on Sundays?"

The woman nodded. "I believe so, and they have a family dinner. His wife insists on getting the clan together once a week. It's wonderful how they're all so close."

And close-mouthed, Marla thought. Prying secrets out of them wouldn't be easy. Or perhaps the other family members didn't know whatever Zach did about the farm's status. She really had to talk to the man in charge.

"Let's stop by his house," Dalton suggested when she told him the results of her discussion. "I still want him to look over the list of contestants to see if any names pop out at him as persons of interest. His family should be back from church by now."

Dalton had returned from the fields hot and sweaty and was glad to cool off inside the market. Brianna added a jar of dilled mustard, a package of organic sliced turkey, and a bunch of arugula to their bag, for her school lunches.

They packed the bundles into their car trunk and then headed off in a cloud of dust. Zach Kinsdale's residence wasn't too far away. He lived in a quiet residential community bordered by a canal system. His property must be at least an acre, Marla thought, viewing the expanse of grass dotted with spindly evergreens. The sprawling one-story house had a white tile roof and sand-colored exterior.

"You again," the farmer exclaimed as he answered their summons at the front door. Dressed in a shirt and tie with belted black pants, he appeared to have come home directly from church.

"Sorry to bother you on a Sunday, but we were in the area and I have a few more questions," Dalton explained. "This is my wife, Marla, and our daughter, Brianna."

"Nice to meet you, ladies. Come in then. We're relaxing before we begin meal preparations. Grace, we have company," he hollered.

A woman bustled in from the kitchen, judging from the apron she hastily discarded. Zach did the introductions. Evidently, she hadn't met Dalton before.

74

They took seats in the living room while Marla surreptitiously studied the man's wife. She wore a pretty lavender dress with pearl jewelry and black heeled sandals. Her blond hair, styled in a bob, was a bit too brassy. Marla's gaze wandered to a shelving unit. It held cat figurines, framed photos, and a porcelain tea set in addition to books. A built-in bar took up another corner. As though noticing her scrutiny, a black cat with white paws and a snowy tail slinked into view.

Marla crossed her legs when the cat nudged her ankles. She smoothed her jeans, aware of how rumpled the three of them must look.

"I was hoping you'd glance over this list and tell me if any names jump out at you as significant to Francine's case." Dalton handed Zach a crumpled piece of paper he'd taken from his pocket. "It's all the people from the bake-off and Find Franny competitions."

"I can't believe that poor woman died at our farm," Grace said in a cultured tone. With her elegant manner and slender form, she didn't appear the way Marla pictured a farmer's wife.

"It's a terrible tragedy," Marla agreed. "Had you ever met Francine?"

"No, I hadn't the pleasure. Wasn't she editor of some magazine?"

"She was publisher of *Eat Well Now.*"

"Oh, I don't subscribe to those journals that tell people how to eat. If you listen to all the advice about what's bad for you, you'd have nothing on your plate." Grace gave a low chuckle to emphasize her point.

"I understand your farm uses sustainable growing techniques and natural pest management," Marla commented to Zach.

"We do our best to guard the environment, Mrs. Vail. Our planet is a fragile thing. People should do everything possible to preserve it for future generations."

"I agree. So who do you think might have wanted to harm Francine? Was it somebody who disagreed with her magazine's philosophy about healthy eating habits?"

Zach snickered. "You'll probably find half a dozen people who had a grudge against her. I'm not saying I know who or why, but nobody is universally well-liked. There's always someone who is jealous or wants what the other person has."

"Or it could have been somebody protecting a secret. Did Francine know your farm was in trouble?"

CHAPTER FIVE

"Where the hell did you hear that?" Zach demanded, his shoulders tensing.

Marla waved a hand in the air. "Your son Rory is friends with my pal, Arnie Hartman. Arnie mentioned to me that Rory seems concerned about the place."

"Rory is a good kid but he's a dreamer. He can get strange ideas in his head, like becoming an hotelier. Did Arnie mention their joint venture to you? My boy doesn't have a mind for business. You should take anything he says with a grain of salt, because he can easily misinterpret things."

Dalton leaned forward, his hands clasped. "Do you make all the decisions for the family?"

"I'll get my brothers' advice but they're happy to let me take charge. We're equal partners in terms of ownership."

Marla glanced at Brianna, who was texting on her cell phone. No doubt the teen was avidly listening, though. Maybe she'd pick up some pointers for her school debate team.

"How many siblings do you have?" Marla asked Zach in a friendly tone.

Zach dashed a hand through his sandy hair. "Two brothers and a sister."

Dalton took out his notebook and flipped through the pages. "Let's see. Janet is married to Tony Winters, correct? And he's vice president of Amalfi Consolidated that sponsored the bake-off. Janet organized the day's events."

Marla's jaw dropped. She hadn't realized their sponsor's wife was related to the farm family.

Zach's walnut eyes darkened. "We're happy to have Tony's support. Where are you going with this, Detective?"

Dalton pointed to the list he'd given Zach. "Does Tony have any interest in the farm besides selling his company's products in your store?"

"Of course he's interested. His sister has a stake in the farm's ownership."

Dalton shook his head. "I mean, does he have an actual financial interest in the place?"

"Oh, you mean like a loan? Certainly not. Our property is free and clear. We inherited it from our Pa." His gaze flickered between Dalton and Marla as though he challenged them to refute his statement.

Was there an element of fear hidden there? Dalton could easily look up the farm's title information. Had he already done so?

"How about the judges?" Dalton persisted. "Did any of them have a beef with Francine that you knew about?"

Zach's mouth thinned. "I don't know all these people personally, Detective. But let's see. Carlton Paige is the food critic, yes? He writes his column for the newspaper, so I can't see what problem he'd have with the lady's magazine. She might have disagreed with his reviews but that wouldn't be a motive to kill someone."

"Tristan Marsh is pastry chef at The Royal Palate. Have you ever eaten there?"

"That place is too fancy for us. Right, Grace?" He grinned at his wife, who sat in a lone armchair and looked stiffly poised.

"Their menu choices are too eclectic for our choosing," Grace replied in a smooth tone. "Janet knows the guy, though. They met at a menswear store when she was shopping for her husband. I gathered the pastry chef has expensive taste in clothes."

"Was he ever featured in Francine's magazine?" Marla queried. She couldn't conceive of a connection between the two otherwise.

"I wouldn't know, dear. I don't read the publication. I like the TV show with Raquel Hayes. She's very entertaining and I always learn something new."

"I'll have to watch it more often, although I don't have much time for television. At the end of the day, I'm tired from work and there are chores to do at home."

Dalton shifted restlessly in his chair, and she could tell he was ready to go. Since he didn't seem to have any further questions, Marla continued to hold the conversational ball.

"One more thing, and then we'll be on our way," she said with an amiable smile. "I understand Francine had participated in the Find Franny game before, so she wasn't a first-timer to the festival. Did you either of you speak to her before the scavenger hunt started?"

Zach rose and so did his wife. "I'm afraid not, Mrs. Vail. We were both too busy to greet everyone. The harvest festival is enormously popular, and we give press interviews as well as overseeing the staff and vendors. I'm sure you understand."

Marla understood perfectly as he ushered them to the door. He was lying.

Teri the chocolate lady had identified the handsome man speaking to Francine. It was none other than Zach Kinsdale. This took place after the bake-off contest but before the Find Franny game. Had their encounter slipped Zach's mind in the confusion, or had he fabricated his reply on purpose?

"He knows more than he's letting on," she said during the drive east. The car smelled like ripened strawberries. She couldn't wait to get home and eat some of the fresh fruit.

Dalton focused on the road lined by shrubbery as they sped past an intersection. "I'll check into their finances tomorrow to see if the man is telling the truth about not having any loans. What are you planning to do on your day off?"

"The dogs are due for their annual check-ups at the vet. After that, I thought I'd talk to Carlton Paige. Becky Forest indicated the food critic might be a useful source."

"Hey, Dad, did you consider the wife's role?" Brianna inquired from the back seat. "Maybe her husband was having an affair with Francine, and Grace bumped her off."

"Brianna, you shouldn't be thinking such things," Dalton said with a glance at the rearview mirror.

Marla peered at him. "She has a good point. You should look into Grace's movements the day of the festival. You're the one who's always told me to examine all the angles."

The next morning, Marla examined the pet hairs on the linoleum floor at the veterinarian's office. She held her dogs loosely by their leashes in the waiting room. Her golden retriever explored the perimeter while her poodle played a sniffing game with a smaller canine.

Marla and the owner — a young woman in athletic garb — exchanged understanding smiles. Pet owners shared commonalities that gave them a mutual interest. The room smelled of animal mixed with a cleaning solution scent.

Nearby, a bearded man sat with his cat in a portable cage. Marla suppressed an inner smile. She wouldn't have taken him for a cat person.

Her turn came, and she leapt from her seat to follow the technician. Inside the cubicle assigned to her, she greeted the female doctor and gave a status report on her pets. Dr. Nelson, a pleasant woman with hair a shade darker than Marla's chestnut brown, wore a white lab coat and a friendly smile. She performed the examinations with skilled efficiency. Marla cringed when her precious pets received their annual vaccinations. It hurt her more than it did them.

"Did you go to the harvest festival at Kinsdale Farms this year?" she asked the vet, knowing the woman liked to attend. "I entered the bake-off contest for the first time. A percentage of the proceeds went to the Safety First Alliance where I volunteer. We educate the public about the dangers of leaving children in hot cars, but we also include pets."

"I'm aware of the group. It's a worthy cause. We have their brochures in our front office. I didn't make it to the festival this year, though. Would you believe one of our clients organized the whole thing? That would be an enormous undertaking for anyone, but Janet loves planning social events."

"Do you mean Janet Winters? Her husband's company sponsored our competition and provided the award."

"It was generous of Tony to get his firm involved. I can't imagine why Janet would be worried about him."

"Worried? How so?"

Dr. Nelson bit her lip. "Sorry, I shouldn't repeat things. Your pets look fine. If you'll follow me to the front, we'll renew their heartworm meds and Spooks' eye drops."

Marla wanted to pursue her remark about Janet but dutifully trailed the animal doctor toward the checkout counter. Her dogs, reattached to their leashes, bounded ahead toward freedom. As Dr. Nelson scribbled notes in their charts, Marla posed one more question.

"By any chance, do you know Carlton Paige, the food critic? He was one of our judges at the bake-off contest. The man struck me as a dog lover." *That's because he looks like one,* Marla thought but didn't say aloud.

Dr. Nelson's face split into a grin. "Sure enough. Carlton takes his pets to the dog park every day. You'll never find a more dedicated owner."

"Which park would that be? The one over by Fig Tree Lane?"

"No, it's out west off of Nob Hill."

"Maybe I'll take these guys there. They could use a good run. Thanks for the info."

When she'd called the newspaper where Carlton's restaurant reviews appeared, the person there said he worked from home and emailed in his pieces. Dalton wouldn't approve of her going alone to his residence, so this would give her the perfect opportunity to encounter him on a casual basis.

She released the dogs in the enclosure at

the dog park, smiling at their high spirits as they charged around the grassy area. Unfortunately, Marla had no idea what time of day Carlton usually showed up. It was not quite ten, but he might have been there earlier.

She struck up a conversation with another dog owner while watching her pets cavort on the field. Spooks chased after another small animal while Lucky ran from one corner to the next. Once the woman left, Marla stayed on the bench. The tranquil park lulled her into shedding her concerns. A soft breeze rustled through the trees and caressed her skin. She inhaled the freshly-mown grass scent, and observed the fluffy clouds scudding overhead in a bright blue sky.

"Marla Vail? Fancy meeting you here," said a familiar nasal voice.

Startled, she jerked upright. She'd become so mesmerized by the peacefulness of the place that she'd forgotten her purpose in coming. Carlton Paige stared at her from his rotund face, his complexion reddened. A black lab and a smaller dog with a pug face strained on their leashes held in his hand. He let them go into the fenced field and rolled up the restraints.

"Hello, Mr. Paige. Nice to see you again."

"Likewise. Which dog is yours?"

They discussed canines for a bit, and then Marla steered the conversation to the harvest festival. "It's a shame what happened there. We were having such a good time until Francine was found."

"Weren't you the person who discovered her body?"

"Yes, it was horrible. Would you like a seat on the bench? There's plenty of room, and our dogs don't want to leave anytime soon. Your lab is getting quite friendly with our golden retriever."

"Thanks, and please call me Carlton."

"Can you think of anyone who might have wanted to harm Francine?" she asked him, wishing she'd worn a hat. The scorching sun warmed her scalp.

"Beats me. Her magazine is popular. You're married to that police detective, aren't you? What does he say?"

Dalton is wondering if Francine was meant to be the target. She'd been wearing Alyce's jacket and got hit from behind. Maybe the killer attacked the wrong person.

"He doesn't share those details," she replied. "I noticed how you were startled to see Alyce at the festival bandstand. Didn't you expect her to be there when the winners were announced?"

Carlton's face blanched. "I thought she would have left already."

"Really? When the judge's verdict had yet to be shared with the crowd?"

"I'd told my wife about her, you see. Sally was supposed to get her off my back."

"What do you mean?"

His lips thinned. "Can I count on you to keep this confidential?"

"Aside from sharing it with my husband, yes."

"Thanks to bloggers like Alyce Greene, my readership is eroding. Her online site is so popular that it's stolen my audience. I'm aiming to become editor of the newspaper's entertainment section. That won't happen unless I can increase my followers."

"So you begrudge Alyce her success?"

"She's undermining my ratings. Now I know this doesn't sound nice, but my wife figured out a way to discredit Alyce. She knew something about her. Francine and Sally are acquainted from the gym. I suggested that Sally put a bug in Francine's ear about Alyce."

"What did you hope to accomplish?"

He avoided eye contact, staring at the ground. "I thought when Alyce heard the rumor going around, she'd get upset and would leave the festival early."

"What information does your wife have on Alyce?" Marla asked, appalled by his intent.

"She didn't share it with me. You can talk to Sally if you want to learn more."

"I will, thanks. Do you have any theories about who might have bashed Francine on the head?"

Her mild tone didn't fool him, because he stiffened. "I hope you don't think it was me. I'm not a violent person. My talent is using words, not implements, to get my points across."

Implements? Did he know a shovel was used as the murder weapon? Or was it a guess, since the police had issued a public statement that a blunt instrument was involved?

Or perhaps his wife, fearful of him losing his job, took matters into her own hands. A visit to the woman rose to the top of her to-do list.

"What gym does Sally attend?" she asked.

Carlton stroked his double chin. "She goes to Perfect Fit Sports Club."

Doesn't everyone? Marla thought with a cynical twist to her mouth. She'd had dealings there before.

"Which days?"

Carlton rose to his feet and whistled for

his dogs to return. "She'll be at the club on Monday, Wednesday, and Friday. She likes to go from ten until noon, and then she'll often head out to lunch with a friend."

"I appreciate your honesty, Carlton. This has been helpful." He wasn't a nice person to urge his wife to start a malicious rumor about a rival, but would he resort to murder? Or was he not the violent type as he'd claimed?

She stood to allow a couple of newcomers to take their seats. "If you become editor of the entertainment page, does that mean you'll give up your food critic column?" He must enjoy his job, judging from his pudgy figure. And even though his remarks might offend some people, he had his loyal fans.

"I'd assign it to someone else," he replied with a frown. "In truth, I'm at the stage in life where I'd rather go out to eat and enjoy myself without analyzing every item on the menu. If a particular place strikes me, I can still write it up for the syndicates."

"I hope you achieve your dream, Carlton."

"Me, too, but I also want your husband to catch the bad guy so Francine can find peace."

They parted ways, and Marla took her pets home. She did a quick check for voice mail and other messages, grabbed a snack, and then headed out again.

Her stomach clenched as she approached Perfect Fit Sports Club. Memories surged of unpleasant encounters from the past. Nonetheless, based on prior experience, she knew the staff.

It wasn't long before she located Sally Paige at one of the machines. A hunky guy in a logo shirt and shorts appeared to be showing her how to operate the controls. He had a hand on her butt and his other one stroked her arm. Sally laughed and muttered something into his ear and then she flicked her tongue at his lobe.

They broke apart as Marla approached.

"Hi, I'm Marla Vail," she said, introducing herself. "Your husband said I should talk to you about Francine Dodger. Francine and I were entrants in the farm festival bake-off contest."

"Really? Oh, I'm sorry, this is Jorge, my personal trainer. We'll just be a few minutes, dear," she told him.

He gave Marla a nod and strode toward another lady wrestling with a torture device, as Marla perceived the machinery.

"I can't believe Francine is gone. What a horrible tragedy." Sally wiped her neck with a towel. She wore her acorn brown hair in a short bob as Marla had done before she'd

90

grown her hair longer.

"Dying in an accident is a tragedy. This was murder," she stated.

"What's your interest in the case?" Sally asked in a curt tone.

"My husband is the lead investigator. I'm making inquiries on his behalf."

"What is it you want to know?" Sally gestured for Marla to accompany her to a padded bench against the wall.

Marla waited until Sally took a seat and then followed suit. "Carlton mentioned you knew something about Alyce Greene that could discredit her, and you were going to give Francine this information."

Sally shook her head. "I decided it wasn't a good idea to speak to Francine at the fair. She knew things about me, too, you see. If I wanted to spread gossip, I'd have to be prepared for it to lash back in return."

Marla's glance flickered to the personal trainer who kept looking their way. *I can see what it is you have to hide, pal.* "What is it you know about Alyce? I'll keep whatever you tell me in strict confidence except for my husband."

"It's not so much about Alyce as the woman's brother."

"What about him? Was he present at the festival?"

"We've never met, so I wouldn't know." Sally wrung her hands together. "Look, I love Carlton, but I don't want to spread rumors that will cause trouble. I know he blames the food blogger for his falling ratings, but I'm not so sure that's the root of his problem."

"Do you think newspaper readership is down in general, and that's the reason? More people are going online for news and entertainment these days."

"That's true, but Carlton's posts are available on the newspaper's website. He has his fans. Lately some of his reviews have been — how can I say this tactfully — not quite up to par."

"Can you elaborate?" Marla gritted her teeth. Gaining information from Sally was like coaxing a stubborn curl into place.

Sally leaned forward. "At the last restaurant where we ate, I thought the food was mediocre. And yet Carlton gave it five stars."

"So you're saying his judgment is unreliable?" *Or were his palms getting greased by restaurateurs who wanted better ratings?*

"I'm saying readers might be looking elsewhere for an honest opinion."

"And Alyce Greene fills that void?"

"She supports the farm-to-table movement that is wildly popular right now. Her posts mention sustainable farms and organic food sources, among other topics."

"Does she do restaurant reviews?"

"Only on occasion, and her slant differs from what Carlton does. He used to be more discerning in his tastes. That's what gave him his reputation."

"Do you believe people like Alyce threaten the existence of food critics?"

"Not necessarily. People are more conscious of conservation efforts and green grocer practices. Organically grown and locally produced foods are popular and so are restaurants that use these resources. Maybe Carlton just needs to change his focus."

While Marla paused to consider what to say next, sounds from their surroundings impinged on her awareness. Chatter from the mob of exercise enthusiasts mingled with clunks and clanks from the machinery.

"Francine was wearing Alyce's jacket that day," Marla ventured, watching Sally for a reaction. "Do you suppose her death could have been a case of mistaken identity?"

Sally's brows arched. "How should I know? It could have been a piece Francine was working on for her magazine that riled someone. Or maybe a colleague at work had a grudge against her. What does Alyce say? Have you spoken to her?"

"Not since the festival. Would it have been within Francine's range to challenge Carlton about his reviews? Were they on friendly enough terms to talk openly that way?"

"They met at industry functions as far I know. Their relationship didn't go any further." Sally's mouth compressed. "I know someone else you should interview. At the festival, I overheard Zach and Francine talking near one of those tractor sheds. Francine said she'd learned something about the farm that could cause Zach to lose the property."

CHAPTER SIX

"Sally's statement corroborates what Arnie told me," Marla said to Dalton that evening after dinner. "And yet, Zach denied anything being wrong with the farm's ownership. Maybe we should talk to Rory, his oldest son. I could ask Arnie to set up a meeting since he'd mentioned Rory to me in the first place. Or have you already interviewed the guy?"

"I've asked him some preliminary questions, but I have more to follow up on."

"Would you mind if I tagged along?"

He gave her a thoughtful glance. "It might disarm the fellow to bring you with me. Speak to Arnie and see what he can do. In fact, tell him to make it seem as though you'll be interviewing Rory as a favor to him. I'll come along as escort. That way, my questions will seem less like a planned interrogation."

"Great, I can ask Arnie tomorrow. Did

you learn anything new about the property today?" She hadn't wanted to bother Dalton at work earlier, waiting until they were seated at the kitchen table and had finished dinner. She'd chatted instead about her visit to the vet and the other Monday errands she'd accomplished, while Brianna had described her school day. Once the teen had left the kitchen to do her homework, Marla told Dalton her findings.

His brow creased as he regarded her from across the table. "Interestingly enough, there's another man's name listed as the farm owner. I had to dig deep to find the information. But locating this person is a dead end. I'm not even sure he exists. Zach has been the one paying property taxes, and his father before that. So there must have been a change of ownership somewhere along the way that failed to get recorded. I have my staff researching the item."

"Let's ask Rory about it when we speak to him. He can see if there's a deed in his family's vaults. Otherwise, Dr. Nelson mentioned Janet Winters to me today. She said Janet is worried about her husband in some way. He's the guy who sponsored the bake-off competition," she reminded Dalton.

"Yes, I've spoken to Tony Winters but not

96

to his wife. You might work that angle."

"Okay, but I won't have time until later in the week. My schedule is full."

Her schedule got fuller when Becky Forest walked through the salon door on Wednesday. Marla recognized the history museum curator and put down the spray bottle in her hand. While waiting for her next client, she'd been cleaning her station. She hastened over to the reception desk to meet the new arrival. Becky looked smart in a tailored jacket dress and subtle makeup.

"I have a great idea for your salon if you're interested," Becky said, after they'd exchanged greetings. "Since this is Pioneer Women's History Month, it would a perfect time for you to participate in a fundraiser benefitting the museum."

Marla stared at her. "You must have been reading my mind. I've been thinking of doing a bad hair day clinic as a charity benefit. Here's how it would work. Our stylists would give free consultations to people on their hair problems. New customers would get twenty percent off any services they book that day. We'd give the museum thirty percent of proceeds from those bookings."

Becky clapped her hands while Robyn, the receptionist, listened in to their conversation.

"I could help with the promotional end of things," Robyn offered, her prior experience as a marketing executive kicking in.

Marla grinned at her good fortune in snagging Robyn to work at the salon. After she'd been laid off from her high-paying position, Marla's neighbor had decided the corporate world could live without her. She'd snapped up the offer of a receptionist job at Marla's salon as a fun place to work with less pressure. An inheritance meant she didn't have to worry about the mortgage.

"Can I leave you two to work out the details?" Marla said, ready for her next client who had appeared in the parking lot.

"Wait, Marla, there's one more thing," Becky replied. "Did you ever speak to Carlton?"

"Yes, I did. Oh, I'm sorry. I forgot to mention your cookbook to him. Did you want me to put in a good word for you?"

Becky propped a hand on her hip. "It would certainly help if that lout reviewed my books in his column and mentioned our rotating museum exhibits."

"Maybe it's better if he doesn't mention you. I've heard his ratings are down, although it may be a rumor going around. He's still widely respected."

"I wouldn't be surprised. That guy is out for his own gain."

Oh, and you're not? Why are you really here? "I know you wanted me to talk to Raquel, but I haven't had the chance. I'm leaving the interviews to my husband."

"And what has he learned? Is he any closer to identifying Francine's killer?"

"He doesn't share that information with me."

"I suppose not." Becky surveyed the salon. "Hey, as long as I'm here, maybe I should do something to cover up my gray hair."

Marla gave her a genuine smile. "Now you're talking my subject. I'd love to help you, but I'm fully booked today. However, Nicole might have a free spot."

"That would be awesome. I've been meaning to make a hair appointment."

"Robyn will set you up." Marla gestured toward the receptionist. "Now please excuse me, but my next customer has arrived."

Marla ruminated on their conversation while cutting the client's hair. She'd wanted to offer a bad hair day clinic for a while now, thinking it could support the Safety First Alliance. But this being Pioneer Women's History Month made the museum a good cause.

Was that the only reason Becky had

99

stopped by? The curator had sniffed around for information on Dalton's case. Was she afraid he might discover something shady about her? Becky certainly had it in for Carlton Paige. Was it mere professional resentment as she implied, or were deeper roots involved?

At their earlier meeting, Becky had also urged her to see Raquel in person. Marla would have to make it a point to visit the celebrity chef as well as Alyce, the food blogger. If only she had more free time. After work, she drove Brianna around to her various after-school activities. And Saturdays were out of the picture, since she worked all day.

Hey, wait. She hadn't spoken to Tristan Marsh, the pastry chef, since the bake-off event. Maybe she and Dalton should make a reservation to dine at The Royal Palate. They could bring Brianna along, ostensibly to celebrate her dad's birthday, even though it wouldn't happen until next month. Marla had other plans in mind for Dalton's special occasion, but nobody said they couldn't celebrate twice.

When she had a break in her schedule, Marla opened the restaurant reservation app on her cell phone and booked a table for Saturday night. They'd meant to spend a quiet evening at home, but it would be fun to go out and try a new place.

"Marla, thanks for giving Becky over to me. She liked the way her hair turned out," Nicole said later from the next station. The cinnamon-skinned stylist looked as sleek as always in a maxi-dress with her hair clipped back from her forehead.

"You did a great job. That color was perfect for her. I like the cut you did, too."

"She said you two had met at the bake-off contest. Was she there that day when you found the body?"

"Yes, Becky had entered the competition. She's curator of the history museum and a scientist who studies food practices of early Florida natives. She's written several cookbooks based on pioneer recipes."

Nicole's eyes brightened. "Do tell what you've learned about her, girlfriend. Is she a suspect? Why would she need the award money?"

Marla laughed at Nicole's expression. It reminded her of a squirrel that had just discovered a stash of acorns. Her mystery-lover friend wouldn't let this go.

"Look, I need to head over to Bagel Busters for a few minutes. We can talk later. Do you want anything to eat for lunch?"

"No, thanks, I brought my own today."

"Okay, I'll fill you in when we get another break."

Marla hustled over to Bagel Busters to speak to Arnie. He grinned at her when he caught her arrival. Signaling for one of the staff to take over the cash register, he hurried in her direction. His moustache quivered as he gave her a quick hug.

"Marla, what brings you in today? I already gave your daily order over to Robyn."

"I know. I'm here to give you an update." They sat at an empty table and she offered him a brief summary of their findings within Dalton's allowable parameters.

"You should talk to Rory. Has your husband interviewed him yet?"

"Yes, but Dalton has more questions." She hadn't mentioned the other owner's name on the property records. There could be an explanation, and she didn't want word to get around in the meantime.

"I'll set up a meeting. When are you available?"

"Thursdays are my late day at the salon. I don't go in until one o'clock, so tomorrow morning would work for me. Make it sound as though I'm doing you a favor by talking to him. Dalton will come along as a matter of form."

"Let me see what I can arrange." Arnie

102

withdrew a cell phone from his pocket and sent a text message. A few minutes later, he got a response.

"Rory will see you and Dalton at his house if you can come at eight sharp."

She winced. That would give her hardly any time to get ready for the day. Never mind. She knew farm hands started work at the crack of dawn. This was a concession on his part, and Dalton shouldn't have any trouble with the early hour.

"Okay. At least traffic will be headed in the other direction." And if her husband couldn't make it for some reason, she'd go alone. Dalton would know her whereabouts. Then she'd have the rest of the morning free for other errands.

Arnie gave her the address and thanked her for taking action that would help his friend.

"Sorry I don't have more news to share," she said.

"No worries. I'm glad you were able to speak to Zach, even though you didn't clarify what Rory overheard him say on the phone. I appreciate your efforts and hope you can clear up the issues with the farm. It's Rory's livelihood, and I don't know what he'd do if it was taken from him."

"There's always the hotel business," she

replied in a wry tone.

Arnie's expression soured. "After our spectacular failure? I don't think so."

"Neither of you had any training. These days you need education in the hospitality industry. Maybe Rory could get a scholarship and attend college if that's his dream."

"You can talk to him about it." Arnie rose, his attitude clearly one of dismissal.

Back at the salon, Marla took Nicole aside in a free moment and gave her friend a quick rundown on the case. She cut their conversation short when her next client walked in. Laurianne was a new customer with medium blond hair who wanted to do something different.

"I can see you with bronze lowlights," Marla told the young woman after studying her facial structure and hair texture. "They'd complement your natural shade. I'd also give you more lift with some added layers. However, if you don't want to mess with the color, we'll just do the cut for now."

Nicole butted in from the next station. "Marla is not known for what she cuts out of hair, but for the love she puts into it. I agree with her assessment. You'd look stunning with a touch of bronze, but it's your call."

"All right, I'll give it a try," Laurianne

decided. "You're the experts."

Robyn approached, a frown on her face. "Marla, I forgot to tell you a wrong order came in. They sent us the shampoos with sulfates instead of the sulfate-free ones."

"Did you send it back?" They needed the latter to use with chemically straightened hair.

"Yes, and they'll expedite the next shipment."

"Good, our stock is getting low so we need that delivery." Marla got busy with her customer and soon the afternoon had zipped by.

She scurried out of the salon as soon as she finished her last client. While ferrying Brianna to her debate team practice, she told the teen about their dinner reservation.

"I can't go with you on Saturday. I have plans with friends."

"Oh? Which friends?" She didn't like how Brianna was sharing less than in the past. Was this normal when kids become independent?

"It's the usual gang. We're going to Las Olas to hang out," Brianna replied in a defiant tone.

Marla pursed her lips. "Your dad will want more details. Where are you going exactly? You can't go to a bar." *Not unless you have a fake ID.* Marla had played a few tricks like that in her youth. But she had to trust her stepdaughter or she'd end up suspicious about everyone, same as Dalton. Brianna was a bright girl who knew right from wrong. And while she'd had a rebellious streak earlier in their relationship, she'd mellowed considerably. Marla would do her a disservice to lose faith in her character now.

"There's a new jazz club we want to try," Brianna admitted while staring out the side window. "Jason's older brother plays in the band. They serve coffee drinks, not liquor."

"It sounds like an old-fashioned coffee house. Who's driving?"

"Cassie is picking me up. You know, if you loaned me your car, I could drive myself places. You wouldn't have to chauffeur me around."

"Uh huh. Talk to your father about it."

"I'm going to save up for my own car. You'll see."

"Oh yeah? How do you propose to do that unless you get a job? You're too busy with extracurricular activities. If it's not softball or acting class or drama club, your debate team has a big competition coming up this year."

Brianna's face turned sullen. "So I'll get a

106

job when I'm in college."

"You won't need a car if you get into the school of your choice in Boston. So who's Jason?" she asked, hoping to catch the girl off-guard.

"He's a friend. Who's going to take me to the school bus stop tomorrow if you and Dad have to leave so early?"

Marla smiled inwardly. The girl was adept at changing topics. "There is such a thing as walking, you know."

Brianna rolled her eyes. "You're becoming as old-fashioned as Dad."

When Thursday morning arrived, Marla took care of the dogs and waved to Brianna before she and Dalton got in the car. They headed west toward the development where Rory Kinsdale lived with his family. The address wasn't far from where his parents resided, although his gated community had newer homes and plots of land packed closer together.

"Detective, it's good to see you," Rory said, greeting them at the door. He shook Dalton's hand and waved them inside.

Was it really good to see them, or did he hide his true feelings? Most people weren't pleased to see a homicide investigator on their doorstep. She studied the tall man with muscled arms, broad shoulders, and rust-colored hair. Now where did that come from? She remembered his dad's sandy brown shade and his mother's brassy blond tones.

"You have a lovely home," Marla said in a friendly voice after Dalton introduced her. They took seats in the living room. She noted the high ceilings, tasteful paintings on the walls, and screened-in pool patio facing a lake in back. Someone had an artistic touch, judging from the expensive knick-knacks placed strategically throughout the room. Laughter and children's voices came from a bedroom wing.

"Thanks. We're lucky to be able to afford the place," Rory said with a sheepish grin. "It's mostly thanks to my wife who's a corporate litigation attorney. Hey, Sherry, come out here and meet our guests," he hollered.

A brunette strode into the room. She wore a black pencil skirt, cream shell, and royal blue blazer. Gold jewelry completed her outfit. "I have to get the kids ready for school."

"Detective Vail is here about the woman who died at the farm. This is his wife, Marla. She owns a beauty salon in the same shopping strip as Arnie's deli."

"Is that so?" Sherry's interested gaze swung toward her.

"I was also present at the festival that day," Marla explained. "I'm the one who found Francine's body."

Sherry gave a visible shudder. "How horrible. Why did you come to see Rory? Haven't you already interviewed him, Detective?"

"Marla is friends with Arnie Hartman. He wanted her to have a chat with Rory."

"Well, unless I'm needed here, I'd like to finish with the boys. Please excuse me."

After ten minutes or so of letting Dalton lead the conversation, Marla rose and asked for restroom directions. But when she got to a junction in the hallway, she couldn't remember which way to go. Hearing voices down the hall, she wandered in that direction.

The voices emanated from a kids' room with twin beds. Toys, shoes, and clothing covered every surface. Two young boys stuffed items into their backpacks while their mother supervised. Sherry glanced up at Marla's entrance and flushed beet red.

"Hello again. Can I help you?"

"Sorry, I was looking for the bathroom."

"It's down the hall in the opposite direction. Forgive the mess. I haven't straightened up in here yet."

Marla chuckled. "No problem. You should see my salon storeroom after we get in a new load of supplies."

Sherry stooped to tuck in one of her boys' shirts. "This is Gary, and that's Andrew. Do you and the detective have children?"

"It's a second marriage for us both, so I have a teenage stepdaughter. We're trying for our own, but it hasn't happened yet."

"You'll get pregnant when you least expect it. Enjoy the peace and quiet while it lasts."

"You seem to be doing quite well managing a career and a family. Do you mind my asking how a farmer's son and a lawyer hooked up together?"

Sherry straightened, her face easing into a wistful smile. "Believe it or not, I'm a country music fan. We met at a concert through a mutual friend. When Rory told me what he did for a living, I wanted to run in the opposite direction. I'd always pictured myself marrying another attorney. But he had a romantic streak and persisted in pursuing me. In the end, it's the man that matters and not what he does."

"So true. Did he mention to you his dream of operating a hotel?"

"Hell, yes. I've offered to help him get financial aid if he wanted to get a degree in

110

hospitality management. But he doesn't have enough confidence in himself. It breaks my heart, because he'd be much happier than he is now."

"Oh? He doesn't like working on the farm?" The air-conditioning kicked in, sending a cooling blast her way and dispersing the dirty socks aroma from the kids' room.

"He's never been cut out to be a farmer like the rest of his family. But I can't get him to break away from his heritage, as he calls it. And he doesn't care to disappoint his father again."

"That's understandable. Hey, I have an idea. Has he ever thought of opening a bed-and-breakfast? It wouldn't require extra training and he could be his own boss. It's not that far removed from a small boutique hotel."

Sherry shooed the boys off to pack their lunches. "That's an interesting possibility, but it would require a huge investment on our part. Besides, Rory would need someone to handle the business aspects. He doesn't have a detail-oriented bone in his body."

"No, but you do. Maybe you'll think about it after your kids are grown." She paused. "In the meantime, is Rory concerned about his future on the farm? Arnie had indicated

111

your husband was worried because of a phone conversation he'd overheard."

Sherry's mouth compressed. "Rory heard his father make a remark about the farm, but he might have taken it out of context."

"Has Rory ever seen a deed to the place? Like, who is listed as the actual owner?"

"Zach and his siblings are equal partners. As for a deed, Zach would know where it's kept."

"Has Rory shared his concerns with his uncles?"

"He's talked to them, plus his cousins and brothers. Nobody knows about any threat against the farm. The business is doing well financially, and there aren't any debts to my knowledge. Any mortgage has been paid off by now. I suppose Zach might have borrowed against the equity. That's something your husband could determine, isn't it?"

"I'll mention it to him. Who does the bookkeeping for the farm?"

Sherry stuck the worn clothes into a hamper. "Zach works with an accountant, plus his brothers have access to the accounts. I'm not worried about the financial end of things, though. Rory should think about leaving the farm for other reasons. I'm always afraid for him when he goes to work there. Farms can be dangerous places with all the hazards on the property."

CHAPTER SEVEN

"What kind of hazards?" Marla asked Rory's wife. Did Sherry believe a murderer hid among the farmhands? Or was she talking about something else?

Sherry waved a hand. "Oh, you know. Accidents happen all the time on farms. And there was that one incident . . . but I don't want to bore you. You should rejoin the men. I've got to drop the kids off at the school bus stop and head to work."

Marla waggled her brows at Dalton as she reentered the living room. He gave a subtle nod indicating he understood she'd had a productive conversation.

"Rory has been telling me about his family," Dalton said with a welcoming grin. "They have quite an extended group."

"Does everyone work on the farm?" she inquired, taking a seat on the couch next to her husband.

Rory's forehead wrinkled. "As I explained,

we like to keep things in the family, so my answer is yes. Except for Aunt Janet, of course."

Marla folded her hands together. "I understand she's married to Tony Winters. His firm sponsored our bake-off contest. It was most generous of him to get involved."

Rory gave a low chuckle. "Aunt Janet loves planning social events, so I'm sure it was mostly her idea. She coordinated the whole thing. But yes, Tony is vice president of Amalfi Consolidated. He sells their imported olive oils and other goods to us for our fresh market."

"If he's the VP, who's in charge?" Marla asked.

"His relatives from Italy. Every now and then, he'll come around with a bunch of them. They're a lot less polished than Tony." Rory stroked his jaw. "If I had to guess, I'd never see them as being related. Let's say they're not people I'd want to meet in a dark alley at night."

"Do they stay with Tony when they come to visit?"

"I don't think Aunt Janet would put up with them, but you can talk to her about it. She's reluctant to discuss the subject. It makes her uneasy."

"If they're coming to evaluate her husband's work, I can understand her discomfort. Or does it stem from another reason?"

Rory gave her a frank stare. "My aunt avoids the topic when I ask her how things are going at home. She loves doing her society events and rattles on about their kids, but I get the impression she's not being entirely truthful."

"How do you feel about her husband's import company?"

"People like their products, so I guess that counts for something. As for the guy himself, I've always gotten an odd vibe around him. I mean, he loves his kids, and he treats Aunt Janet with respect. Maybe it's me, because I'm just a farmer and he has money. Rich people tend to look down on folks like us who labor for a living."

"We wouldn't have food without our agricultural roots," she said in a soothing tone. "Has your farm ever been featured in Alyce Greene's blog?" From the corner of her eye, she noticed Dalton's piqued interest. He seemed content to allow her to guide the conversation.

"Alyce is a true friend to our family. She mentions our sustainable farming techniques and the value of local produce on her site all the time."

"Not everyone likes her. Carlton Paige,

the food critic, implied she's stealing his readership."

Rory snorted. "Carlton's reviews have gone downhill. We've eaten at some of the restaurants he recommends. They're not worthy of four or five stars."

"How about The Royal Palate? Have you been there? We have a reservation for Saturday. That's where Tristan Marsh works as pastry chef. He was a contest judge at the bake-off."

"We like the place, although it can be expensive. You have to try Tristan's desserts. Each one is an artistic creation." He frowned as he glanced at his watch. "You'll have to forgive me, but it's getting late. I'm needed at work. Honey, are you still here?" he yelled to his wife.

"We're leaving now. Bye!" Sherry shouted back from the kitchen. A door slammed, and the garage door rumbled open.

Rory stood, and Marla and Dalton followed suit. Marla slung her cross-body purse strap over one shoulder. This visit had been fruitful, but she was ready to move on.

"Thanks for seeing us." Dalton offered his hand to Rory for a firm shake. "I'll let you know if anything significant turns up on the case."

"Ask your wife about an idea I gave her,"

Marla added. "It's been a pleasure meeting you. You have a lovely home and family." She pointed to his hair. "By the way, where did your unusual shade come from? Your dad has sandy brown hair and your mom is a blonde. Does anyone else in the family have red hair like you do?"

Rory laughed and ran his fingers through his thick hair. "Mom says it's our Irish ancestry. Seems I'm the only lucky one in the family to have a carrot top, not to mention these freckles. I have to be careful in the sun since I burn more easily than my brothers."

"I'm sure you wear a hat when you're working the fields." Marla shook his hand on the way out. The day had warmed, and the sun was already heating the pavement. She sniffed the chemical scent of insecticide from a neighbor's lawn.

Once she and Dalton were ensconced in their car, he shot her a glance. "I have to go into the office. What are you planning for the rest of the day?"

"I'd like to pay a visit to Janet if she's home. You have her address, yes? Then I'll grab a bite to eat and head to the salon."

"What were you and Sherry discussing? You took a long time to return from the restroom, so I assume you chatted her up."

She sank back into the seat cushion while they drove east. "I asked Sherry how she'd met Rory. They were both at a country music concert. She seemed to feel bad for him that his dream of owning a hotel didn't work out. She's offered to help him get financial aid if he'd like to apply to hospitality school, but he won't risk disappointing his father again."

"Rory told me about his family and how they loved the farm. I didn't get the sense he was unhappy there."

"He may be resigned to his fate. Sherry said he wasn't cut out to be a farmer. I suggested they consider opening a bed-and-breakfast place in the future, perhaps when the kids are grown. He wouldn't need any special training, and Sherry could handle the business details."

Dalton gave her an admiring glance. "That's a great idea."

"She seemed agreeable to the possibility. As for a threat against the farm, the mortgage is paid off. Could Zach have taken out a loan against the equity?"

"I can check on it. I asked Rory about a deed to the property. He hasn't seen it. He'll ask his family members before confronting Zach for more information."

"Sherry wishes he'd leave the farm. She

119

said working there can be dangerous, as in job hazards. She'd mentioned some incident but then changed the subject."

A brooding look came over Dalton's face. "It's annoying how nobody seems to have any definitive answers. Maybe you'll learn something new when you talk to Janet. Her husband might be generous in donating his company's money to your cause, but he kept glancing away when we spoke. He also scratched his head a lot. That man is hiding something."

"His wife might be more forthcoming. I'll text you if I learn anything important."

By the time he dropped her off at home, it was already ten o'clock. Marla would need a half hour to drive downtown in traffic and locate Janet's waterfront residence. With her first client scheduled for one o'clock, she'd be cutting it close if she hoped to stop for lunch. She should grab take-out at Arnie's deli on the way back. Then she could fill him in on their interview with Rory.

Before leaving again, Marla phoned Janet to make sure she'd be home and amenable to a visit. Janet had sounded wary until Marla gave an excuse. She could use Janet's help regarding the salon fundraiser. Pleased to be included, Janet had said Marla should stop by.

Soon she was on her way east toward downtown Fort Lauderdale. Janet's address was located off Las Olas Boulevard in the Seven Isles neighborhood.

She found the proper bridge and crossed the canal, admiring a row of gleaming yachts lined up by the waterway. Fort Lauderdale was called the Venice of America for a reason. These people lived a lifestyle she could only imagine but didn't envy. She liked being a business owner and feeling useful. Her job allowed her to help other women by making them feel better about themselves, and she wouldn't give that up for any amount of money.

Janet and Tony Winters lived in a McMansion, as other residents termed the spectacular homes that tour boat guides pointed out to guests. Marla pulled into a circular driveway, turned off the ignition, and emerged to gaze at the house's façade.

The Mediterranean style appealed to her sense of aesthetics along with the structure's terra-cotta exterior and rolled tile roof. Sand-colored columns rose to a second-story balcony, while hurricane impact windows stared back at her.

She strode to the entry, enjoying the tropical landscaping, which included pygmy date palms, colorful crotons, and flowering hibiscus shrubs. Maybe she wouldn't mind living in a place like this after all. You'd need a bevy of staff members to maintain it, though. At least the owners saved on boat dockage fees.

"Hello," she told the uniformed maid who opened the door. "I'm Marla Vail here to see Janet. I called ahead of time, so she's expecting me." Marla attempted to peer past the woman into the marbled foyer but her line of vision was blocked.

"Come inside, please, and follow me."

Marla stepped into the air-cooled interior and shut the door. The housekeeper led her into an enormous living room with contemporary furnishings and expensive art works. A mouth-watering aroma of bacon and French toast wafted her way, presumably from a kitchen somewhere in the rear. Marla should wait in the living room, the maid said, before vanishing up a curved staircase.

A few minutes later, Janet bustled down the stairs along with her housekeeper. After giving the woman an order and watching her bustle off toward another part of the house, Janet turned to Marla. She was dressed in a royal blue sheath dress, a diamond pendant shining from her neck.

Matching earrings dangled from her ears. Marla's gaze swept to her blond hair knotted in a chignon.

Feeling out of place, Marla smoothed her floral-patterned skirt, glad she'd worn a work outfit rather than casual attire.

"It's nice to see you again, Marla. Did you have fun at the bake-off?" Janet's face reddened. "I mean, before you, um . . ." Her voice trailed off.

"Yes, it was a blast," Marla hastened to reassure her. "You did a fabulous job organizing the whole thing. Before we discuss my salon fundraiser, I'd hoped to talk to you about the farm. I have a few questions to ask."

"Aren't you married to that police detective? He's already interviewed us."

"I'd like to get your perspective on things. It will help me process Francine's death."

"All right; let's go into the parlor in back. It's more comfortable. I've asked Tabitha to bring us a tray of pastries and some glasses of fresh-squeezed orange juice."

"That would be lovely, thanks." Marla followed Janet to a sunny room decorated in yellows and greens with potted plants. French glass doors led outside to a terraced patio with an outdoor kitchen. A huge yacht sat by the dock, its white hull reflecting the sunlight.

"I have a lunch date at noon, so we can't take too long," Janet said, after they'd both taken seats. A Pekinese dog ambled into the room. It circled Marla's feet and sniffed her ankles. "Sherlock, stop that. Oh, I'm so sorry. He'll calm down after a few minutes. Or would you rather I lock him away?"

"No problem. He probably sniffs my two dogs. We have a golden retriever and a miniature poodle. I believe you and I go to the same vet."

Janet's face cracked a smile. "I still go to the animal hospital there even though we live east now. I love Dr. Nelson. She's so sweet and always patient about explaining things."

Marla let the dog smell her hand and then petted his neck. She liked his name. Was Janet fond of mystery novels?

"I'm a volunteer for the Safety First Alliance," Marla said. "They appreciated the generous donation from the bake-off contest."

Janet nodded. "I prefer to tie social events to a charitable fundraiser, and preventing hot car deaths is an important issue in Florida. Why not raise money to help people while we're having fun?"

"Our group gave out a lot of brochures at

the festival, so thank you for your support."

"Oh, I love organizing these events. Otherwise, I'd be bored out of my mind." Janet chuckled but then her face sobered. "Most of my friends don't know about my origins. They believe I came from wealth like my husband. But I grew up accustomed to being useful and carrying my weight."

"It was generous of your husband's firm to offer the prize money. Was that your idea?"

"I might have suggested it to him. I'm sorry you didn't win, Marla. Your coconut fudge pie was fantastic."

"Thanks, it's one of my mother's recipes. Speaking of family, I understand Amalfi Consolidated supplies its gourmet imports to the farm's marketplace. Are you the liaison between your husband's company and the farm?"

"No, that's Tony's doing. He sold my brothers on the idea after we were married."

"They must be proud of you. The festival brings a lot of publicity to the farm as well as the sponsors. Has Zach said anything to you about the place being in trouble? Rory overheard a conversation involving his father that caused him to worry. He's afraid of losing his livelihood."

"Is he? Rory never wanted to work there

in the first place. It's a shame he gave up on his dream to operate a hotel. I told him to go to hospitality school and make a career of it, but he won't disappoint my brother again. As for the farm having problems, I haven't heard about it. Zach keeps things tight, though."

"Meaning what?"

Janet tucked a strand of hair behind her ear. "He doesn't always share his concerns. I've gotten the impression the farm is doing well. That's not what's on my mind these days."

"Oh no?" Marla leaned forward in her eagerness to hear what came next.

Just then the maid interrupted, bringing in a tray of pastries and juice. Marla helped herself, her stomach growling despite her preoccupation with their conversation.

Fortunately, Janet resumed talking after the housekeeper left. She might be lonely, Marla surmised, if she couldn't speak frankly to her friends about her extended family.

"Someday I might want to open an event planning business," Janet confessed after taking a few hearty gulps of orange juice. "In case something ever happens and I need to fend for myself, it would be a good venture for me."

"Is your husband's company doing okay?" Marla asked, surprised by her admission.

Janet cast a glance toward the entry and lowered her voice. "Yes, but his relatives are coming over from Italy. It doesn't bode well if they feel the need to inspect things in person. They speak in Italian and make me uncomfortable."

"How are they involved?"

"They manufacture the products that Tony imports. He's in charge of sales in the States. We've never visited his overseas relations. Tony brushes them off, saying they don't like Americans and disapprove of his marriage to an outsider, but I don't think that's really the reason. It's too coincidental that they're coming after Tony told them about Francine's magazine exposé. And now she's dead."

Marla gaped at her. "Surely, you don't believe there's a connection?"

"Mind you, please don't repeat this to anyone. Tony is also upset with Tristan Marsh, the pastry chef. I wish I knew what was going on, but I'm afraid to find out."

"Maybe you're worrying about problems that don't exist."

"Who's worried about what?" Tony's harsh voice demanded as he strode into the room.

Janet cringed visibly at his stern tone. "You remember Marla Vail from the harvest festival, don't you, dearest? She wanted to thank us for sponsoring the bake-off event."

"That's right," Marla said in a sugary tone. "Janet has such a gift for planning social events that I need her talents for my salon. We're planning a bad hair day clinic as a fundraiser for the history museum," she told them, explaining her idea.

Janet clapped her hands. "It sounds wonderful. I'd love to get involved. Tony, you could ask Tristan to donate some of his desserts. You cross paths on occasion." She turned to Marla. "His restaurant buys vegetables from our farm. They like to advertise how their dishes contain ingredients from sustainable food sources."

"That would be amazing if his restaurant would get involved in our charity event. They'd benefit from the publicity as well."

Tony frowned, deepening the crow's feet by his eyes. "Likely you'd need to get permission from the owner, and Mr. Romano isn't too pleased with Chef Marsh these days. The pastry chef should mind his own business if he wants to keep his job."

Janet rose and snagged his arm. "But you'll ask him about Marla's event, won't you, dear?" she asked in a coy tone.

He patted her hand. "I'll do it for you, lovey."

"Actually, I can ask him myself," Marla said. "Dalton and I have a dinner reservation at The Royal Palate for Saturday. It'll be our first time dining there. Has Carlton Paige ever written a review on their place?"

Tony stared down his hooked nose at her. "He gives them five stars. It's Alyce Greene who disses them in her blog. She makes unfounded claims that have no basis in truth."

"Oh, really? What sort of claims?"

"Read her posts, and you'll see for yourself. Half of what she says is a bunch of lies. If she doesn't watch her big mouth, she could very well end up like Francine Dodger."

CHAPTER EIGHT

Marla rose, put her empty dessert plate on a table, and gathered her purse. Tony's words of warning disturbed her, but she didn't want to rouse him further. She'd rather follow up directly with Alyce and see what the food blogger had to say about his accusation.

"Thanks for the hospitality," she told the couple. "I have to head to work. Janet, let me know when we can get together for a planning session regarding our event."

The other woman's eyes sparkled with excitement. "How about if you email me your media list so I can add it to my own? I'll help with publicity and community outreach. Think about how you want to notify your individual customers. Flyers in your salon? A direct mail-out? Or do you send email newsletters?"

Marla gave her a startled glance. "Who'd want to read a newsletter from a salon?"

"You'd be surprised. The place where I go sends me one every month. It includes sales specials, seasonal features, hair care tips, and even healthful recipes."

"I'll mention it to our receptionist. Robyn is a former marketing executive. She'll love the idea."

"Also consider if you'd like to have other vendors at your affair. Like, how about face-painting to occupy children while their mothers get free consultations? And if Tristan supplies desserts, what will you offer to drink?"

"We'll have our usual coffeepot. I could enlist Arnie from the deli next-door. He'd be happy to contribute some snacks as well."

"You mentioned this will be a benefit for the historical museum. Do you want me to coordinate with the curator?" Janet asked, while Tony appeared bored by their conversation.

"Sure, that would be one item off my list. But we still have to set a date."

"True. Contact me once you have more definitive plans, and I'll get to work on it."

Marla said her farewells and left, eager to share these ideas with Robyn at the salon. Outside in the fresh air, she felt as though a cloud had lifted from her shoulders. Was it because Tony made her uneasy with his brooding attitude? Or because she'd needed a new focus after the disaster at the farm? The contacts she'd made there would prove useful for this project. And if she involved the day spa, Tally might want to do a trunk show in their lounge.

Her thoughts jumbled once she was in her car and heading west toward Palm Haven. No time left to stop at the deli and see Arnie. She'd have to pay him a visit another day.

Saturday night could be fruitful if she and Dalton got the chance to talk to Tristan Marsh. She'd ask him about participating in the fundraiser. Plus, she remembered another excuse for a chat with the chef. Cousin Cynthia held Taste of the World every year at her Fort Lauderdale seaside estate. She was always looking for chefs to participate, and Tristan would fit the bill perfectly.

Back at the salon, she related Janet's advice to their receptionist.

"I love it," Robyn said, when Marla proposed offering a newsletter. "I'll design an opt-in form for our clients to add their email addresses. In the meantime, I can contact Becky to set a target date for the fundraiser event. Then I'll get in touch with Janet to coordinate our efforts in terms of publicity."

Marla happily agreed to leave the arrangements in Robyn's capable hands. Work occupied her for the rest of the day and through the weekend, until dinner with Dalton on Saturday evening.

They found The Royal Palate without much trouble. The restaurant was located in a former residence on a side street near Las Olas Boulevard. They secured a quiet table by a wall in one room where Dalton could sit facing the entrance.

She noted the location of the exits like he'd trained her to do, then met his gaze across the white-clothed table. It held a glass-enclosed candle and a vase with a fresh peach rose.

"Nice place," he remarked, giving her a lopsided grin. He looked dapper in a dark brown sport coat with a beige dress shirt open at the collar. His eyes glinted in the soft lighting from recessed lights overhead. "Have I told you how lovely you look tonight?"

"Thank you," she answered with a demure smile. His compliment made her heartbeat quicken. She smoothed her teal dress. Other patrons had spiffed up for the occasion as well.

A waiter dressed all in black bustled over

to take their drink order. Dalton consulted the wine list before ordering for both of them. Then he picked up the menu to peruse the selections. A frown creased his forehead.

"I don't see anything here that I like. You didn't tell me the menu was this eclectic."

Marla took a look. Crawfish cocktail, conch fritters, gator bites, deviled crabs. Those didn't appeal to her, either. "How about the guacamole?" she asked in a less than enthusiastic tone. It wouldn't be her appetizer of choice.

"The dip comes with pita bread. And what's this pawpaw martini?" Dalton asked.

"Some kind of fruit drink, maybe? We could always get a salad to start."

"That seems like the best bet. I wouldn't want the sunray salad. That's got oranges and onions and cream cheese balls. Ugh."

"I'm not fond of kumquats either," Marla added. "Jellied lime salad with papaya? Fish rounds in avocado shells? Spiced tongue? Or tossed greens with conch bites?"

While they were deciding, the waiter brought over a basket with crispy seeded flatbreads. Another guy delivered their drinks and filled their water glasses.

"We could just ask to see Tristan," Marla suggested.

"No, we're here. We have to eat. I think I'll skip straight to the entrée. The grouper Creole is probably our safest choice."

Marla agreed. She wouldn't want the crawfish enchilada, the sweetbreads supreme, or the kidney stew. Did people really like these things?

"Is Tristan Marsh here tonight?" Dalton asked the waiter after placing their order. "If so, we'd like to talk to him when he has a spare moment." He handed over a business card.

Marla knew he'd confirmed the pastry chef's schedule after she'd made their reservations. Too bad they couldn't go straight to dessert. At least there they couldn't go wrong.

They'd finished their meals and had asked for the dessert menu when Tristan came into view. He headed to their table and bobbed his head in greeting. His white chef's uniform seemed large on his slim figure.

They shook hands and exchanged pleasantries before Marla offered her excuse for their visit. "My hair salon is doing a fundraiser for the history museum. Would you be interested in donating desserts? It would be great publicity for the restaurant."

Tristan stroked his clean-shaven jaw.

135

"That wouldn't be my decision. I'd have to ask my boss if he'd be interested in participating."

"Would that be the owner, or the executive chef?"

"Paolo is the new head chef, but I don't take orders from him," Tristan said with a disdainful sniff. "He got hired after Jeff quit. We had no warning. One day Jeff tells me his suspicions about things, and the next day he's gone."

"What sort of suspicions?" Dalton asked in a mild tone.

"I can't talk about it here."

"Wait, I've another offer for you," Marla said as Tristan looked about to turn away. "You won't need anyone's permission, either. My cousin Cynthia runs Taste of the World each December. Would you be interested in being one of the featured chefs? She'd be thrilled to have you."

Tristan's eyes brightened. "Let me know the exact dates for these events, and I'll let you know."

The host chose that moment to lead another couple to a nearby table. Tristan spoke in a loud voice meant to be overheard.

"I'll send you a sampling of my best desserts. After you've finished your meal, I'd be happy to give you a tour of the kitchen.

Thanks for suggesting me for the fundraisers."

Marla enjoyed the exquisite confections he sent their way. The Key lime tartlet melted on her tongue. The guava dumplings served with brandy sauce left a trail of fire mixed with sweetness down her throat. And the chocolate rum torte left her craving more. They should have skipped the entrées and ordered a selection from the dessert menu for dinner.

Once Dalton had paid the check, which came to a substantial amount even without the sweets, they wound through the different rooms toward the rear kitchen. Marla held her stomach, eager to go home. She'd eaten too much, and it made her feel uncomfortably bloated.

Tristan, holding a spatula, gestured to them from a back corner of the kitchen. He proceeded to give them a tour, explaining what went on at each station. The place bustled with activity. Marla got an impression of gleaming stainless steel counters, steaming pots, and stacks of plates. A variety of cooking smells met her nose, which didn't help her unsettled state.

"What were you saying about the executive chef?" Dalton said once they'd relocated to the pastry station. Flour covered the surface, and Marla noted dough in a nearby bowl.

Tristan leaned inward after casting a nervous glance over his shoulder. "Jeff was a good guy. He and I got along well. It wasn't until Paolo arrived that things got tense. Paolo is friendly with Mr. Romano, the owner. They buy supplies from Amalfi Consolidated. It's not my fault if I have to use inferior ingredients. Jeff protested, and look where it got him. I don't want to get fired."

"I don't understand," Marla replied. "Are you saying these inferior products come from Tony Winters' specialty import company?"

"I'll show you what I mean." He went to a shelf and withdrew a bottle of extra virgin olive oil. "Let me give you a taste, but don't let anyone see us."

Dalton tasted first, his expression thoughtful. "It tastes all right to me."

Tristan waved a hand in an effeminate gesture. "Perhaps you lack a discerning palate. Marla, dear, what do you think?"

The spoonful of oil sank to her stomach, which roiled in protest.

"I'm afraid this isn't agreeing with my dinner. Is it outdated, do you think?"

"No, that's not the problem." Tristan

frowned at her, as though she should know what he meant.

"I don't follow, but it doesn't matter right now. You'll have to excuse us, Tristan. I need to go home," Marla said.

"We'll be in touch," Dalton promised the fellow. He put a hand to Marla's back to guide her toward the exit. "What's wrong?" he asked.

"My stomach is upset all of a sudden. I think this place is off my list. The menu is too weird for my tastes. Tristan's desserts are the only good thing about it."

He opened the front door for her. "Olive oil on top of those sweets wasn't the best idea."

As Marla swung into the passenger seat of their car, she wondered if that was the case. Something had made her feel queasy.

She didn't feel quite herself the next day, either. Dalton went into work on Sunday to make inquiries into Amalfi Consolidated. Marla took a walk in the park with Brianna in the morning and then tried to relax when the teen went to do her homework.

Her appetite had fled, and she barely picked at her lunch salad. Maybe that piece of fish from the restaurant had been under-cooked, but Dalton had eaten the same item and he'd had no ill effects. Hopefully, things would resolve within the next few days. She took the afternoon off and ignored her chores to watch TV and read her salon magazines.

On Monday, she'd planned to stay home and rest until Tally called. "I thought I'd drop by Raquel's studio today. How about joining me?"

Marla sat up straight in the desk chair where she'd been catching up on household bookkeeping. "I'd like to interview her about the bake-off contest, but what reason do you have for going?"

"Becky gave me a couple of tickets for the studio audience. They have vacancies at today's filming. Besides, Raquel knows I'm a fan of her show. She said I could come by anytime, and she'd find me a seat. I gather they hold some in reserve for VIPs."

"I didn't realize the show had a live audience. I've watched it but can't remember the details."

"Can you be ready by ten? We have to get there a half-hour early for check-in. I'll pick you up."

Marla winced. She'd have to change her clothes, fix her hair, and grab something to eat. Her stomach churned at the thought. "Okay. Have you taken Luke to day care already?"

"Yes, we got an early start today. See you soon."

Tally showed up on time, and shortly thereafter they headed south down the highway toward the film studio. Marla filled her in on last weekend's restaurant date with Dalton.

"Did the olive oil taste off to you?" Tally asked, after Marla complained about her queasiness since then.

"It had no taste at all. Isn't extra virgin olive oil supposed to have more flavor? From what I've read, it's first-pressed oil and may contain bits of olive. Regular olive oil, on the other hand, is refined through charcoal or chemical filters. Sometimes producers add a bit of virgin grade product to enhance it."

"Are you certain which one Tristan gave you?"

"I saw the label. It said extra virgin olive oil. Maybe it was old. It didn't seem rancid, though, and Tristan indicated it wasn't outdated."

"And you're still not feeling up to par? Maybe you picked up a stomach bug."

"That's possible. Dalton is okay, so it couldn't be what we ate. We had the same meal. And we had wine with dinner. You'd think the alcohol would kill off any germs."

"Let's hope you get over it quickly. I'm excited about seeing Raquel in action. She reminds me of Julia Child back in the day."

"How did she get this gig?"

"She said the producer liked her pitch and gave her a slot that had opened. Her cookbooks are popular, and her shows get high ratings. I expect they'll renew her contract when the time comes."

"Isn't she in competition with Becky regarding their recipe books?"

Tally shook her head, blond waves of hair fanning her face. "Not really. Becky's focus is on historical lore along with recipes derived from early Florida settlers. Raquel's emphasis is on modern techniques and using locally produced ingredients."

More questions hovered on Marla's tongue, but she held them back through the show. Raquel kept up a running banter while slicing and dicing in front of a live audience. Marla was interested to learn about the different varieties of salmon while the chef demonstrated how to prepare an Alaskan salmon terrine with asparagus sauce. The accompanying dish, a corn and cilantro couscous, didn't appeal to her because she had a distaste for the herb.

"If you're one of the few people who don't like cilantro, blame it on your genes,"

Raquel said in her Southern accent. "You have an olfactory gene that allows you to detect the smell of aldehyde chemicals, found in both cilantro and soap. So to you unfortunates, cilantro has a soapy taste. You can avoid the issue by using parsley instead of cilantro in your recipes."

"I'm glad to know it's not just me," Marla murmured to Tally, sitting beside her.

"Now here's a handy tip for removing corn kernels," Raquel continued, picking up a knife. "Take your freshly cooked ear of corn and hold it over the hole in a bundt pan like this. Scrape down the sides of the corn, and voilà. No mess!"

Marla watched entranced until Raquel finished production and had a free moment.

"Your show was wonderful," she told the chef. "And this kitchen set is amazing." She gestured to the cherry wood cabinets, granite countertops, and stainless steel appliances that were surrounded by a bevy of stage lights, wiring, and other production equipment. The seating area, now darkened, faced the stage.

"Thanks, although the clean-up is a bitch. Thank goodness for Carlos. Isn't that right?" Raquel flicked a seductive smile toward her assistant, scrubbing dirty dishes in the sink. The lanky man didn't bother to turn around and respond.

"It was generous of you to participate in the bake-off contest at the fall harvest festival," Marla mentioned.

"Sorry you two didn't win. Your entries were really quite good." Raquel took off her apron and tossed it onto a counter. She wore a flowery top with a straight skirt and costume jewelry with jade stones that enhanced her green eyes.

Marla glanced at the woman's piled-high blond hair. Darker roots were coming in that would better match the woman's olive complexion. She should offer her salon's services in case Raquel needed a colorist.

"Tally and I had a good time at the event, at least until I found Francine," Marla replied instead.

Raquel's eyes narrowed. "That woman got what she deserved. Too bad Alyce didn't join her. Neither one of them is . . . or was . . . on my friend list."

"Why is that?" Marla asked, while Tally wandered off to examine the fine points of the kitchen studio. She leaned against a counter, aware that Carlos might be listening.

"Alyce has accused me of using shortcuts for my behind-the-scenes preparation methods."

144

"You perform the demos in front of a live audience," Marla pointed out. "We can see how you do everything."

"Yes, but then I pull out my previously prepared dishes to show TV viewers and to give audience members a taste."

"Does it really matter how you complete those dishes?"

"It does to me. I won't have anyone damage my good name. No one, you hear?"

"O-kay. How about Francine? Had she ever featured you in her magazine?"

Raquel lifted her chin. "Sometimes, such as when I've had a guest chef, but she didn't go out of her way to feature my show. That woman rubbed lots of people the wrong way."

"Oh? Like who?"

"Talk to Tristan about her, and ask him what she said about his restaurant. It wasn't complimentary. But I suppose your detective husband has been learning all this on his own."

"He's been interviewing everyone present that day."

"I didn't like it when he showed up at my door. I won't have this nasty business affecting my daughter, you hear? None of the rumors floating around about me are true.

145

People are jealous of my popularity, that's all."

Marla raised an eyebrow. "I hadn't realized you were married."

"I'm divorced. It isn't easy putting my child through private school. Her father doesn't have enough money to pay child support. Occasionally, I'll get a publicity gig that pays a hefty fee. I like those events, because I can meet more high rollers. Otherwise, I've been fortunate with this show and my cookbook sales."

And the producer? Marla wanted to ask but didn't. The fellow had been present during the filming that morning but had vanished since then along with the rest of the crew.

"I'm a business owner, so I know what it's like to make your way in the world," Marla commented. "Here's my card. Please stop by if you're in the area, and I'll give you a discount on your first service. Do you happen to know who will take over *Eat Well Now* magazine with Francine gone?"

Raquel snorted. "Francine was listed as editorial director and publisher, but a conglomerate owns the publication. It'll be up to them to appoint a successor. Since we're being open with each other, Francine made a remark at the festival that bothers

146

me. She said Kinsdale Farms might not host the event next season. Bless their hearts, those family members are always so supportive of our community. Do you know what she meant?"

"Sorry, I'm in the dark in that regard," Marla hedged. "I overheard *you* speaking to Alyce that day. You stated that Francine wouldn't win the competition despite her threats."

Raquel leaned inward and lowered her voice. "Francine tried to blackmail the judges into voting for her. None of us would have it. We try to play fair, you understand, or we wouldn't be asked back again."

"Who invited you to be a judge? Was it Janet Winters?"

"She's a peach, that one. I love her to death. She's so good at organizing these affairs. Too bad her old man is such a snob."

And you're not? Marla fumbled with which thread to follow up on. "What did Francine have on Carlton Paige that would rile him?"

"Have you read his column lately?" Raquel asked with a snicker.

"I'm afraid not. I did speak privately to him, however. He acts resentful toward Alyce, not Francine."

"Just so." Raquel tapped her chin with a painted fingernail. "Am I mistaken, or was

Francine wearing Alyce's jacket when you found her?"

"How did you — ?"

"It was on the news. And I have an eye for detail."

Was it public knowledge? Marla didn't remember if Dalton had mentioned that tidbit in his media updates.

"I'm leaving," Carlos announced, approaching them. "You'll turn out the lights, yes?" he reminded Raquel.

"Naturally." Raquel stroked his head like a pet. "See you later, hot stuff. Don't forget to get those supplies I ordered." She gazed after him as he left, undisguised interest in her eyes.

Tally rejoined them and addressed Raquel. "I have a message for you from Becky who says hello. She'd like to treat you for lunch as thanks for endorsing her latest book."

Raquel gave a wide grin. "Becky is a sweetheart. I love what she does at the museum. Her research is fascinating, and she has a talent for transcribing it into her recipe books to share with readers."

"We heard one of her lectures," Marla remarked. "It's too bad she didn't win the bake-off contest. She'd planned on using the prize money to purchase a new collection for the museum. I agreed to help her with a fundraiser. We're going to do a bad hair day clinic at the salon."

"That's very kind of you, Marla. Becky is one of my strongest supporters. She needs all the help she can get."

"Really? I thought she was doing well between her curator position and her authorship."

"Things aren't always what they seem. Now if you'll excuse me, I have a radio interview in thirty minutes, and I need to prepare," Raquel said with an air of dismissal.

Tally's cell phone rang. Her gaze clouded as she glanced at the caller ID. "It's the day care center. Hello?" A brief silence ensued while Tally listened. "Okay, I'll be there shortly." She hung up and turned to Marla. "Luke is fussing. He might have a fever. I have to go pick him up."

Raquel grabbed Tally's arm. "You shouldn't leave your kid at those places. Hire a nanny and keep him home until he's school age."

"Excuse me?" Tally shook her off. "I have a career to restart. Besides, Luke likes having other people around. It helps with his socialization."

"Like they know the difference at that age? Heed my warning. One little mistake and . . ." Raquel seemed to recover herself and straightened her spine. "Never mind. What you do with your child is your business. It was good seeing you, ladies."

Marla noticed Raquel's accent became less pronounced when she got emotional.

"Thanks for speaking to us," she replied with a polite smile. She grasped Tally's elbow and herded her toward the door. "What was that about?" she asked in a hushed tone.

Tally gave her a troubled glance. "I don't know, but I believe Raquel is right in one regard. None of these people are what they seem. I wouldn't trust any of them past the door."

CHAPTER NINE

Marla had the rest of the day free once Tally dropped her off at home. She didn't want to sit idle when she could learn more about the suspects in Dalton's case. The sooner he put the killer behind bars, the sooner their life could return to normal. She decided to pay a visit to Alyce Greene, the food blogger. She took off in her car once she'd freshened up and let the dogs out.

Alyce's address led her to a single-story ranch house in Cooper City. She resided in one of those gated communities where lines of service people waited to get in and the guards swiped your driver's license. Marla appreciated the added security layer but knew from Dalton that smart burglars could jump the surrounding hedge or enter the community via the lake in the back. A barking dog was the best deterrent.

Alyce answered the door at her summons. She wore an apron over tan shorts and a clover top. "Marla! I was surprised when the guard notified me you were here."

"Sorry, I should have called first, but I was in the neighborhood and thought I would stop by. Is this a good time?"

"I'm in the middle of making a vegetable gumbo for dinner, but come on in. I just have to set the timer."

Marla trailed her into the kitchen, noting high ceilings, an open flowing design, and a screened-in pool patio facing a lake in the back. She scanned the cluttered counter-tops and the refrigerator decorated with children's art work. Her nose sniffed sautéed onions. Instead of appealing to her, the aroma caused her to feel queasy.

"You have two kids, right?" she asked to get her mind off bodily functions.

Alyce programmed the timer and then gestured for Marla to take a seat at the kitchen table. "Yes, Jed and Jackie. They're my pride and joy. How about you?"

"We don't have any children of our own yet, but Dalton has a teenage daughter from a previous marriage."

"Enjoy the time you have together, be-cause if you have a baby, it changes every-thing. Can I offer you a cup of coffee?" Alyce pointed to a single-serve brewer on the counter.

"I'd love one, thanks." Maybe it would help settle her stomach. "How are you doing since the bake-off contest?"

"I was having fun until . . . you know. I'd met a lot of my readers at the fair."

"That must have been gratifying. It's too bad things had to end on such a sad note."

"Poor Francine. Has your husband discovered any viable leads in his investigation?" Alyce removed her apron and tossed it onto a vacant chair. She inserted a K-cup after filling the coffeemaker with water.

"If he has, he's not sharing them with me. I'm friends with Arnie Hartman who owns Bagel Busters in the same shopping strip as my salon and day spa. Arnie has known Rory Kinsdale since his school days. He says Rory is worried about the farm's future."

"I'd hate to see anything happen to them. They supply organic produce to restaurants in the area. The farm-to-table movement is so important to our country's health."

"I'm familiar with the term, but what does it mean to you?" Marla accepted a mug of coffee from Alyce, who settled in a chair across from her after putting cream and sugar on the table.

Alyce brushed a wisp of short hair off her face. Her pixie cut looked as though she'd applied mousse and finger-fluffed it. "People prefer fresh fruits and vegetables grown with minimal use of pesticides and chemical fertilizers. Green farmers rely on crop diversity, beneficial insects, and pest-resistant plants to control insects and weeds. Soil conservation is important, too. They'll use sugar cane as windbreakers, cover crops, and low-impact cultivation methods to prevent erosion."

"That sounds better than wearing the land down."

"It's healthier for you, too. Locally raised food decreases the time it sits around before reaching your plate. It has a higher nutrient value and retains its flavor more than items you buy at the chains. Chefs love to buy local when they have a choice. That's why we have to support independent farmers like the Kinsdales."

"So you haven't heard anything about their farm being in trouble?" Marla asked, wrapping her fingers around the mug. The coffee was rich and flavorful, although her stomach seemed more sensitive than normal. Perhaps this roast was stronger than the one she made at home. She added a tad more cream to dilute it further.

"Kinsdale Farms doesn't have any blots on its record to my knowledge. I investigate all of my sources thoroughly, you understand." Alyce paused to frown at Marla. "Well, there was that one time when a worker vanished."

Marla straightened her spine. "What happened?"

"Rumor said he had a silo accident, but if so, it wasn't reported. That's not an uncommon occurrence on a farm. Hazards are everywhere, from silos to machinery to animals."

"They don't raise cattle at Kinsdale Farms," Marla pointed out. "But when I spoke to Rory's wife, she was concerned for his safety."

"Tractor accidents are the leading cause of deaths and injuries on farms. She should be worried about him. It's a dangerous place to work, unless you know what you're doing."

"Rory was raised on the farm. I'm sure those boys are well aware of the dangers. But you gave me a good idea. I'll ask my husband to look into the farm's accident record."

If Zach had covered up one death on his property, there could be more. And she'd also advise Dalton to check into the hired help to see if they had proper documentation. He should be able to confirm their citizenship status and see who was around on the day of the bake-off.

Alyce jabbed a finger at her. "Make sure your husband doesn't jeopardize that farm in any way. We need more places like Kinsdale Farms to grow our food."

"Do you think Francine knew something about them that got her killed?"

"Francine could have riled anyone. It would have been easy to follow her into the fields if that's where she went to hide for the scavenger hunt. Or maybe she went there to meet someone."

Marla gave her a startled glance. That possibility would make her death less of a crime of chance. "Did you notice anyone missing during the game?"

"No, I was too busy schmoozing. But if you're looking to cast blame, check out Raquel Hayes. She takes shortcuts on her show and deceives viewers."

"How so?" Marla asked in an innocent tone, as though Raquel hadn't already told her about Alyce's accusations.

"She doesn't make things from scratch or use the products she claims. It's no surprise, since Raquel couldn't make it on her own as a chef. She only got this gig by sleeping with the producer. If she doesn't do something to raise her ratings, her show could be cancelled."

Wow, you don't mince words. "That would upset Becky, the museum curator. Becky likes the publicity when Raquel has her on the show to talk about her new cookbooks."

"I'll bet she does. Sometimes I wonder about those two, at least from Becky's angle. Raquel may be straight as a page margin, but Becky is still single."

Marla's mouth gaped. "Are you saying Becky has a thing for the TV chef?"

"Stranger people have gotten together, luv."

"I thought Raquel's show was doing well. She didn't give me the impression otherwise."

"Shows are cancelled on television all the time. If she drops out of favor with the producer, she's toast. And I wouldn't count on Becky bailing her out. Her job isn't safe, either."

Were these claims true, or was Alyce merely casting aspersions on others to take the heat off herself? "Becky said she wanted the prize money to buy a collection of artifacts for the museum," Marla stated. "She must feel her position is stable to be so generous."

"That's a load of hogwash. The curator lied if she told you the cash was meant to purchase a new exhibit. She's hoping to save the museum from its creditors."

Marla stared at Alyce. Had Dalton verified the bake-off contestants' job status and business plan proposals? The more she learned about them, the less she trusted these people.

"My husband hasn't mentioned anything about the museum's status being in jeopardy," Marla admitted. "What do you know that we don't?"

Alyce pecked at a smudge on the table with her unpainted fingernail. "The city's budget cuts have hurt the museum. They need to pay back their last construction loan. Otherwise, they could default on it. If Becky filed a business plan that says otherwise, she's lying to appease her board of directors."

"Where did you get this information?" Marla asked with a note of skepticism. Who was telling tales here — Alyce the food blogger or Becky the museum curator?

"My brother, Steve, is an investment advisor. His firm provided the loan. But I realize Becky means well. She does a good job of educating the public with her lectures. If she'd meant to pay back the borrowed money and save the museum, good for her. Raquel, on the other hand, deserves to be derailed." Alyce's lips twisted in a derisive smile.

Marla had an insight and pounced on it. "Did your brother's company also provide the starter loan for your husband's food truck operation?"

"Yep, and Steve isn't pressuring us or anything, but that loan weighs heavily on our minds. We'd like to pay it off and move on."

"I can imagine so." Marla floundered for what to say next. Alyce seemed eager to talk, so she should take advantage. Maybe the woman got lonely working from home. She decided to introduce a touchy topic. "You know, Francine was wearing your jacket that day. Do you suppose the killer meant to get you instead? I mean, the woman was hit from behind, and you'd be tough to tell apart with your similar statures and haircuts."

Alyce's gaze hardened. "What are you saying, Marla?"

"I can't help wondering if you were the intended target that day and not Francine."

Alyce shot to her feet and raked her fingers through her short hair. "That's absurd. Who would want to do me in? Francine had her share of enemies."

"Like who? Do you have any suspicions

besides the people you've already mentioned?"

"Steve's firm manages Tony Winters' accounts. Steve has hinted there's something fishy about Amalfi Consolidated. I have an idea what it is, but I need evidence. Maybe Francine got wind of it and threatened to expose them."

"Can you tell me what this involves?"

Alyce's lips pursed. "Not until I can back up my theory with hard proof."

Marla, sensing a dead end in that direction, changed tactics. "How does Carlton Paige feel about your blog? Aren't you two rivals for the same audience?"

"That pompous ass blows a lot of hot air. His reviews are questionable, if you get my drift. If anyone's job is in jeopardy, it's probably his."

"He gave a high rating to The Royal Palate. Dalton and I ate there over the weekend. Their menu items were too eclectic for our tastes. Tristan was kind to give us a tour of his kitchen and a taste of his desserts."

"Tristan suspects the truth but he's afraid to say anything. The restaurant's ads claim they buy their ingredients from sustainable resources. That's baloney. Lots of restaurants claim they buy from environmentally-friendly green farms. Maybe they start out that way, but then they go for cheaper choices. They have to offer food at a price consumers will pay, while buying the best ingredients they can afford. But soon it becomes buy low and sell high."

"Like seafood that's mislabeled? I've read about that. It's a common occurrence."

"You're buying a cheaper brand, and you don't know it. Same goes for locally grown heirloom tomatoes that are really from Mexico, or chickens supposedly raised by humane methods. How can you, as a diner, tell where your food really originated? And do you care?"

"It's clear that you do."

Alyce gave a firm nod. "That's my job. I'll actually call the source when a restaurant or food market makes a claim that seems doubtful. That Florida blue crab you might enjoy? It likely comes from the Indian Ocean. I've discovered farmed trout from Idaho, beef from Colorado, and yellowfin tuna from the northern East Coast. They're from as far away as you can get but restaurants claim they are Florida-sourced. I even once found Parmesan cheese bulked up with wood pulp."

"Eww, that's gross. So how can we know what we're eating?"

"You can't. I have a friend who works in a

161

lab. He does DNA testing for me. Plus, I trace bills of sale back to their origins. Restaurant owners and market vendors lie in their ads all the time. Take wild Alaskan Pollock, for example. In one organic market, it was actually made from frozen Chinese fish treated with preservatives. Their Florida-caught shrimp? It came from a fish farm in India. The homemade chocolate cake that looked lip-smacking good? Out of a box you could buy in the supermarket. And let's not forget the drinks. One fancy restaurant I know refills their Evian bottles with tap water and has a house wine that's a dump from leftover bottles."

"I think I'll eat at home for a while." Marla would have to subscribe to Alyce's blog. It appeared she did a service to consumers, but how many providers had she offended along the way? Did she inadvertently ruin someone's business without being aware of the damage she'd caused? Dalton should view the comments on her blog to see if any of them were particularly vitriolic.

Alyce had given her much to think about, but her brain was getting too addled to sort it all out. With a stretch, Marla rose. Her limbs had gone stiff, and she had other errands to do.

The timer on the range chose that moment to beep its conclusion. Alyce bustled over to turn off the burner. "Wait, Marla. How about a taste of my vegetable gumbo? It's a healthy main dish."

"Okay, sure." She had to admit to being curious about Alyce's cooking skills. Did she offer recipes on her blog?

Alyce handed her a bowl. Marla accepted a spoon and dug in. She detected baby corn, onions, peppers, red kidney beans, and zucchini among other ingredients.

"It's delicious," Marla said, but before another word came out, her stomach revolted. "Excuse me, can I use your bathroom?"

She put the bowl down and rushed in the direction Alyce indicated. Her stomach heaved but nothing came out. Great, she must still have a virus in her system. Or perhaps she'd developed a food allergy.

Did the gumbo contain olive oil? Maybe a batch of imported oil had become contaminated and should be recalled. But then a lot more people would have gotten sick, wouldn't they?

"I'm sorry. It wasn't your food. I must still have a touch of a stomach bug. I'd better leave," Marla said to Alyce upon her return to the kitchen.

Alyce showed her to the door. "Take care of yourself. And Marla, let me know if you learn anything more about Francine. It makes me nervous to know a killer is running around town."

That's understandable, Marla thought, *especially because the murderer might have been after you.*

CHAPTER TEN

Marla pulled into her driveway just as her neighbor Susan was bringing her kids home from school. The Feinbergs lived two doors down on the east side of the street. Susan drove a silver model SUV, had a smoky-colored cat that detested the outdoors, and baked the best brownies on the block. A twinge of envy hit Marla. They were the same age, and yet Susan was way ahead of her in the children department.

Wait a minute. Susan worked as a consulting editor for a women's magazine and she wrote a blog. Could she be acquainted with Francine or Alyce by any chance?

Marla rushed inside her house, greeted the dogs, and let them out into the fenced backyard. Then she hurriedly refreshed herself before exiting once again. The mild October air entered her lungs. Soon it would get cold by her standards, and she'd freeze as soon as she walked out the door.

Any temperature below seventy qualified as chilly.

She should be enjoying the drier weather instead of running to and fro like a mad hatter. Dalton had told her that expression originated from the days of early hat makers. They had used mercury to stabilize wool during the felting process and didn't realize exposure to these vapors could be toxic. They'd suffered neurologic impairment as a result. That part didn't apply to her, but she certainly felt frazzled.

Outside, she paused on the sidewalk to admire a pink bougainvillea bush across the street. Was it really her business to chase down suspects? Dalton appreciated her input but could get by without it. Shouldn't she focus on the things that mattered most, like family?

Brianna would be going to college soon. What would Marla do if having children wasn't in her cards?

An empty future yawned in front of her. While she kept occupied with her salon and day spa, she'd cast aside her ambitions to become an educator. Her dreams of traveling could become a reality, but Dalton wouldn't be able to retire for a number of years. In the meantime, shouldn't she assist him in every way possible so he would have more quality time for family events?

In a thoughtful mood, she turned toward Susan's house. The woman wrote a blog filled with wisdom and inspiring messages for other housewives. Maybe Susan could offer some advice.

"Hey, Marla, how are you?" Susan said upon greeting her at the door.

Marla's glance rose to Susan's hair, layered and wavy at shoulder length. She came to Marla's salon for her highlights every other month. "I'm good, thanks. I know you just got home, but do you have a few minutes to talk? I can follow you around if you have things to do."

"No problem. We're eating leftovers tonight, so I don't have to fix dinner. Come on in."

Their cat sidled up to Marla as she stepped inside the house, which smelled from lemon furniture polish. Susan led her past the kitchen into the family room.

"Donny and Jess, come say hello to Mrs. Vail," Susan called. The children, ages ten and seven respectively, dutifully obeyed. Then Donny and his sister ran off, chasing the cat.

Marla took a seat on the sofa as indicated and refused an offered drink. She folded her hands, her posture stiff. Although comfortable chatting at the salon with the woman, she felt awkward here. "I'm helping my husband with another case," she began, sticking to safe ground. "You've heard about the fall harvest festival at Kinsdale Farms?"

Susan nodded, her brown eyes regarding Marla shrewdly. "You found another body, right? I can't imagine how you keep doing that and stay so calm."

Marla wove her fingers together. "I'm not, really. It bothers me each time, but I put it aside in another part of my brain so the images don't haunt me."

"I'm still haunted by Alan Krabber's death next door."

"Me, too. It doesn't seem to bother the young couple that moved in there. Are you friendly with them?" Marla had only exchanged polite words with their new neighbors.

"They keep to themselves pretty much," Susan replied. "I'd rather not be invited inside their place anyway."

Marla winced. "I know what you mean. I'm wondering if you knew Francine Dodger, publisher of *Eat Well Now* magazine. She's the person who was killed at the harvest festival."

Susan's face sobered, and she crossed her legs. She wore jeans and a loose top and kept her figure trim at the gym. "I've met her, but we weren't friends if that's what you mean. She seemed a no-nonsense type. I got the impression people respected her and the magazine did well. Who's taking over her position?"

"I have no idea, but I plan to make a visit there one of these days to talk to the staff." Could rivalries at the publication have played a role in Francine's death? She'd have to ask Dalton how far he'd gotten in interviewing their personnel.

Jess ran into the room and clutched her mother's legs. "Mommy, Donny took my string bracelet. Make him give it back."

Jess's two front teeth were missing. A cascade of acorn brown hair hung down her back. The kid would be a looker when she grew up. A pang of longing struck Marla. What would it be like to have a miniature version of herself running around? Jess bore a distinct resemblance to her mom.

"Donny," Susan yelled, "I've warned you not to take your sister's things. Give it back right now, or you'll lose your iPad privileges."

The boy stumbled into the room with a contrite look on his face. "Here, take it." He thrust the bracelet at his sibling. "Next time, don't steal my favorite comics."

The pair ran off, pushing at each other and grousing. Susan gave Marla an exasperated grin. "See what you have to look forward to if you and Dalton ever have children."

Marla allowed a morose expression to cross her face. "Believe me, I'd like to have that problem. After years of not wanting kids of my own, now I can't wait. We're trying, but nothing is happening."

"How long have you been working on it?"

"It's been over six months since I've gone off the pill. Our families would love it if Dalton and I had kids together."

"Be sure it's what you want. Once you have a baby, your entire life changes."

"Dalton knows what it's like. His daughter will be going to college soon. Maybe I should give up chasing crooks to focus on our family while she still lives with us. I could be overburdening myself with too many activities, and that's inhibiting me from conceiving."

Susan wagged a finger at her. "Don't stop what you are doing. You're a crime-solver as well as a salon owner. Heck, if not for you, Alan Krabber's killer might still be terrorizing the neighborhood. You're good at sleuthing. And you help your husband with his cases. Have you ever thought that maybe it's your true calling?"

Marla's skin prickled. She'd been told so by a psychic in Cassadaga.

"My bat mitzvah portion was about pursuing justice. I do feel strongly about finding closure for families of crime victims. But it drains my energy for other things, like getting pregnant."

"Don't be absurd. It's not any of your activities causing a lack of conception. Go get tested. You'll feel better when you receive solid results."

"You're right. I'll talk to Dalton about it, but not until he solves Francine's murder. Don't you work for a magazine besides writing a blog?"

Susan nodded, petting her cat that had sidled up to her and rubbed her ankles. "I'm a consulting editor for *Ladies Town Post*. We cover social events in the tri-county area and include women's interest articles. Fortunately, it's a job I can do from home. I also write a blog called Count Your Blessings. My slant is a humorous view of our daily hassles. It amazes me how my readership has grown when I don't make any effort to publicize the site."

Marla tilted her head. "Alyce Greene writes a food blog. She was a contestant at the bake-off. She's very enthusiastic about the farm-to-table movement and sustainable farming techniques. Do you follow her posts?"

"I'm a fan of hers. I love her chatty writing style, and she infuses her articles with humor. It's such a contrast to Carlton Paige's acerbic remarks. Have you seen his column? We don't go to the restaurants he reviews. They're too expensive and not family-friendly places."

"Guess I'll have to start reading the Sunday newspaper. Dalton likes to do the crosswords."

"Really? So does David. We should go out together sometime without the kids."

"That's a wonderful idea. Let's check our calendars and get back to each other to set a date." Marla stood, not wishing to outstay her welcome. "Look, if you hear anything in the rumor mill about any of these people, can you let me know?"

"Of course." Susan rose to accompany her to the door. "Listen, Marla, you need to keep doing what you do. Don't doubt yourself. You're being led down this path for a reason."

"So I should have faith. Is that what you're saying?" Marla gave her a rueful glance. Susan and David went to temple on a regular basis, while Marla's religious practices had lapsed. She made holiday dinners, but that was about it. Susan seemed more in touch with her spiritual side, whereas Marla continually questioned her purpose.

Susan tapped her arm. "Our streets are safer due to your diligence. And you make us women look good in the process," she added with a laugh. "Follow your instincts, and you'll be true to yourself."

Susan's words echoed in her mind as Marla trudged home. *Follow your instincts.* She hadn't yet visited Francine's magazine offices. And what about the newspaper where Carlton worked? Did he have any issues with his colleagues? His co-workers might know how he felt about Alyce and if he had any anger management problems.

She put both of those items on her mental to-do list but couldn't act on them for the next few days. Work kept her busy, and so did commitments to Brianna's after-school activities.

On Wednesday, she and Dalton finally had the chance to exchange news.

"What puzzles me," he said over the dinner table, before he had to take Brianna to a debate team meeting, "is that the trail runs cold on Raquel Hayes. She showed up on the cooking scene like a tornado, but I can't get anything on her before she became a chef. She's not in any of the databases. It's like she didn't exist beforehand."

"That's odd. Where did she get her training?"

"Johnson and Wales in Miami. They have her school records, but I can't trace anything back before her prior jobs in the field." His brow wrinkled as he stuck a forkful of chicken tenderloin into his mouth.

"So what are you thinking?"

He chewed and swallowed. "I'm not sure Raquel Hayes is her real name."

"Can't you ask the woman for documentation?" Marla asked, passing him the mashed potatoes for a second helping.

"I have, and she gave me some excuse. I'll have to dig deeper, but it bothers me."

"Your hunches are usually accurate. What about the other suspects?" She glanced at the dogs. Lucky had settled onto his bed in the family room, while Spooks roamed at their feet hoping for a morsel. Brianna had downed a quick meal and was getting ready for her meeting.

"They all seem to point the finger at somebody else."

"Tell me about it. Carlton Paige blames Alyce for his drop in readership. If the killer meant to get her instead of Francine, he'd

174

be at the top of my list. Did Alyce tell you about her husband's business? He owns a food truck enterprise. His starter loan came from Alyce's brother, Steve, who is an investment advisor. Steve's firm manages Tony Winters' accounts. Does this mean he handles the guy's personal investments, or their company's business?"

"He could manage both accounts," Dalton suggested.

"Steve hinted to his sister that something seemed off about Amalfi Consolidated, so he must have insider knowledge where they're concerned. Carlton's wife, Sally, knows something that would smudge Alyce's reputation. Maybe it's not about Alyce as much as Steve. He could be cooking the books for Tony's company, or perhaps he suspects somebody else at his firm of doing the same." Marla rubbed her temples. Her forehead throbbed from so many complexities.

Dalton's mouth tightened in frustration. "These people are all connected. My focus at the moment is on the victim, not Alyce Greene. Ms. Dodger could have been researching an article for her magazine and hit pay dirt. I interviewed the staff at her publication. She'd been excited about an exposé she had been writing. We took her

175

hard drive, but our techs haven't found anything meaningful. Nor did she keep notes on this article, at least none that I could find."

"I'd like to stop by their offices to have a chat with her colleagues. I might learn something new."

He nodded, his warm gaze sweeping her. "It's worth a try. What else have you come across?"

She gave a weary sigh. "I can't remember right now. Were you able to find out any more about the farm's ownership?"

"The property tax record shows the Kinsdales making payments, and yet the deed is registered to another man. Some sales records were lost back in the 1960s, although I believe the Kinsdales arrived a decade earlier."

"If they did buy the property, could the record have gotten lost then? It doesn't make sense otherwise. They should have a copy of the new deed."

"We're still looking into it."

Marla got up to take their empty dishes to the sink. "I need to have another chat with the history museum curator. According to Alyce, Becky lied when she said she'd meant to donate her prize money toward purchasing a new collection. The city's budget cuts have hurt the museum. They have to pay back their last construction loan, or they could default on it. If Becky filed a business plan that claimed otherwise, she was lying."

Dalton stood and stretched. "How does Alyce know about this?"

"Her brother's investment firm supplied the loan."

"I need to interview him. But that's enough on the case for now. We'll look at things again in the morning when we have a fresh viewpoint."

The next day, Marla finally had time to consult Becky Forest at the historical museum. She sat in the woman's office, ostensibly to discuss their mutual fundraiser. Crossing her legs, she swung her foot back and forth while debating how to start. Becky looked frazzled, her hair clipped off her face. The cream top she wore complemented her caramel skin, but the knitted brown skirt made her appear frumpy. It was like she'd gotten up on the wrong side of the bed.

"Janet Winters has volunteered to help publicize our event," Marla began. "She's a whiz at social events, so she'll know who to contact for publicity. My staff is excited. We'll put a poster in our window and can hand out flyers to our customers. Our receptionist is collecting emails to start a newsletter."

"Don't forget the library. You can put notices there, too," Becky said, her face easing into a smile and erasing her lines of concern.

"I saw Tristan Marsh the other day. Dalton and I ate at his restaurant, and I asked him about donating desserts. He said he'd have to get permission, but I haven't heard back from him. I could stop by there again to push for an answer."

Becky picked up a ballpoint pen and clicked it on and off. "Did you like his place? It's too high class for me. I don't care for their menu."

"I agree, although we did like our fish entrée. Tristan gave us a tour of the kitchen after we'd finished our meals. He said the executive chef was hired by Mr. Romano, the owner, after the previous man was fired. Their restaurant buys supplies from Amalfi Consolidated."

Becky tilted her head, a look of puzzlement in her eyes. "Isn't that the company run by Janet's husband?"

"Yes, and she isn't fond of Tony's Italian relatives who are planning a trip here. I wonder what's going on with them."

"I wouldn't know. Doubtless your husband has interviewed Mr. Winters."

"Tristan gave me a taste of their extra virgin olive oil at the restaurant." Marla rubbed her stomach with a grimace. "I haven't felt quite right ever since and am wondering if it was rancid."

"Unless you're an expert on those things, you might not be able to tell the difference. Who knows what's in most of those bottles at the supermarket? Do you read the labels to see if they're outdated?"

"Not always. Anyway, what else have you done for the fundraiser?"

Becky's dark eyes lit with enthusiasm. "I'll be promoting the event in our museum newsletter. And I plan to ask the city for support as well. After all, they subsidize the museum."

At last, here's the opening I need. "Just how invested is the town in this place?" Marla asked. "I mean, don't our taxes go toward supporting the museum? Is there a mortgage on the building?"

"The mortgage is fully paid off."

"Maybe so, but I understand the construction loan for the new wing has a balance due."

Becky put her pen down. "Where did you hear that? From your detective husband? If you must know, I didn't want the prize money for the collection I'd mentioned, although I'd love to purchase it for our exhibits. However, we won't be open much longer if we can't pay off that loan. The city's contribution doesn't cover it. Their budget cuts have threatened our solvency."

"Along with your job, I would imagine," Marla added with a cynical twist to her lips.

Becky's mouth thinned as she regarded Marla from across her desk. "This museum serves an important purpose in the community. I'd hate to see it close its doors. If that happens, I could probably make it on my own with the royalties from my cookbooks and with teaching gigs. But I need Raquel's continued support to publicize my books and raise my profile. Being on her TV show provides me with credible references. I get offers to speak at places afterward that I wouldn't receive otherwise. And I always put in a plug for the museum on those occasions. It draws in visitors who leave donations."

"So you admit that you lied on your business proposal to the bake-off committee?"

Becky hung her head. "I would buy the collector's entire repertoire if we could afford it. Call it wishful thinking. But the loan has to be paid off first. I meant well, Marla."

"Did Francine know? I mean, would the

article she'd intended to write for her magazine be about the museum?"

"I doubt it. Francine had never set foot inside of here."

"How about Alyce? Did she ever interview you for her food blog? She'd be a good source of publicity for your cookbooks, I'd think."

"She's not into history. However, she is into gossip. That woman should stop sticking her nose into everyone's business," Becky said with a touch of venom.

"Oh? What's she been doing?"

"That little do-gooder has been spreading rumors about Raquel. Alyce isn't all honey and sweets like she'd let you believe. She can have a nasty streak."

Marla pretended innocence. "What does she have against the TV chef?"

"You know how Alyce tracks people's food sources in the industry? She asked the producer for a list of supplies Raquel requisitioned for her show. Would you believe that busybody said Raquel uses prepared mixes for the samples she gives her audience?"

"So what? She makes her recipes from scratch for the live demo on her show."

"Exactly, but consumers expect her to be blemish-free. No one is that pure. Who cares if Raquel takes a few shortcuts off-camera? She was hopping mad when she heard about Alyce's request. Raquel and the producer have a thing, and she didn't like it when he questioned her."

"Raquel told you all this?" Marla scratched her arm where a small red welt appeared. She must have let in a mosquito at her entrance.

"We're friends outside of the studio. Friends support each other, Marla. They don't look for ways to tear each other down."

"Did you know Raquel before she got her gig? Dalton has been having a hard time tracing her background prior to culinary school."

Becky's gaze shuttered. "We don't talk about the past when we're together. By the way, I hear Alyce had a row with Sally Paige at the gym the other day. One of my friends told me about it. She couldn't hear what they were saying. Did you ever speak to Carlton like I'd suggested?"

Marla knew very well that Becky meant to distract her. "Yes, and he hinted that Sally knew something unsavory about Alyce." Or Alyce's brother, but Marla didn't say that aloud. "You're sure you didn't notice anyone missing between the time when our contest members dispersed at the harvest festival and when the awards were announced?"

"Nope, I was busy talking to people." Becky's eyes widened. "Hey, I just had a brilliant idea. Instead of relying on Tristan for desserts, why don't you approach Teri from the artisan chocolate factory? She might like to participate in our fundraiser. Her treats would be a big hit, and she'd benefit from the publicity. You could always tell Tristan someone else had volunteered in his place."

Marla's mood lifted. "That's a wonderful suggestion. I'll ask Tally to come with me when I go to see Teri. She's a big chocolate fan." And it would give the two of them a chance to catch up. She couldn't wait to share the latest news with her best friend.

CHAPTER ELEVEN

Tally squealed on the phone when Marla mentioned a trip to the chocolate factory. "I'd love to go. I've been doing paperwork all morning, and it's so tedious. Do you have time for me to show you the location I've picked out for my new shop?"

Marla glanced at her watch with a frown. "It's eleven, and I have to be at work by one. I doubt we'll have time to do both. I can approach Teri about the fundraiser another time. I'd rather see your new place."

After Tally's accident, Marla had told herself their friendship would come first, no matter the imperatives with her job or her crime-solving exploits. If she'd been a better listener, she might have learned her friend's secrets before they had harmed people she loved.

"I'm excited about this site," Tally said a short while later upon hopping into Marla's car. "There's a restaurant on one corner that draws customers from the nearby mall and a couple of upscale gift shops in the strip. My dress boutique with a café at the other end will be a good fit. The landlord agrees and has offered me a discount on the deposit."

"Have you signed a contract already?" Marla asked, alarmed about her friend making hasty decisions.

"No, just a letter of agreement. I'm having my lawyer look over the terms. You can examine the lease too, if you'd like. I would value your opinion."

"Have you found a chef who's willing to partner with you on the café aspect?" Marla turned west on Sunrise Boulevard, heading toward the Sawgrass Mills complex.

Tally grimaced. "Not yet. Maybe Teri knows somebody. I wish we had time to visit her place now."

"I could take a break at lunch tomorrow and run over there with you," Marla offered.

"All right, you've got a date. Did I tell you what Luke's doing now?" Tally launched into a description of her fourteen-month-old son's latest antics, while Marla's heart squeezed. She missed seeing Luke on a daily basis.

"Earth to Marla. Are you listening?" Tally's face crumpled. "Oh, I'm sorry. I know you miss Luke. You can come over anytime, Marla. He'd love for you to visit."

"I know. I've been busy talking to people involved in Dalton's case."

"How is that coming? Any leads you can share?"

Marla reflected back to the days when she would eagerly call Tally to discuss a case and review the various suspects. Now with child care as Tally's priority and a career move to plan, Marla didn't want to bother her. She had Robyn and Nicole at work who both took an interest in her sleuthing adventures.

Then again, Tally was invested in this case since she'd been at the bake-off and knew the contestants. Plus, she was always good at seeing things from a new perspective. Maybe Marla had been too quick to dismiss her participation.

"Here's what I've learned so far," she said, reviewing her findings to date.

"You should ask Teri if she noticed anyone missing from the bake-off group before the contest winners were announced," Tally remarked upon Marla's conclusion. "What time will you be available to visit her shop?"

"I'll be free at noon. How about if I swing by your house and pick you up?"

"Sounds good. I need to feed my choco-

186

late addiction. It'll hasten my recovery."

"Don't let me buy anything. I don't need the extra calories."

Nonetheless, when Marla entered the shop with Tally on Friday, the scent of chocolate overpowered her. Maybe she would get a treat for Dalton.

They'd arrived just as Teri was wrapping up a tour. When the owner spied them, she signaled for her salesgirl to manage the café, which offered hot beverages and desserts. Teri moved behind the display counter where her artisan chocolates were available for purchase.

"I didn't play the Find Franny game," Teri said after Marla explained their purpose.

"So what did you do after you'd put away your supplies from the bake-off contest?" she asked, while Tally scrutinized the day's specialties for sale.

Teri straightened the white lab coat she wore over her street clothes. "I spoke to Zach Kinsdale about carrying my desserts in their marketplace in addition to my artisan pieces. They'd appeal to the upscale crowd he gets there."

"Did he agree?" Marla's gaze rose to the back wall where wrappers from international chocolate bars made an impressive work of art.

"He said he would try a few of them to start. If people bought the items, we could expand the order."

"Did he give any indication of how things were going for them? I'd like to see their farm succeed. We have so few places left in Broward County with U-pick fields."

"Francine's death will put a pall on future events, that's for sure."

"I'd observed her talking to Zach. Do you remember? You identified him for me."

Teri stared at her. "Yes, I recall. But you're not implying Zach Kinsdale —"

"Not at all. I'm hoping for a clearer picture of who was doing what that day."

A customer, wanting a selection of chocolates, interrupted their conversation. After Teri rang up the order, she turned back to Marla. Tally, meanwhile, had acquired a dish of chocolate mousse and was spooning it into her mouth with a heavenly expression on her face.

Teri chuckled. "I did see Tristan almost make a fool of himself. The idiot wasn't looking where he was going and walked into a wheelbarrow. A pile of dirt tumbled onto his boots. He staggered away, his face crimson as a red velvet cake."

"He was lucky it wasn't a load of manure," Marla added with a smile. "So that explains why he showed up with a limp on his way to the judging stand." The pastry chef had lied, stating he'd twisted his ankle at a dip in the grass. Likely he didn't care to admit his clumsiness.

"Too bad none of us won the competition," Teri said. "I'm trying to get an investor interested in my business plan. I still think a line of chocolate-based beauty products would have appeal."

"I'd buy them," Tally inserted, sauntering over. She'd finished her treat and placed the empty dish on the counter. "I've been meaning to ask you. Would you know anybody who'd like to run the café at my dress boutique? I tried the culinary school, but none of their candidates are interested."

Teri nodded sagely. "You might have more luck once your place is established. Have you found a new location?"

"Tally took me there yesterday," Marla said. "The site is perfect. It's close to the day care center where her son goes and is located in a busy shopping strip. The space is big enough for clothing racks and accessories on one side and a snack bar along the opposite wall."

"My goal is to encourage customers to linger," Tally added.

Teri pointed to the tables and chairs filled

with guests. "I understand completely. It really does help to boost sales. Do you have a theme, like a coffee bar or tea shop?"

"I've put a deposit on a lease agreement, but that's as far as I've gotten."

"Don't worry. The right partner will come along. Florida draws chefs same as crooks and tourists. They're looking for a place to get started."

Tally's blue eyes sparkled. "I can't wait to open my doors again. Marla has been so good about showcasing my collections at her day spa in the meantime. I haven't lost too many customers in my absence."

"You're fortunate to have such a good friend," Teri said.

"I need to decide if I should sell the same fashions or specialize in social occasions. It might be fun to try something different. The shop would be more of a destination that way."

"You mean, like prom dresses and mother-of-the-bride gowns? That could be fun, especially if you offered champagne like at bridal shops."

"Or your café could sell pastries and lunch items," Marla suggested. "If you don't get a chef, consider outsourcing the food instead."

"I have a lot to consider," Tally agreed.

Marla sought more questions to ask Teri about the harvest festival. "What else did you observe the day of the contest?" she finally asked the chocolatier. "Any detail might be important. I'd like my husband to solve this case so we can move on."

Tally strolled away while the other woman regarded her with a thoughtful expression. "Now that you mention it, I don't know where Raquel went. I didn't see her while I was working the crowd. Was she doing the scavenger hunt?"

"I figured she was schmoozing like you. If you didn't notice her, she could have been inside the marketplace."

"Or she might have been hanging out at the barbecue hut or vendor alley. I hope they do the spring festival next year. I love their corn maze."

"We'll have to see. Did you run into Alyce during this time?"

"She was busy chatting up the lady from Francine's magazine. You know, the features editor. I'd proposed an article to them once on the health benefits of dark chocolate, but Lynette turned me down. I didn't have any scientific credentials. She was nice about it, though."

Marla hadn't realized someone else from Francine's publication had attended. "Was this woman still there when the winners were announced?"

"I don't recall seeing her around. She must have left. It's Lynette Wilde if you want to look her up. Maybe Alyce was proposing an article for the magazine."

"That's possible." Surely Dalton had interviewed this person. He'd been to their offices and talked to Francine's colleagues.

Tally poked her in the ribs when she rejoined them. "You're forgetting the other reason we came here, Marla."

Marla slapped a hand to her mouth. "Lord save me, I almost forgot." She explained about her bad hair day clinic to benefit the historical museum. "Would you be interested in donating desserts? It would be great publicity for your chocolate factory."

Teri bounced on her heels. "I'd love to be included. You're sweet for thinking of me."

"*Your* sweets are what made us consider you," Tally said with a laugh. "I can't resist wanting to try everything when I'm here."

Marla's stomach knotted at the strong chocolate aroma in the shop. It hadn't bothered her earlier, but now she needed some fresh air. "Come on, Tally. I have to get back to work."

"Sure. Aren't you getting anything?" Tally wagged her eyebrows, as though indicating

Marla should make a purchase to support their friend's enterprise.

"Oh, thanks for reminding me. Teri, I'll take a half pound of the dark chocolate almond bark. That's my husband's favorite." Marla waited by the cash register to pay for her item. "Our salon receptionist will be in touch with more details about the fund-raiser," she promised, taking her bagged item.

Tally praised the chocolatier during their drive home. "Teri is an artist with her individual pieces. Her desserts will be a hit at your event. Will you be working on it this weekend or taking some time off?"

Marla pulled into Tally's driveway and put the car into Park. "I have a full schedule on Saturday, so I'll let Robyn handle the details. Tomorrow night, Dalton and I are double-dating with Ma and her boyfriend."

Tally's gaze scrutinized her. "That should be interesting. You like Reed, don't you?"

"I do, especially since Dalton's background check on him came back clear. He's a retired literature professor whose academic credentials are respected. And he makes Ma happy, which is all that counts. She misses seeing Luke."

Tally put her hand on the door handle. "Tell her I said hello and that she's welcome

193

to visit us anytime."

Back at the salon, Marla got busy with clients and didn't have a break until that evening. Brianna had plans for Friday night, and Dalton decided to work late at the office, so she had some free time on her own. She spent it researching gastrointestinal ailments on the computer. Maybe she'd contracted a virus that took a long time to resolve. Or it could be she'd developed food allergies. It wasn't unusual for people to have sudden sensitivities later in life.

One other possibility reared its head. She could be pregnant. The idea both excited and alarmed her. But if this were the case, wouldn't she have more symptoms than a sensitive stomach? She shoved this notion to the back of her mind, preferring to shift her focus to the murder investigation. Besides, she wouldn't want to get her hopes up prematurely.

Speaking of food problems, didn't Dalton's suspects relate to the industry in some manner? This seemed to be a connecting link between all of them. And yet, a vital part appeared to be missing.

"I can't figure it out," Marla said to her mother and Reed the following evening. "No one appears to have a strong enough motive to do away with Francine."

"And yet, someone cracked her on the head at the fall festival," Dalton pointed out between bites of garlic bread.

They'd met at a local Italian restaurant and sat sipping Chianti while waiting for their salads. Anita looked radiant in a sunshine yellow ensemble, while Reed appeared his usual dignified self in a dress shirt and belted dark gray pants. Since their cruise together, they'd grown closer. But although they spent most of their free time in each other's company, Anita still kept her modest two-bedroom home and Reed maintained his townhouse.

Marla wondered how much longer her mother would be able to keep up the house once she turned seventy. Another decade? Or would she and Reed decide to merge their households and move into a senior community at some point?

"Marla, why don't you let your husband pursue the case?" Anita suggested in her singsong tone. "You need to focus on more important things."

"Like what? Brianna will be going to college soon. If we don't have any children by then, I'd cut back my hours at the salon so we could travel. But Dalton won't be able to retire for some time yet."

"What about the expansion plans for your

salon? Didn't you want to add a snack bar at the day spa?"

"The space will be free once Tally opens her new shop and removes her stock from our lounge. She found a great location near Luke's day care center. She's planning to sell her house and move closer to her store's site."

"How is Luke? I miss the little guy." Anita's gaze grew wistful.

"That kid gets feistier every day. Tally has her hands full with him."

"You need a lot of energy to raise children. You'd better hurry up and have a baby before you hit forty."

"I'm trying, Ma. I don't need the added pressure, thanks."

Reed cleared his throat. The retired literature professor's hair had grayed more since she'd met him, but streaks of his boyish red still showed through. He aimed his piercing green eyes at her.

"So you still don't have a strong lead on the culprit in your case?" he asked, knowing talk of the crime would divert their attention.

Marla broke apart a piece of garlic bread. Familiar Italian melodies played in the background. "I still mean to visit Francine's magazine office and talk to her colleagues," she replied.

Dalton, seated on her right, tapped her arm. "Get this. Francine had a boyfriend. I only learned about him earlier today."

She gaped at him. "What? That's news to me. How did you discover this gem of information?"

"Francine's cell phone records showed them texting each other. The man teaches Middle Eastern history at NSU."

Reed's brows lifted. "What's his name? Maybe I know him."

"Colin Abubakar. It's hard to forget that one."

"I think I've heard of the fellow, although I don't know him personally. Would you like me to ask my former colleagues about the guy?"

"Sure, it couldn't hurt," Dalton agreed.

"So no one who knew Francine has mentioned this man?" Marla took a sip of water.

"That's correct. I'd like to track his movements to see if he was at the festival that day. We can triangulate his position from his cell phone records, but I would have to get a warrant to obtain them."

"Did you speak to him? Maybe he'll be cooperative."

"When I asked where he was at the time of Francine's death, he said he had to run

197

to a meeting and we could discuss things later."

"Did he appear upset about losing his girlfriend?"

"I'd say he was more agitated than grieving. I'm wondering how deep their relationship went if Francine didn't mention him to her friends."

"Did he have any theories about who might have harmed her?" Reed asked, his intelligent eyes regarding Dalton.

"He said her colleagues might have been jealous. But they indicated the article she'd been researching could be relevant to the case."

"I really have to get over there and talk to them," Marla said.

Their salads arrived, and they got busy eating. Conversation drifted to other mundane topics, while she mused over this new revelation. What was Francine's connection to this alleged boyfriend, and why hadn't she told anyone about him? Were they secret lovers, or was something else going on?

On Sunday, Dalton took the morning off from work. With a hot case, he couldn't stay away from the office for too long. After walking the dogs, he pulled the car from the garage. Marla and Brianna piled inside, and they headed to the local park for their usual

Sunday walk.

"Can I borrow a car?" Brianna asked as they strolled under a canopy of tall pine trees. "It's Amy's birthday today, and the restaurant where she's having her party is over by the beach. I thought I'd hang out there afterward with the gang."

Marla noticed Dalton's brow furrowing so she forestalled his retort. "You can use mine. I was planning to stay home and get caught up on things."

Brianna cast her a grateful glance. "Thanks, Marla. I should be back in time for dinner."

Glad to have some time alone that afternoon, Marla did the laundry, paid the bills, and took the dogs out again. She was back in the desk chair checking her emails when she noted a new message from Reed.

"I spoke to my friends at the university," he wrote. "They said this Abubakar fellow is always spouting off about Egyptian gods. Egyptology is his niche, so that doesn't surprise me. But one of the people in his department believes the guy's involvement goes deeper. He might be participating in ancient rituals. Perhaps that's why his girlfriend kept quiet about their relationship."

199

CHAPTER TWELVE

"My hands are tied until I can get a warrant," Dalton said later Sunday afternoon after he'd come home from work. She had forwarded Reed's message to him earlier. "I think the judge will grant it since this guy isn't being forthcoming about his movements that day."

Marla regarded him from the chaise lounge on their patio, where they sat enjoying glasses of lemonade and admiring the aqua water in their pool. Lucky and Spooks whined from inside the family room by the sliding glass door, but Marla had let them out earlier. After receiving no response, the dogs settled down.

"What about Francine's messages to the guy?" Marla asked. "Did you get any vibes about the nature of their relationship?"

"The texts and emails seemed innocent enough, like two friends talking. It was more the frequency that tipped me off they might have a closer connection."

"Take another look. You might learn which dates and times they got together."

He finished his drink, put down the glass, and rose. "I'll go get my laptop. Wait here."

Marla glanced at her watch. She'd have to put the eggplant rollatini into the oven pretty soon. She'd assembled the dish but had left off baking it until an hour before dinnertime. Dalton would make the salad when they were ready to eat, and Brianna — who'd come home — had already set the table.

Marla rarely had time to relax, and here they were talking crime-solving again. Would it always be this way, or would their mindsets change if she and Dalton had a baby?

He returned and opened his laptop. "Hey, listen to this," he said a few minutes later. "Abubakar's last message to Francine mentions tonight's date."

She sat up straight. "How so?"

"It says, 'Meet me at midnight by the Living Tree. All Hail Osiris.' "

"Osiris? Isn't he one of the Egyptian gods?"

"Yes, he's the god of the underworld. But what's the living tree? I'm not familiar with that term."

"Lots of cultures have a tree of life. Maybe it's a banyan."

"You could be right. There's one at the local park with a hollowed-out central core. Let's see if this tree relates to Egyptian mythology." Dalton touch-typed on his computer keys. "The banyan is featured in Asian creation stories and fertility rites. It's the national tree of India, where the biggest specimen covers more than four acres. In the United States, Thomas Edison planted the first banyan tree in Fort Myers in 1925. It grew from a seedling and now covers an entire acre of the estate."

Marla had seen the big trees throughout Florida parks. Its branches wrapped around other tree trunks and strangled them. "I believe the banyan is also known as the strangler fig," she mentioned.

Dalton continued reading. "The trees grow from seeds dropped onto leafy canopies by birds and mammals. The seedlings send down aerial roots. These woody vines encase and smother their hosts."

"Does a banyan produce fruit?"

"Yes, it's pollinated by a species of wasps that breed inside the figs. The trees need to produce on a continual basis to keep these pollinator wasps alive. As a source of fiber, vitamins, and minerals, figs support many species of wildlife. They've been an important food staple as far back as ancient Egypt. Pharaohs took dried figs to their graves to sustain their souls during the journey to the afterlife."

"What about the tree of life? Was the banyan part of Egyptian mythology in that regard?" Marla sipped her drink, listening to birds warbling and the occasional squawk of a neighborhood duck. She and Dalton should relax on the patio more often.

"Here we go. According to legend, Osiris was born from an *Acacia Nilotica* tree, and so he's believed to live inside the spirit of these trees. It's also called the gum arabic tree. Supposedly, the tree that God set on fire in front of Moses was an acacia tree. Hebrews used the wood from these sacred trees to build their temples."

Marla arched her brows. "You know the superstitious phrase, 'knock on wood'? Early believers felt spirits dwelled in trees. By knocking on wood, you could alert them to help you. Today we use the phrase to ward off evil. Lots of cultures revere trees in their early myths."

"Listen to this," Dalton said, squinting at the screen. "The acacia tree is the source of a chemical compound called Dimethyltryptamine, or DMT. Amazonians use it in a drink for shamanic rituals to induce a mind-altering experience."

"So this substance has psychedelic properties? Does the acacia tree grow in Florida?"

"Yes, but I'd say a banyan tree is more likely to be a meetup site, especially the one with a hollowed-out center at a local park."

Marla finished her lemonade in one gulp and rose. "I have to start dinner. What do you plan to do with this information?"

He put aside his laptop, stood, and stretched. "If people are gathering tonight by this tree, I should talk to them. They might have known Francine."

"You're not going alone. I'll come as your cover story in case you run into trouble. Who would question a couple out for a romantic stroll in the moonlight?"

"No way. It could be dangerous."

"Exactly. You need me as backup. No arguments, Dalton. We're a team, remember?"

He glanced heavenward, as though seeking guidance. "I doubt I'll dissuade you, so you can join me, but you'll head back to the car immediately if the situation goes south."

Several hours later, the two of them drove silently toward the park. It was dead of night, but in this metropolitan area, the sky wasn't fully dark. City lights gave the heavens an unnatural glow, obliterating all but the brightest stars. They'd left Brianna at a friend's house with a ride to school in the morning in case they were late in getting home.

Marla, hands clasped in her lap, gave Dalton a nervous glance. "What if the park gate is closed? Could we be wrong about the location?"

Dalton set his mouth in a grim line. "We'll find out soon enough. We might have to park down the road and go on foot. Are you sure you're up for it?"

"I'm ready." She checked the zipper on her black hoodie and the dark sneakers on her feet. She'd doused herself in bug spray before they left and hoped her chemical scent wouldn't draw human predators instead. Her sturdy jeans should provide a barrier against mosquitoes.

Dalton, too, had dressed all in black. The evening had cooled, and it actually might be quite pleasant in the woods except for the darkness and whatever creatures lurked there. She shivered at the idea, hoping their foolhardy scheme wouldn't be a bad choice.

Sure enough, the gate was closed for the night. They halted by the entrance, wondering which way to go.

"There's another entry point," Marla

205

reminded her husband. "You know, the walkway over the ridge?"

"True, but I don't recall any parking lot at that site. It leads past a housing development."

"Let's circle around. We might find something. If we're right about the meeting, people have to park close by. And where do you suppose this tree exists? I don't recall seeing a big banyan on our walks there."

"That's because we tend to stay on the designated trails." He turned the car around and drove along the park's perimeter. His headlights illuminated the darkened road ahead. No other cars plied the streets at this late hour.

They were nearly at the opposite end when Marla pointed. "Look at the cars parked by that playground. A trail leads toward the higher ridge above."

"There must be a park entrance that way." Dalton found an empty space and pulled in. Armed with flashlights, they headed along the curving concrete path on an uphill incline.

Marla marveled at the silence, broken only by crickets and the occasional bird cry. This grassy area led over the Pine Island Ridge. The archaeological site was twenty-nine feet above sea level, making it the highest natural elevation in Broward County. However, the scarcity of trees made her feel exposed. She hurried along the trail toward the forest in the distance. She'd always preferred walking under the tree canopy or strolling along the boardwalk across the wetland marsh to this sparser region. It could get blazing hot during the daytime.

After what seemed like an endless trek, they reached the northern entrance into the monitored park section. The metal gate swung open at their touch. Somebody must have unlocked it. A park employee, perhaps?

A creepy hush descended as they entered the forest proper. Living things slithered under rocks and rustled the shrubbery, while Marla imagined bobcats waiting for prey to pass or snakes hanging overhead. The hairs on her arms stood up, while a prickle of unease tickled her nape.

"Could the banyan tree be over by the picnic tables?" she asked in a low tone. "It would make for a shady canopy, and we don't usually go that way."

"You could be right. I doubt it's near the marina by the lake or the kiddie section. Let's skirt the usual trails and head toward the picnic shelters. I think there's an old campfire ring in that direction as well."

Their feet crunched dead leaves underfoot

until they reached a wood chip trail. She winced when one of Dalton's boots creaked.

"They'll probably hear us coming from a mile away," she remarked. "What's our excuse if we're caught?"

His eyes gleamed in the light from a full moon. "We could be out for a romantic stroll as you suggested."

"Let's hope they believe us." She scratched an itch on her arm. Despite the cooler air, she was sweating under her jacket. Her scent would attract insects, but hopefully most of them would be chased away by the insecticide.

A creature hooted nearby, making her jump. When a large rustle sounded to her left, she quickened her pace. Her heart pounded as she imagined all sorts of hidden terrors in the woods.

They came to the end of the trail and crossed a road. The picnic areas would be farther along. "Should we just follow the signs to the pavilions?" she asked, glad they could see better in the clearing.

"Yes, but let's steer clear of the asphalt so we're less exposed."

After another long hike during which Marla wished she were back at home in bed, Dalton pointed toward a shady grove. "There, do you see the glow?"

She squinted, making out a barely discernable source of light ahead. "What is it?"

"I think it's our group. Go quietly, now." He paced forward like a panther, steady but light on his feet without making a sound.

Marla, on the other hand, stepped on a branch that made a loud crack. Both of them halted, waiting with bated breaths until the stillness of the night returned.

Finally, Dalton signaled for them to move on. As they neared the site, Marla could make out the distinctive light from lanterns. It seemed to come from inside a big spreading tree.

Voices chanted as they drew nearer. Marla could hear them more distinctly now.

"Hear us, Lady Isis, and receive our prayers. We invoke thee to awaken our souls. Speak to us and save us from the darkness. May our words be a spell and a link to thy great light, O Queen and Mother. Let your Divine goodness arise within us and bring thy truth."

Their volume rose in unison. "I am Isis, and from my life come the suns and the moons, the rain showers and the streams, the living and the dead. I am the Mother and the Earth. All glories of the universe bow to me as I am the priest, the sacrifice, the shrine. I am thy queen enraptured by a love that shall encompass thee."

Their pitch changed again, becoming more pleading. "Hear us, Lady Isis, and accept our prayers. We worship and invoke thy greatness. Hail to thee, Mother of our humble lives."

"You there, stop where you are," a man hollered from behind Marla and Dalton.

Great, the group had left a lookout. Marla would never have succeeded as an Indian scout. The Native Americans would know how to proceed through the forest with stealth.

Slowly, with both hands in view, they turned around. Facing them was a guy in a turban with a swarthy face. He glowered at them but didn't carry any firearms that she could see.

"Oh hello," she said. "We didn't realize anyone was out here tonight."

"You're interrupting a meeting. Guys, we have visitors," the man shouted. He ushered them towards an opening in the giant tree's main trunk.

Inside, a circle of men and women stared at them. Each person had a lantern at their feet. They wore robes and had black streaks on their faces.

"Is this some sort of pagan ritual?" Dalton asked in an interested tone like a tourist.

One guy broke off and approached them. He had dark eyes in an olive complexion, thick lips, and a goatee. "Who are you and what are you doing here?"

"Actually, we're looking for a man named Colin Abubakar."

"What do you want with him?"

"We'd like to ask him some questions about his girlfriend."

So much for our excuse of a moonlit stroll, Marla thought, wondering why Dalton was revealing their purpose so readily. Did he perceive these people as being harmless? Or did he hope honesty might produce quicker results?

A bearded man with beady eyes and a scowl stepped forward. "How did you find this place, Detective?" he said, evidently recognizing Dalton from their prior meeting.

"Mr. Abubakar, this is my wife, Marla. I have a few more questions to ask you about Francine Dodger."

"And you couldn't wait for my office hours at the university?"

"Your friends might have known Francine. Would you like to introduce us and tell me what you're doing here . . . other than trespassing on park grounds after hours, that is."

Marla heard the implied threat in his words and inwardly cringed. He shouldn't rile these people. She pressed her lips tight and refrained from commenting.

Colin Abubakar's eyes narrowed as he regarded them. "We're not doing anything illegal. This tree is sacred. It's where we hold our rites of renewal."

"What kind of rites? Is this, like, where you worship some satanic deity and make human sacrifices?" Dalton asked.

"We celebrate the Entry of Osiris into the Moon with the Invocation of Isis," Colin responded in a calm tone, while the others stood around in clusters, speaking to each other in low voices.

"What's that?" Marla asked. "Isn't Osiris the god of the underworld in Egyptian mythology?"

He swung his gaze towards her. "I see you've done your homework, young lady, but it isn't complete. Isis raises Osiris from the dead. He is symbolically the sun as he enters into and unites with the full moon, which is Isis. Thus the moon is impregnated by the sun. Isis gives birth to Horus ten months later. She is our divine Mother."

Understanding dawned. "This is a fertility rite, isn't it?"

"Fall is a time of harvest. It's celebrated

in many ways by different cultures. Why don't you join us and see for yourselves?"

He stomped off, and Dalton started after him. "Wait, we need to talk about Francine." But the others closed in and drew the two of them into their reformed circle. A cup was produced and passed around. Carved from wood, it looked old and venerated, judging by the careful way the participants took it. Each one sipped the liquid inside before handing it to their neighbor.

When the cup reached Marla's hands, Colin gripped her arm. "Not you," he said. "Give it to your husband. It would not be wise for you to drink the sacrament in your condition." He snatched the cup from her grip and reached past her to hand it to Dalton.

Marla didn't have time to ponder his remark. It was Dalton's turn to take a sip of the sacramental brew.

He sniffed the liquid inside and wrinkled his nose. "What is it?"

"The elixir of life. It brings rebirth during this season of harvesting and replanting. Drink now, and then I'll answer your questions about Francine."

Dalton raised the cup and took a tentative sip, rolling the liquid on his tongue. "Not bad. It tastes like fruit juice."

Marla couldn't tell if he'd swallowed much before he passed it on.

"Were you and Francine dating?" she asked, while the others began their chant again. Leaves rustled in the nighttime breeze, while moonlight filtered through the overhead canopy.

"Yes, we'd met at a food and wine event. Doing tastings together was an interest of ours. Francine guarded her privacy and didn't care to air her social life in public, so she didn't talk about us."

"Was she also interested in ancient Egyptology?" Dalton asked.

"Francine intended to do an article on seasonal rites. I invited her here to see what we do to celebrate the fall renewal. Unfortunately, she never made it."

Marla shivered as robed individuals muttered their incantation in unison. It reminded her of a witch's circle. Could this group's aims really be so innocent?

"Did you attend the harvest festival at Kinsdale Farms the day she died?" Dalton added.

Colin shook his head. "I wish I had gone. Then maybe I could have prevented what happened. I was at a popular culture conference in New Orleans that weekend."

"Do you know anyone who might have

wished to harm Ms. Dodger?" Dalton swayed slightly on his feet as he spoke.

Marla gave him a sharp glance. Was the incessant chanting getting to him, or was it the drink he'd ingested?

Colin tented his hands together in prayer formation. "Francine did sound excited about an article she'd been researching. 'Now I'll finally get my revenge' are the exact words she said to me. But when I pressed her for details, she wouldn't say more." He scrubbed a hand over his face. "I can't believe she's gone. We were good together, and now . . ."

"I'm sorry for your loss," Marla told him in a soothing tone. "Is there anything else you can tell us that may be helpful? I'm sure you want to see justice done for Francine same as we do. Even something seemingly irrelevant might be important."

"Her colleagues might have more information, especially the lady who took over her job. Maybe she orchestrated the whole thing to get a promotion."

"I've interviewed them," Dalton said, "and no one seemed to bear Francine any ill will that I noticed. As for the topic she'd been pursuing for her alleged exposé, she was keeping it a closely guarded secret, same as her relationship to you."

As soon as those words left his mouth, Dalton's legs folded. He sank to the ground in a sliver of lantern light that illuminated his senseless form.

CHAPTER THIRTEEN

"Dalton, what's wrong? Wake up," Marla shouted. Crouching, she shook him. He moaned and twisted to his side, muttering words she couldn't decipher. By then, several of the others had collapsed onto the grass as well.

"Don't worry," Colin said, patting her head. "He's going on a little trip. He'll be fine once the drug wears off." The rest of the circle sank to the ground as he spoke.

She stood and glared at him. "What drug? You mean that drink was spiked?" Her pitch rose along with her panic.

"He'll have visions and then will experience a rebirth. We will all do the same. It's part of the rite of renewal. You can watch over us."

"Wait, is this the stuff that derives from the acacia tree? Dalton called it DMT and said it's a psychedelic agent."

"That's right. We buy the ingredients on

the Internet. It'll wear off in a few hours. Do not fret, my dear. We do this every year, and it has no ill effects. Your man will have a spiritual experience that will give him a renewed sense of purpose." Colin wobbled on his feet, and his eyes took on a distant glaze.

"Your bodies may be accustomed to it, but not Dalton. Oh my God, what should I do?"

"I suggest you wait it out and don't call the authorities. Watch his breathing, that's all. You can be the sitter for all of us." His nostrils flared. "Look, it's Francine. She's calling to me." And then without another word, he joined the unconscious bodies on nature's floor.

Why did he leave me standing? And is he right? Will they come out of this unscathed?

Shivering as she stood alone among the acolytes, Marla considered her options. Should she call for help on her cell phone? That would land them all in the hospital, where they'd undergo unnecessary and expensive tests until they slept it off. Maybe Colin was right, and she should stay the course. Dalton writhed and muttered to himself, but he was breathing and alive. She could make sure he didn't hit anything sharp like a rock or a tree branch.

She positioned him on the soft cushion of grass, took a pee break among the trees, and then settled onto the bench of a nearby picnic shelter. Withdrawing her cell phone, she engaged the browser and looked up DMT for more details. It was the same compound used in Amazonian shamanic rituals via a drink called Ayahuasca. Effects could last several hours when orally ingested along with a monoamine oxidase inhibitor derived from the ayahuasca vine.

Wait, wasn't this similar to the substance that had killed a woman in a case she'd investigated? The lady had been taking anti-depressants, and she'd been slipped a monoamine oxidase inhibitor in a glass of wine. The drug interaction had caused a lethal elevation in blood pressure. How did these people know what medications each individual took? They could have a fatality if they weren't careful.

She read on. During the spiritual journey, out-of-body states were common. It had even been theorized that the human pineal gland produced DMT and released it when you died, accounting for people's near-death experiences. The drug could induce a plane of existence where the person communicated with other intelligent beings. Some drug takers claimed a "mother spirit" guided them on this trip and taught them what they needed to learn, while others saw entities like dwarfs or aliens. These were colloquially called machine elves.

Depending on the visions, the effect could be either terrifying, or it could bring greater mindfulness, decreases in self-judgment, a sense of connection to the world, heightened spirituality, and compassion for all living beings.

Well, that didn't sound so terrible. Marla couldn't imagine Dalton becoming more spiritual, however. She gnawed her lower lip as she stretched out on the bench. If he took a turn for the worse, she could still summon help. That would bring a swarm of police cars and rescue vehicles. She didn't care to embarrass him that way unless it became necessary.

Her thoughts drifted to her own father and how she'd wanted a sign he was okay after he'd died. Nothing had come to her until she'd seen the psychic in Cassadaga. That experience had given meaning to her sleuthing when she'd doubted herself. Perhaps Dalton would learn something from this after all. If nothing else, he might be more sympathetic to the drug addicts he dealt with every day.

She closed her eyes, letting her body relax

and using an arm for a pillow. She'd just drift off for a few minutes.

"Marla, are you there?" Dalton called from somewhere far away.

She sat upright, her mind groggy. How much time had passed since she'd lain down?

Dawn heralded the approach of day. Her gaze zeroed in on the lone person by the banyan tree. Dalton stood, gazing around in confusion. The group members had gone.

Realizing they'd been abandoned, Marla staggered to her feet. "I'm coming," she yelled, none too steady herself. She took a few steps and found her balance. Her nose sniffed the morning air, redolent with dew. "Are you all right?" she asked as she got closer.

"What happened? Where are we?" Dalton riffled his fingers through his tousled hair.

"We're at the park. We spoke to Colin last night. How much do you remember?"

He shook his head, a bewildered look in his eyes. "I had the most amazing dream. It was so real. Pam was there. She told me what I need to do."

"You saw your dead wife?"

"Yes, and she likes you, Marla. She's happy I found you. I understand things more clearly now. It's not only about us. We're part of something bigger."

"You took a drug, Dalton. It gave you hallucinations. Do you think you can make it to the car? We should get you checked out at the hospital."

He gazed at Marla as though seeing her for the first time. His glance raked over her in astonishment. "You've stayed here the entire time? My God, we need to get you home. You shouldn't have risked your health that way."

She snorted. "You're the one who sampled a psychedelic drink. Come on, let's go to the car. I'm freezing." Her body shook, partially from the cooler air and partially from the shock of events. Was Dalton in his right mind? She took him by the elbow and steered him toward the trail leading to the exit by the ridge.

Birds warbled and crickets intoned their chorus as they stumbled through the woods in the early morning light. Her stomach rumbled, and she realized it had been over twelve hours since they'd eaten. Maybe if Dalton got something solid in his stomach, it would help metabolize the drug in his system.

"How do you feel?" she asked out of concern. "Any nausea, racing heart, headache or other physical symptoms?"

He gave her a troubled glance. "My head hurts like I have the worst hangover. But I also feel an odd sense of connectedness. The trees, the plants, the animals in the woods . . . we're all part of the same universe. We're all part of the One. It's wondrous. I didn't realize —"

"Don't tell me you've found religion all of a sudden," she scoffed, skirting past a fallen branch in their path.

"No, this goes beyond religion. Those are man-made constructs. It's hard to explain, but I feel as though I've been somewhere else, and I've seen the truth."

"Whatever you say. Let's just get you home for now. Or do you want to see a doctor first? You might still be under the influence of that ceremonial beverage."

A thoughtful frown creased his brow. "The others left earlier. They must be more accustomed to the stuff for it to wear off so quickly."

"No doubt you're right." She gave a sigh of relief once they'd reached the gate and entered the high ridge section. Her parched throat cried out for a drink of water. Her hip ached from lying on a hard bench all night, and her temples throbbed. Thank goodness it was Monday and her day off

223

from work.

"You'll have to call in sick today," she told her husband once they were en route to their house. "You're in no condition to drive. You might still be experiencing after-effects from the drug."

Dalton fell into a brooding silence while she concentrated on driving. Finally, they reached their garage, and Marla switched off the engine. She texted Brianna as soon as they entered the kitchen. The teen responded that she was fine. Her friend's mother was taking them to school.

That matter settled, Marla let the dogs out into the fenced backyard. She put on a fresh pot of coffee before hastening to the bathroom for a long overdue shower and grooming session. Meanwhile, Dalton sent a message in to work that he'd be late today.

"I am not calling in sick," he told her as they faced each other across the kitchen table, both of them clean and in fresh clothing. "I'll be all right in a little while. I have to process this experience, that's all."

"I read about the spiritual journey and the beings you might have encountered. It relates to a chemical process in your brain, Dalton."

"Does it?" His brow wrinkled. "I've learned things I couldn't have known otherwise. About myself, and about you."

"Me? What do I have to do with it?"

His lips curved in a secretive smile. "You'll find out. How's your stomach, by the way? Still feeling unsettled?"

"Yes. I hear these GI upsets can take a month or two to go away. But this isn't about me. How do you view things now that's so different? You've always appreciated nature before."

"I see our oneness more clearly. I've been wrong to judge people based on outward appearances. We're all God's chosen. We need to respect each other."

She wrapped a hand around her mug of hot coffee. "Okay. Aren't you doing this already?"

"Not in my heart. I see the dregs of humanity every day. The crooks I bring in are misguided souls who've been led down the wrong path."

"Oh, come on. You told me once that you believed in evil."

"Pam helped me expand my view. She told me why my mother acts so distant sometimes. Mom suffered a trauma when her little brother died in that cave-in out in Arizona. Grandma Hannah took her away from their family. They became estranged from Uncle Ray, who Mom blamed for the accident."

"We know all this already." Marla had learned his family history when they'd visited Arizona for their belated honeymoon.

"Yes, but my mother still experiences fear of loss. She can be afraid to get close to people because they might die like her younger brother. I had a good childhood, but Mom wasn't always attentive. She focused her fears on me and withdrew to avoid the pain of loss. I rebelled by becoming a police officer and putting myself in danger."

"You joined the force so you could catch bad guys. At least, that's what you told me."

"Right, after a friend's father was robbed and beaten one night and nearly killed. But don't you understand? These incidents are all related. We're all related."

She reached across the table and grasped his hand. "Yes, but that doesn't mean you should forgive the bad guys out of a new sense of spirituality. It'll affect your work as a cop."

"Demons exist, Marla. Bad entities are out there. They're the source of evil."

Dear Lord, he was sounding more and more off his rocker. "How about if you take a nap, and then we'll see how you feel? I need to lie down myself."

What did it mean that Pam had been his spiritual guide on this journey? Where did that leave her? And what was it he'd learned about her that he wouldn't relate?

Marla didn't care to deal with esoteric teachings. She had more practical matters on her mind, like solving Francine's murder. That's what they should be discussing, but she left it alone for now. Dalton seriously needed to get some rest.

He seemed to feel better after he awoke at lunchtime. Marla had been up earlier and had fixed him a sandwich. She handed him the plate when he reappeared in the kitchen in his dress shirt and trousers.

"We haven't talked about what Colin said last night," she told him, hoping he wouldn't spout off his nonsense at the office today. The quieter he kept about his experience, the better for everyone. Otherwise, the captain might send him for a psych evaluation.

"I forgot all about it," he said between bites of his turkey sandwich. "Mr. Abubakar did say he'd been attending a conference in New Orleans at the time of the harvest festival. That's easy enough to check on."

"He also said Francine meant to get revenge on someone, and that the article she'd been researching might be related.

Are you sure your boys haven't found anything in the files they brought back from her office?"

"Nothing that would raise my interest. I can check with them again to see if anything new has surfaced."

"You do that. I still need to go over there and talk to her colleagues."

As Dalton left for work, he seemed much more like his normal self, which gave her a measure of comfort. She ran a few errands and was about to look up the magazine's address in Boca Raton when her cell phone rang.

"Hi, dear, it's Kate," said Dalton's mother in a pleasant voice. "We're in the area and wondered if we could drop by for a brief visit."

"Oh, um, I'm actually not home. Where are you? We could meet for coffee," she offered instead. She hadn't seen her in-laws in a while and welcomed the opportunity. It would give her a chance to confirm what Dalton had said he'd learned from his mind-altered state.

Kate and John looked well when Marla greeted them inside a local Starbucks. Kate's auburn hair looked freshly touched up and styled. John had grayed a bit more, but the silver in his hair matched his pewter eyes. They both wore resort wear suitable to the senior generation.

After getting their drinks at the counter, they found an empty table outside on the sidewalk. Planters on the walkway provided spots of greenery.

"I bought some supplies for my stained glass work," John explained. "There's a new shop that opened in Palm Haven, and it had a pattern I'd wanted."

"Good for you. How did your last show go?" she asked politely. He'd been displaying his artistic creations at local art fairs.

"I sold four pieces, so that made it worthwhile."

"I'm glad to hear it. Kate, how are your bridge games? Any trips planned with your group?"

"Not with Thanksgiving coming up, I'm afraid." The older woman gave a heavy sigh. "I'm glad you're having us over for holiday dinner. We never see Brianna often enough, and soon she'll be going off to college. We'll be lucky to get a glimpse of her on vacations."

Marla was well aware Dalton's parents craved more grandchildren. "Listen, I've been meaning to ask you about my husband's childhood. What was he like growing up? Was he a rambunctious kid or a nerdy type?"

"Is there a particular reason why you're interested in this now, dear?" Kate asked with a hopeful note.

Marla sipped her iced coffee via a straw before replying. "He had a weird dream last night. I'm wondering how much of it was true."

Kate pursed her lips. "He wasn't the wild sort, but he would act out to get my attention. You see, he was an only child. I'd had some difficulty with my pregnancy, and the doctor said it might be dangerous for me to have another baby. Plus, John and I wanted to travel. It was easier to leave Dalton with a nanny than if we had two kids."

"I thought you didn't like travelling so much," Marla said. When John retired from his career as an attorney, he meant to participate in art shows. Kate had been less than thrilled with that idea. She preferred to stay home where she had friends and activities.

"We've been to most of places where I wanted to go," Kate explained. "I'm tired of living out of suitcases. At this stage in my life, I prefer convenience."

"So you hired a nanny when Dalton was growing up?"

"That's right." Kate fingered her cup of black coffee. "He told me later that I'd been emotionally distant. That's why he behaved so crazy sometimes, because he needed my attention. I loved him, but I thought if I didn't care so deeply, it might not hurt so badly if anything happened to him."

"You were afraid," Marla concluded. "You'd lost your younger brother, and that loss carried over to your relationship with your son."

Kate nodded, her gaze misting. "Even now, I'm terrified for him. You never know who's going to pull out a gun and shoot him."

"He doesn't do patrol anymore, and he isn't in uniform. He's at risk chasing down suspects, but he usually has backup." Marla didn't share that she was just as scared. It was part of being a cop's wife, but she understood the risks. If you dwelled on it, it could paralyze you.

She'd learned this hard lesson after little Tammy's death. The toddler had drowned in a backyard pool while under Marla's care as a nineteen-year-old babysitter. For years, she'd blamed herself. She didn't foresee ever having children in her future, because she wouldn't be a capable mother. Nor could she risk the pain of loss after viewing the devastation of Tammy's parents. Only through time and with Dalton's love had Marla come to forgive herself and change her mind.

Tears filled her eyes, and she blinked rapidly. What was the matter with her? She hadn't gotten emotional over her past in a long time. She'd atoned for her mistakes and moved on.

"I'm glad Dalton has you to look after him." Kate reached across the table and gave her hand a momentary squeeze. "We gave him everything as a child, I want you to know. Despite my attitude, he didn't lack for privilege. He was a good kid. His grades were decent, if not as high as I would have liked."

"Yeah, and you nagged him on that point," John said. He appeared bored, observing the cars coming and going as though more interested in the vehicle models than in their conversation. He'd had his own problems with Kate after his retirement. It had been an adjustment for both of them, but they'd survived.

Kate wagged her finger at him. "Don't criticize me. You weren't the one driving him to his baseball games, karate lessons, and tennis club meetings."

"He took karate? And played tennis?" This

was news to Marla.

"Dalton did a lot of things in those days, as did we when younger. Right, John?"

He averted his gaze. Clearly, his youthful days weren't available for discussion.

Their conversation segued into more mundane topics until Marla took her leave. She got into her car, realizing she'd forgotten Pam's presence in Dalton's dream. So the part about Kate fearing loss was true, but hadn't her husband known this on a subliminal level?

What mattered to her lived on the physical plane. She glanced at her watch. It was already three o'clock. Would she have enough time to drive to Boca to visit Francine's office?

She'd just put her car in gear when Dalton rang on the car's Bluetooth system. "Marla, where are you? I have bad news. Alyce Greene is dead in a hit-and-run accident."

CHAPTER FOURTEEN

"What happened?" Marla asked beyond a suddenly thick tongue. Alyce was dead? How was this possible? No, it couldn't be true. But even as Marla half-heard Dalton's reply on the preliminary details, she accepted his report.

"Unfortunately, we don't have any witnesses," he concluded.

"I can't believe it. Where did this happen?"

"Near where she lives. She'd been out jogging."

"Did her neighbors report any strangers in the community?" she asked as her sense of pragmatism returned. She'd deal with the horror later.

Unable to drive and concentrate on their conversation at the same time, she pulled the car over to the curb on a side street and idled the engine.

"You're thinking someone was watching

her place?" Dalton replied. "I haven't had a chance to canvass the neighborhood yet, but that's a good point. It would mean this wasn't an accident."

"Do you have any evidence on the make or model of the vehicle that hit her?"

"It's too early, Marla. I won't be home until later tonight. Don't wait on dinner for me."

"Will you let me know if you learn anything important?" Her mind drifted to the field where she had found Francine, and she gasped. "Oh, my. Do you think her death is related to Francine's? Francine was wearing Alyce's jacket, and she'd been struck from behind. Is this the killer completing the job he'd meant to do that day?"

"Or, Alyce uncovered the same dirt on somebody as Francine, and that got her killed," Dalton replied in his wry tone. "I'm aware of the possibilities, thanks. What are your plans for the afternoon?"

"I met your parents for coffee earlier. They were in the area, and your mom called me. We had a nice chat. I'd been planning to visit Francine's office, but it's getting late. I think I'll go home instead. I can't face a bunch of strangers right now."

"Watch your back. This could be a terrible accident or not. Alyce might have riled

235

one of the folks we've interviewed."

She let his remark pass, more concerned about the deceased woman's family. "Her poor husband. He'll be devastated, along with their two kids. Oh, gosh." Marla put a hand to her stomach, not feeling too well.

"I've sent Sergeant Langley over there to speak to Jon Greene. Go home, Marla. We'll deal with this. I need to know that you're safe."

"All right. I'll talk to you later. Love you." She rang off and put the car into Drive. A pall hung over her as she drove home.

Thank goodness Dalton hadn't suffered any ill effects from his mind-altering episode last night. Or at least, none that showed. He seemed back to his normally logical self. She wouldn't want the drug-induced experience to change his outlook. He was good at what he did, but his attention needed to stay focused. It would hinder him to ponder the meaning of life while on a case. If he had any more thoughts about his spiritual journey, he'd kept them to himself.

The rest of the day loomed in front of her like a malevolent specter. She didn't have the heart to do household chores, so she answered email until Brianna came home from school.

"Hey, Marla, what's wrong?" the teen

236

asked after she'd plopped her backpack down on the kitchen counter. She had foresworn her ponytail to wear her hair down, using the curling iron to twist the ends. It made her look more grown-up and gave Marla a pang that she'd be leaving for college soon.

"You can tell, huh? Your dad called with bad news. Another woman is his case was found dead."

"Oh, no. You can talk to me about it if it'll make you feel better," Brianna offered. The dogs bounced at her heels. She stooped to scratch them behind their ears.

"Maybe later. Why don't you get comfortable? I have to start preparing dinner. Your dad won't be home until after dark, so he can reheat his portion then."

Fifteen minutes passed before Brianna ensconced herself at the kitchen table. She opened a school book in front of her and frowned at the pages. Marla stood by the sink, in the midst of gathering ingredients for chicken cacciatore.

"How was your day?" she asked with a glance at the teen. Brianna had changed into distressed black jeans and a blousy top.

"Boring. I don't see the relevance of learning the periodic table."

"I didn't like chemistry either, but I had

237

to take it again when I went to cosmetology school. We have to mix chemicals often in the salon business. Chemistry helps us at home, too. For example, when you get rid of stains on clothing, knowing which ones are acidic or not can point you toward the right solution. It's relevant in baking and other everyday tasks you wouldn't expect. So while these subjects may seem unimportant to you now, they'll become relevant later."

Brianna pushed her book away. "You sound like my teacher. So tell me about this person who died."

"It's Alyce Greene, the food blogger."

"No way. How did it happen?"

"Hit-and-run accident. She was out jogging in her neighborhood."

"An accident seems too coincidental with her involvement in Francine's case. Didn't you say the two of them had similar haircuts and body builds?"

Marla selected bottles of dried oregano and dried basil from the pantry and placed them on the counter next to the extra virgin olive oil. "Yes, and don't forget the issue of the jacket. Francine had borrowed Alyce's outerwear at the farm festival. She'd been hit from behind. The killer might have mistaken her for Alyce."

Brianna studied Marla with serious dark eyes. "Dad believes Francine must have been followed out into the fields. How else would the killer have known she was there? Otherwise, this person would have trailed the food blogger instead."

"That's true." Marla pulled packages of pre-chopped fresh peppers and onions from the refrigerator. She opened the lids and set them next to a twenty-eight ounce can of diced tomatoes. "Teri the chocolatier told me she'd seen Alyce chatting at the festival with Lynette Wilde, the features editor from Francine's magazine. I hadn't realized any of the publisher's colleagues had been there, or that Alyce had been acquainted with this woman."

"How do you know Alyce didn't whack Francine, and then somebody offed her in revenge? Didn't you say Francine had a boyfriend?"

"Yes, and we never told you what happened with him." Marla related their adventures at the fall ritual.

"Holy crap," Brianna said. "I hope Dad's all right."

"I hate to say it, but this new murder — if it proves to be a homicide — may have set him straight."

"The boyfriend's claim of spiritual peace

could be a ruse to deflect suspicion. Maybe it's a bunch of hogwash and he's your killer," Brianna suggested with a thoughtful expression.

"The effects of that drug were real enough." Marla opened the can of tomatoes, tossing the lid into the trash. Then she retrieved her electric skillet from the pantry floor. As she stood, a wave of dizziness struck her. "I should let your dad solve the case. I'm getting too old to chase after suspects."

"Are you all right?" Brianna half-rose from her chair.

Marla waved her back as her equilibrium returned. "I must have gotten up too fast. I'm okay." She clonked the frypan onto the kitchen counter and plugged the wire into the outlet. Then she got herself a drink of water and took a few gulps. "Maybe I'm dehydrated. I've been running around all day."

"Or maybe you're still not over your weird stomach ailment. You should see a doctor," Brianna said with a look of concern.

"I've no time. My schedule is fully booked this week. I'd been hoping to interview Francine's co-workers, but I doubt I'll have the chance."

"Don't worry about it. Dad will solve both

cases like he always does."

Yes, he would, but Marla wanted them solved sooner rather than later as she regarded his empty seat at the dinner table an hour later. She chewed on a piece of chicken cacciatore, sniffing the aroma of sautéed peppers and onions in the air. Brianna worked at her homework in silence, while Marla mulled over their conversation. Too many loose ends about these cases nagged at her. Could she leave well enough alone and let Dalton do his job?

She thought so, at least until Janet Winters strolled into her salon on Wednesday afternoon to report on the progress of their fundraiser. The socialite looked attractive in a black dress with a diamond pendant necklace. She'd swept her blond hair into a twist and wore a set of silver hoop earrings.

"Hi, Marla," Janet greeted her when she had a free moment in between clients. "I was in the area at a charity luncheon and figured I'd stop by. I need to tell you what I've been doing in terms of publicity for our upcoming event."

"Of course. Would you like a tour of the place first? You should see our facilities so you know what you're advertising." Without waiting for a response, Marla took her by the elbow and steered her toward the rear.

241

She proceeded to give the society matron a full tour including the day spa next door. Back at the salon, Marla introduced her to Robyn Piper, their receptionist.

"I've been working on our email newsletter," Robyn said, her brown eyes sharp behind a pair of black-framed eyeglasses. "Our first mail-out should be ready next week. I'll also be designing some ads for the fundraiser."

"That sounds great," Janet replied with a grin. "I've created a mailing list of my friends who might be interested in coming to the event, plus a separate list of media resources. Here's a printout for you." Janet pulled a sheaf of papers from her large purse. "Also, I'd contacted some local merchants. We have offers for gift cards donations and baskets for a silent auction."

"I love that idea. I'll bet Becky could finagle some free passes to the museum for prizes. Can you send me a copy of these files via email?" Robyn asked, accepting the documents. "Or better yet, I'll set up a shared folder for us online."

"Where will we display the auction items?" Marla asked, hoping they weren't going overboard on activities.

"We can use the day spa lounge," Robyn suggested. "I'll add the auction to our flyers and to the window posters we're having printed. But what's this, Janet? I see you've put *Eat Well Now* magazine from Boca on your list. Why would they be interested in our fundraiser?"

Janet spread her hands. "It's where Francine worked. We have a connection to her."

"They don't know that," Marla inserted. "Who's taken over her position?"

"I called and got the name Lynette Wilde from the woman on the phone. Why, do you know her?" Janet asked Marla. "You look surprised."

"Lynette was at the harvest festival. Teri from the chocolate factory saw Alyce speaking to her there."

"Really? I haven't met the woman. Did Francine ever have a memorial service? I assume her colleagues, including this person, would have attended."

"Good question. I've been meaning to visit their office. If I ever get there, I'll ask about Francine's funeral and also if they'd like to send a reporter to cover our event."

"We should approach Alyce, too. She might like to write a piece for her blog," Janet said.

"Dear Lord, you haven't heard the news? Let's go sit on the bench outside so we can have more privacy." Outdoors in the mild

October air, Marla took a seat beside Janet. "I hate to be the bearer of bad tidings, but Alyce was killed in a hit-and-run accident."

Janet slapped a hand to her mouth. "What? Oh my God. I don't believe it."

"I had the same reaction. Her death is suspicious when you consider Francine had been wearing Alyce's jacket at the farm when someone whacked her from behind."

"You believe Alyce was the intended target, and not Francine?"

"Not necessarily." Marla paused to collect her thoughts. "I think Alyce found out why Francine was murdered. That put her on top of the killer's list."

"Marla, that's even worse. Are all of us in danger? The madman could assume Francine had confided in the rest of us."

Marla's heart lurched at the notion. "It's possible, but I'd rather choose to believe something specific triggered the attack on Alyce, if her accident was intentional."

"Do you know what model car was involved?"

"Not yet. Dalton is working on the case. Please don't mention our conversation to anyone," Marla cautioned the other woman.

She stared at the vehicles in the parking lot, wondering what kind of car or truck had mowed Alyce down. Dalton would be tracking the woman's movements and checking out her recent contacts. They could be the same people he and Marla had been interviewing lately, including Janet's husband. She viewed the circling cars with narrowed eyes. Would one of them attempt to charge her as she crossed the asphalt later to her Camry?

Noting her companion's hushed silence, she regarded her with concern. Janet's face had gone pale. The socialite clutched her entwined fingers in her lap.

"Are you all right?" she asked.

Janet shook her head. "I can't get over the shock of this news. It's horrible. Alyce's family must be devastated."

"It'll be hard on them," Marla agreed. She'd rather not think about the sad repercussions right now. "As long as you're here, I have one more question regarding the family farm. Are you aware if a deed exists naming your family as owners?"

Janet gave her a questioning glance. "I imagine Zach has secured the papers somewhere. He's in charge of family documents. I can ask him for a copy if that will help. I've never actually seen the deed myself."

"Thanks. I'm sure your brother has the family's best interests at heart."

"True, although he has been acting strange

lately. Something is bothering him, but he won't say what it is."

"I heard about the silo accident in the past," Marla said in a casual tone. "Have there been any recent incidents like that one, which might have upset him?"

"That was just a rumor. How did you hear about it?" Janet asked, her gaze chilling.

"Alyce mentioned a worker had disappeared, and it's possible he'd fallen into a silo. I'd imagine another such incident would generate bad publicity for the farm if word got out."

"Farms have occupational hazards, like tractor injuries. They have safety rules for a reason."

"That's assuming the farm hands are familiar with them. Where do your seasonal laborers come from? Are they hired for a limited time only? And do they speak English well enough to understand the instructions?" Marla remembered another case she and Dalton had solved involving illegal migrant labor.

"My brothers manage the work force, plus they do a lot of the labor themselves. You'll have to ask them these questions. I'm involved in the marketing end of things."

Marla rose and smoothed down her pants. "Your husband sells his products at the farm's marketplace. What kind of relationship does he have with Zach?"

"They get along fine, although I wouldn't say they're friends otherwise. They come from different worlds. I don't broadcast my origins to my society friends, Marla. Maybe I grew up on a farm, but I couldn't go back there now."

"When we spoke to Rory, he indicated you don't like to talk about your home life. Are you more of a private person, or do you have concerns about your husband that you're reluctant to share?"

Janet leapt up. "I've told you already. Tony is nervous about a visit from his relatives. They're not the sort of people you want to annoy."

"Yes, I remember you said he'd mentioned Francine's name on the phone to them. They made plans to come right after that conversation. You also suggested the possibility of being an events planner in case you ever needed to fend for yourself. Why are you so afraid, Janet?

Janet glared at her. "Wouldn't you be scared if two of your acquaintances ended up dead? I don't want to be next."

CHAPTER FIFTEEN

Marla told Dalton about her conversation with Janet when he returned home later that night. He looked haggard, and she didn't care to bother him about it, but she had to get things off her mind. She waited until he'd showered and crawled into bed before speaking in a soft voice. Brianna had already gone to sleep in her room down the hallway.

"You won't care if I visit Francine's offices, will you? That's one avenue I've been neglecting, and yet those people must know something."

He rolled sideways in bed and leaned on an elbow to regard her. A lock of silver-streaked black hair, still damp, flopped onto his forehead. "We haven't recovered any information about the article she'd been working on before she died. You're welcome to have a go at it."

"Did you interview Lynette Wilde? She seems to be a key figure."

"Yes, she's editorial director now that Francine is gone. She'd seemed happy regarding the promotion but sad by the way it occurred. I wouldn't say she considered Francine a rival. Francine's colleagues respected her and appear to genuinely miss her presence."

"I can visit them tomorrow morning. It'll be Thursday, my late day at work. I can't believe how fast this week is going. Did you ever hear who claimed Francine's body? No one's mentioned a memorial service."

"Her parents aren't living, and she had no siblings. A sister existed once, but she died. I believe a distant aunt decided upon cremation and took responsibility."

"That's sad. Colin might have stepped forward and done something."

"He's not a blood relative. Kinship comes first. Francine must have lived a lonely life without any close family." Dalton trailed his finger up her arm. Her skin tingled in its wake.

"She may have had a lot of friends if she was a social person," Marla suggested.

"That's true. So Janet had no clue as to what Francine's article included?"

"We didn't talk about it. She's more worried about Tony's relatives coming to visit, and apparently, so is he."

"I'll have to do more research into his company. That reminds me; I might want us to take a trip this weekend."

"Oh yeah?" She found it difficult to concentrate when his hand roamed to her lower regions.

"I've discovered a connection between Kinsdale Farms and a plot of land in northern Florida. It's an olive grove owned by Zach's cousin, Ben."

"And this is important because . . . ?"

"Tony sells imported olive oil to Zach's farm. Francine may have been researching a hot topic that got her killed. Janet told you Tony's relatives heard her name on the phone and made plans to visit. I'm sniffing a skunk here."

"So why would this cousin know any more than we do?"

He shrugged, drawing her gaze to his broad shoulders. She never failed to admire his manly form, especially when he was bare-chested like now.

His mouth curved at her glance. "It's just a hunch. If Brie is free, we can make a weekend trip of it and pretend to be tourists interested in the industry."

"Okay, but we'll have to drive up on Sunday, unless I can leave work early the day before. My Saturdays are always booked."

"That's fine," he murmured, snuggling closer as all thoughts of their plans fled her head.

On Thursday morning, Marla headed north to Boca Raton. Traffic was fairly light on the turnpike after rush hour. She'd done a few errands first, so it was nearly ten-thirty by the time she reached the offices of *Eat Well Now* magazine.

Inside the lobby, she gave her name to the receptionist and asked to speak to Lynette Wilde. Without having an appointment, she had to wait a good twenty minutes before being greeted by the thirtyish brunette.

"Hi, I'm Lynette. How can I help you?" Her keen brown eyes regarded Marla with mild curiosity as she offered a handshake. Marla liked the ivory top and cocoa skirt ensemble she wore along with matching pumps. Soft layered waves of hair framed her angular face.

"I was a contestant at the bake-off contest where Francine . . . you know. I'm the one who found her."

Lynette cast a glance at the receptionist before gesturing for Marla to follow her. "Come inside to my office. We can speak privately there."

251

"I'm afraid I don't know much about your publication," Marla began once they were seated inside a glass-walled enclave. Lynette sat behind a wooden desk in a leather swivel chair. "Did Francine work her way up the ranks, or did she come in as publisher?"

Lynette folded her hands on the desk. "May I ask what your interest is in our internal affairs?"

"My husband is Detective Dalton Vail. You may have spoken to him when he visited your offices. We're hoping to learn what article Francine had been meaning to publish. Her research might have upset someone enough to kill her."

"Well then, I'll tell you what I told the detective. Francine worked her way up from editorial assistant. She was dedicated to her job and to our magazine's philosophy. Everyone admired her work ethic and her devotion."

"Was she a proponent of healthy eating like your publication advises?" Marla asked.

"Yes, Francine believed in the 'what you eat is what you are' adage. She wasn't a vegan or a food fanatic, but she believed in healthy choices."

"So Francine ranked above everyone else?"

"That's right. She was a good boss. No

one had any problems with her."

"What was your job before you moved up?"

Lynette studied her fingernails, painted a vibrant coral. "I was features editor."

"Did you actively seek a promotion, or was the offer unexpected? And who made that decision?"

"We're owned by a conglomerate. Their president approached me. It came as a surprise."

"Do you know what Francine had been working on besides her usual pieces?"

"She rarely wrote articles anymore in her position as editorial director. Her job was more management-oriented. But she did mention farm accidents at one time. That kind of startled me because it seemed a diversion from our purpose. Francine said fatalities happened all the time on farms, and no one knew about them. It could have been a topic she'd heard about in the news, because she didn't say anything about writing an article on the subject."

"Did she associate Kinsdale Farms with any specific incidents?"

Lynette shook her head. "Not that I recall."

"Could this be the exposé she'd intended to publish?" Marla persisted. "Maybe it wasn't a coincidence that she entered the bake-off contest."

"You mean, she wanted to check out the farm while there? I suppose it's possible."

"What did Francine plan on doing with the cash reward if she won? She had to present a business proposal for approval by the contest committee."

Lynette glanced toward the door. "Please keep this quiet, but our magazine's readership has been eroding. It could be she was afraid of losing her job. Maybe she hoped to invest the money in our publication to take control."

"She'd need a big nest egg to buy out the magazine," Marla noted.

"Or maybe she meant to broaden our scope. She had talked about our team doing more in-depth investigative articles."

"You could be right. If your publication expanded its focus, a new direction could reverse the slide. She may have been researching the first piece on her own."

"The cops took her hard drive. Have they found anything there?"

"Dalton isn't sharing that information." Marla shifted her position along with her focus. "Is there anyone you can think of who might have wanted to harm your former boss? Was there somebody she'd fired who might have held a grudge against her, or a person whose work contributions she had overlooked?"

"Not really. Francine had her occasional scrapes but mostly she got along with everyone. I understand she had a boyfriend. Did your husband check him out?"

"He's a potential person of interest. He might have attended a memorial service, had there been one."

Lynette's gaze saddened. "I was surprised to hear an aunt came forward to claim the body. Francine had a sister who died when they were young, and her parents were deceased. It's too bad she didn't have more relatives."

"Likely she had enough friends to make up for it. Speaking of acquaintances, another contestant at the bake-off told me she'd seen you at the festival talking to Alyce Greene. I didn't realize you'd attended."

Then again, how had Teri known the other woman was Lynette Wilde? Had they met earlier? Or had someone else identified Lynette?

"Francine had told me about the fair, and it sounded like fun," Lynette said, twisting a strand of hair around her finger. "She'd introduced me to Alyce a while back. The two of them believed that growing sustainable food was important to people's well-being."

"Were you present for the bake-off contest?"

"I didn't buy a plate and fork, if that's what you mean. I waited to greet Francine later, but she'd disappeared. Then I ran into Alyce and we spoke for a few minutes."

"Was this before the judges announced the winners?"

"That's right."

"Did Alyce seem okay? Not out of breath or anything?"

"No, she looked fine. Why would that matter?"

"I'm just trying to fit the pieces together of what happened that day. Did you notice Francine wearing Alyce's jacket earlier? She'd been cold, and Alyce loaned it to her."

Lynette gave her an impatient glance. "No, I'm sorry. Is that significant?"

"It could be. At first, I'd wondered if the bad guy got the wrong person. Maybe he'd meant to knock Alyce on the head, and when he failed, he went after her a second time. Otherwise, Alyce might have learned something new about the case that made her a target."

"I didn't want to believe it when I heard the news about Alyce. Are we in danger, too?" Lynette asked, echoing what Janet had suggested earlier. "The killer might think Francine told us what she'd been working on, if it's related."

"Or her proposed article may have had nothing to do with her death. We need more information before making that determination. Is there any detail you can add that might seem unimportant?"

Lynette pushed to her feet, her expression indicating dismissal. "I've told you all I know, and your husband before this. Will you keep me informed if anything new surfaces? We're going about our business as usual, but we're all upset."

"Of course." They exchanged business cards, and Marla took her leave.

So what had she gained? She reviewed their conversation on her way to work. People had liked Francine. Nobody held a grudge against her or wanted her job. She had mentioned farm accidents, though. Could she have been reviewing the records from Kinsdale Farms and came across something damaging to them? Or maybe she'd discovered who actually owned the title if it wasn't Zach and his siblings.

Marla stopped by Bagel Busters to order a takeout sandwich for lunch. Arnie waved at her from behind the cash register as she approached. He wore his usual apron over a pair of jeans and a tee shirt.

"Hey, pal. Business seems to be hopping," she said to him with a smile. Not an empty seat was to be seen. Locals liked the menu and the reasonable prices. Smells of corned beef and pickles wafted her way as a waitress strode by carrying a laden tray.

Arnie came around the counter to embrace her. His moustache tickled her cheek. "Good to see you, as always. Have you come to give me a report on your investigation?"

"Actually, I came to order lunch. Can get you get me a turkey delight to go? Just the sandwich and nothing on the side."

"Sure. Hey, Ruth!" Arnie shouted the order to a familiar server and then called over another staff member to man the cashier desk. "So, did you talk to Rory? What did he say?"

"Dalton and I have spoken to a lot of people about the case." Marla gave him a quick rundown of the findings that Dalton had said she could share.

"Wow, that's a lot to take in." His somber face regarded her. "Do you really feel Zach is hiding something about the farm? Damn, Rory was right then."

"Has he mentioned any incidents relating to their labor force? As in, accidents involving tractors or silos?"

"No, but he said it's hazardous work. Any job involving machinery can be dangerous." Arnie gestured toward their meat-cutting machine. "Heck, we could easily slice off a finger if we're not careful."

"Dalton is still looking into the land title. It's troubling that Zach can't produce a deed with his family's name on it."

"I hope for Rory's sake that his dad is not involved in Francine's murder."

Standing in a corner, she patted his arm. "Don't worry, we have lots of other suspects. And now with Alyce dead, the plot thickens. Was she meant to be a target in the first place? Or did she learn what Francine knew, making her a fresh threat to the killer?"

"You've done as I asked, Marla. Now be careful and stay out of trouble," Arnie advised.

"I will. On a lighter note, our salon is planning a bad hair day clinic as a fundraiser in conjunction with the history museum. The curator is working with us, as is Janet Winters."

His eyes rounded. "Janet is Rory's aunt. Why would she get involved?"

Marla explained the function. "Janet and Robyn from the salon are doing publicity.

Teri from the chocolate factory is donating desserts. Would you like to contribute appetizers? We'll add your deli to the flyers if you're interested in joining us."

"Sure, I'd love to participate. We can supply whatever you need."

She informed him of the date and details. "This brings to mind another issue I've been considering." Shifting her feet, she put her weight onto her other leg. "Tally has signed a letter of agreement on a new location for her dress boutique. Once she moves her stock out of my lounge, it'll clear the space for another purpose."

"Like what? You had coffee set up in there before you added her fashion line. The latter is still a good idea, by the way. Maybe Tally will let you keep a few items to sell there."

Marla plunged ahead with her proposal. "I've wanted to offer lunch to our day spa guests so they'll stay longer, but I don't want to steal business from your place. It's silly for me to offer meals when your deli is next door. So how about if you supply us with ready-made sandwiches and salads each day? And muffins or Danish for midmorning that we can offer for sale?"

He stroked his moustache. "Next you'll

want a wine bar. That's all the rage, you know."

"No, thanks. I wrote up a business proposal for the bake-off contest. I'll email it so you can see what I had in mind. The changes don't have to be that extensive, since we won't be preparing the food, but I'd like for you to be involved."

He gave her a bow. "I'd be honored. Oh, I think your lunch is ready," he said, indicating a brown bag by the cash register. They exchanged a few more words before Marla paid her tab and left.

Nicole accosted Marla at the salon. The other stylist was waiting for her next customer. "Hey, girlfriend, what's up? You haven't filled me in on your latest case."

"It's Dalton's case, not mine." Marla tucked her purse inside a drawer at her station and plugged in her implements. She sniffed the usual mixture of chemical solutions and hair spray with a sense of pleasure. The splash of water in the background competed with the soft music on their speaker system.

Nicole smirked at her. "Since when? You're more of an unofficial deputy these days."

"Don't let his captain hear you say that. I was just speaking to Arnie. I asked him if he'd supply snacks for sale in our day spa so customers won't leave if they get hungry."

"What about your grand plan to construct a lunch counter?"

"We'll offer prepared foods sourced by the deli instead. I wish we had more space. Arnie suggested we keep some of Tally's fashions to sell. They have been a popular item."

"You could sell accessories instead of the whole line. Add a few display cases for jewelry, scarves, and handbags. Other salons offer more than hair products. We could include holiday gift baskets, too."

Marla gave a weary sigh. "It's a good thing I didn't win the prize at the bake-off contest. Remodeling is a nightmare, and we have limited space available."

"It would be handy if we could eliminate the wall between the salon and day spa."

"The landlord won't permit it," Marla reminded her friend. "You're right about the accessories, though. Those could be fun to sell here. I'll talk to Tally about it." A twinge of queasiness hit her stomach. "I'd better eat. I haven't had anything since this morning."

Nicole followed her into the back storeroom. "I noticed how you changed the subject away from the murders. What's going on in that regard?"

Marla drew a stool over to the counter, sat on the vinyl seat, and unwrapped her sandwich. After taking a few bites, she said, "We have some promising leads, but nobody stands out as the main suspect."

"Who do you have so far? In the mystery novel I just finished, the guilty party was the business partner."

A frown creased Marla's brow. "I visited Francine's office this morning. People there seemed to like her. The current editorial director, Lynette Wilde, said she didn't know anyone who might have held a grudge against Francine. I don't believe she'd knock off the woman to gain her position, either. Hmm, she did mention a conglomerate that owned the publication."

"Oh? I'd gotten the impression Francine was in charge."

"She directed their day-to-day operations, but I guess she answered to a higher boss. I'll have to see if Dalton knows who it is. Lynette said the cops took Francine's hard drive. No one knew what article she'd been researching, but it would help if we could find out. The magazine's readership has been declining, and they need the boost that an exposé might provide. Lynette thinks Francine meant to broaden their scope with more investigative-type pieces."

"What would Francine have used the prize money for if she'd won the contest?"

"Lynette theorized that Francine would have made an effort to buy the magazine from the conglomerate that owns it. Dalton has access to her business plan. I'll ask him about her intentions."

"Did Francine ever have a funeral? You could have attended and met everyone there."

Marla got a can of cola from the fridge and popped the lid. She took a few sips of the cold beverage before answering. "No; her body was released to some aunt who lives elsewhere. She didn't have any close relatives. We did meet her weird boyfriend, though." She told Nicole about that incident, grinning at her friend's horrified expression.

"Holy highlights, Dalton could have been seriously harmed by drinking that stuff."

"Fortunately, he's okay. I'm lucky Colin didn't let me drink it. He assigned me the job of sitter, which meant watching over the group. I fell asleep, and when I woke up, they were all gone." She jabbed a finger at Nicole. "I wonder if Dalton could get them on assault of a police officer."

"He was off-duty, wasn't he?"

"Yes, but he'd identified himself. It would be a good excuse to bring Colin in for more questioning." She resisted the urge to yank out her cell phone and text her husband. There wasn't time now. She'd better finish her sandwich before her first client arrived. "What are your plans for the weekend? Are you seeing Kevin again?" Nicole had been dating the hunky paramedic who worked for the fire department for over a year now.

Nicole's eyes turned the color of warm honey. "Can you keep a secret? I've been spending weekends at his place."

"No kidding? This is getting serious. Why haven't you told me before now?"

"You've had other things on your mind."

Marla clapped her hands. "I'm excited for you. You two make such a great couple. I knew you would hit it off when I introduced you."

"Enough about my personal life. What's your next step in crime-solving?"

"Dalton wants to take a drive north on Sunday. He says the Kinsdales have a cousin in central Florida who owns an olive grove. This man might be able to give us some answers."

Nicole chuckled, a low throaty sound. "Sounds like a good excuse for a day trip. Relax and enjoy the outing. Temps are supposed to be in the seventies. Take advantage of the good weather while it lasts."

Marla should heed her words. Even though the winter months could bring cold air to South Florida, a new hurricane season was always around the next corner . . . same as the killer in their latest crime case.

Chapter Sixteen

When Sunday arrived, Marla and Dalton decided to make an overnighter out of their trip, since it would take five hours or so to reach their destination northwest of Orlando. Brianna chose to stay at a friend's house that night, since she had school the next day. Marla suspected the teen wanted them to enjoy a getaway alone.

"What do you know about Ben Kinsdale?" Marla asked Dalton from the passenger seat of his sedan. She regarded his tall, handsome figure with a proud thrill that he was all hers.

Dalton's brows lifted. "He's related to Zach Kinsdale. He purchased the land in Lakesville eight years ago and appears to have established a thriving olive grove. Before that, he lived in our area and worked the family farm with his other cousins."

"I wonder what made him leave."

"Maybe he knows something we don't.

Let's back up to your visit at the magazine office in Boca. Tell me again your impression."

"As you'd said, Francine seemed to be genuinely liked by their staff. She hadn't fired anyone lately who might hold a grudge, nor did Lynette appear to have been jostling for her position. So nobody there had a burning desire to get Francine out of the way."

"Yet Ms. Wilde gained the editorial director post as a direct result."

"True, but she hadn't been expecting a promotion. Have you found out who actually owns the publication?"

Dalton's mouth compressed. "Not yet. I've been busy working up Alyce Greene's death. I really shouldn't be going away this weekend, except that her case might be connected to Francine's."

"Anything new in regard to her accident?"

"No witnesses. No vehicle tracks. One neighbor heard a brief shriek, but by the time she went outside, a white car was speeding down the street. She called nine-one-one."

"So you've no way of knowing if it was an accident, and the driver fled because he got scared, or if it was a deliberate act to run Alyce down."

"I'm more inclined to believe the latter."

"You'd think Alyce would be more careful. She must have learned something that made her a viable target." Marla stared out the side window at the passing scenery. Mount Trashmore was coming up on their left. She could smell the garbage dump and noted the black birds circling overhead.

"Our tech boys still haven't found anything significant on Francine's hard drive. Did her people tell you what she'd been working on?" Dalton asked, keeping his gaze focused forward.

Marla offered him a package of cheese crackers she'd brought along. After he took it, she opened one of her own. Her stomach rumbled. They'd eaten breakfast earlier, although all she could eat was a piece of cinnamon toast. Breakfast didn't sit well with her these days.

She realized what that might mean. Buying a pregnancy test kit rose to the top of her to-do list. The timing couldn't be worse if the results proved positive. Dalton had to focus on solving his cases. He didn't need distractions.

"Francine's colleagues have no clue about her research topic," she replied to his question, pushing aside her ruminations for now. "The magazine's circulation has been faltering, and Francine may have meant to revive things with more investigative pieces into the food industry. Did you see her business proposal for the bake-off committee?"

"She'd mentioned a buyout to some company. I didn't read the details but assumed it related to the magazine."

"Lynette suggested Francine may have meant to purchase their publication from the conglomerate to gain control, and then she could broaden their focus without needing approval."

"I'll look it over again. In the meantime, let's talk about where we'll eat lunch."

Typical male, Marla thought. "What time did you tell Ben Kinsdale to expect us?"

"Two o'clock. We'll have the chance to grab a quick bite somewhere." They'd left early and traffic was light, but it was still a long distance.

"Is Ben going to tell Zach we're coming to interview him?" Marla had urged Dalton to set up a private tour. She'd never been to an olive grove before and couldn't pass up the opportunity, even though Dalton had revealed the purpose of their visit to Zach's cousin.

"I suggested Ben keep our chat confidential for now. We don't know what prompted his move north. It could be he'd had a falling out with his family. That's one of the things I plan to ask him."

They reviewed their list of questions and then fell into an amiable silence as they passed the orange groves in central Florida and entered the greater metropolitan Orlando area.

They stopped for lunch in Altamonte Springs at the north end of town. Having some time to spare, they found a place where Marla ordered an avocado and crabmeat salad. Dalton got a shrimp and mahi bowl served with rice.

Their stomachs satisfied, they resumed their journey northward and then headed west. The terrain became hilly and shaded with tall trees. Spanish moss hung from tree limbs and graced lakes that glistened in the afternoon sun.

Soon they pulled up in front of a gift shop with a big sign facing street-side to lure visitors. Rows of trees stretched into the distance beyond a collection of outbuildings.

Were the olives picked using mechanical means, Marla wondered, or was it done by seasonal laborers? When was the harvest anyway? She knew nothing about growing olives although she loved to eat the product.

With an eager bounce in her sneakered steps, she accompanied Dalton through the screened front door.

A middle-aged man in a caramel sport shirt and a matching baseball cap stood behind a sales counter. He grinned at their arrival. Both items of clothing bore the grove's logo of an olive branch with green fruits.

"Howdy. You must be Detective and Mrs. Vail. I'm Ben Kinsdale." He came around to shake their hands. Ben had tanned skin, a stocky build, and whitened teeth. His wheat hair seemed a tad too uniform in color to be natural.

"You said you'd like to have a tour of the grove while we talk?" the proprietor said. "I'll give you a taste of our olive oil varieties after we return."

Marla's jaw dropped as she noticed the variety of goods for sale. Shelves filled with bottled olive oils tempted her along with jars of cured green and black olives, olive oil soap, olive leaf tea, olive wood products, tropical fruit jams and jellies, Florida fruit wines, and bottled vinegars, plus freshly baked breads and muffins. Heck, forget about touring. She wanted to shop.

"I'm a big olive fan, and I can't wait to hear how you grow them. It's a relatively new industry in Florida, isn't it?" she asked.

"Hey Amberly, can you man the front

desk?" Ben hollered to someone out of sight past an open inner door. "I've got some folks here for a tour."

After the woman entered, he gestured for them to follow him outside. "With the citrus industry in a slump, growers are looking for an alternative crop," he told Marla in reply to her query. "Our citrus industry has declined more than seventy percent since its peak production in the late 1990s."

"How come? Has demand gone down that much?"

Ben shook his head. "Not at all. The citrus fruits are being destroyed by an incurable greening disease, spread by a sap-sucking insect called the Asian citrus psyllid. Olive growers believe their crop may be the next best thing. Look at how the Florida blueberry industry has taken off."

"Is that why you jumped ship from the family farm to move here?" Facing Ben, Dalton wore a pair of sunglasses on his nose and stood in a patch of shade.

"Both Zach and I saw the future," Ben said with a shrug. "This industry could become big, and we wanted to get in at the ground floor. We're actually partners, although I get a bigger share of our net income since I work the place. But Zach saw it as a safety valve in case something happened to the old homestead."

"Rory told us the farm may be in trouble," Dalton stated, observing the older man.

"That kid should keep his trap shut. He's never been happy working in his daddy's shadow. Rory should have gone to school for hospitality management, but Zach couldn't accept his son's lack of interest in the family business."

"Is there truth in his words?" Dalton asked. "I've been unable to verify your family's ownership as recorded on the deed. Another man's name is on the title, which goes way back. There's no evidence of a later sale although some records have been lost."

Ben peered at him. "Have you asked Zach to produce a deed?"

"Yes, and he's failed to comply. Either he doesn't possess this document, or he isn't willing to show it for reasons of his own. We're unable to track the other person's kin. The prior owner seems to have left no heirs."

"You'd best take that up with my cousin. Or better yet, speak to his lawyer." Ben pointed to the trees extending in rows with sandy aisles in between. "Let's start our tour, if you're really interested and didn't just come here on a fishing expedition."

Marla linked her arm into Dalton's. "I love olives, so I made Dalton request a tour. We like plants and trees, too. We'll often go to parks and see how many we can identify. I wasn't even aware olive trees would grow in Florida."

Ben's chest swelled with pride. "We have twenty acres with over eleven thousand trees planted in high-density rows. That's nearly five hundred and sixty trees to the acre. This includes seven different varieties. If you want to grow your own, we have young trees in containers that are for sale."

"When's the growing season?" Marla asked, wondering what Ben knew about Kinsdale Farms that he wasn't mentioning. He'd given them a good idea, though. They could speak to Zach's attorney. Maybe his family lawyer knew something about the property that he'd be willing to share.

Ben adjusted his cap to shade his face from the bright overhead sun. "The trees blossom from February through April, and the fruit matures over the summer. Harvesting runs from August to early October."

"How come they don't grow in South Florida? Is it too humid?"

Ben started down one of the paths. "Olives need about two hundred hours at forty-seven degrees or lower per year in order to flower. You're not gonna get that further south. It takes two to three years before a new tree produces fruit."

"Are your olives hand-picked?" Marla asked.

"We use mechanical harvesting. We have our own mill, too. It can process up to eight hundred pounds per day via batch or continuous feeding. We only cold press our oil because we want to preserve the nutritional value as much as possible."

"Is it true you can't eat olives raw?" Marla noted the different varieties as he pointed them out. The green leaves were narrow and tapered at the ends. She hadn't realized you could make tea out of them.

"That's correct. They have to be cured, or they're too bitter to eat due to oleuropein, a phenolic compound. You can use the dry salt method or cure them in brine."

"What's the difference between green and black olives?"

"Green olives are picked when they're full size but before they ripen. They can be shades of green to yellow. Semi-ripe olives are picked at the beginning of the ripening cycle. Their color has begun to change from green to shades of red or brown. Black olives are fully ripe. They can be assorted shades of purple or brown to black."

"So that bitter substance is neutralized as the olive matures?" Marla asked for clarification.

"Right. Some olive varieties may be edible off the tree if they are sun dried first. Otherwise, the curing process can take a few days with lye treatment, or a few months with brine or salt packing."

"What do you mean, with lye?" Marla wrinkled her nose at the thought.

"Lye processing is mainly used with green or semi-ripe olives," Ben explained, as they crossed over to another row and then headed back toward the main complex. "The olives are soaked in lye for eight to ten hours to hydrolyse the oleuropein. Then they're washed in water to remove the caustic solution and transferred to fermenting vats filled with brine. Or, you can avoid the lye process and put them directly into fermentation vessels. There are other methods as well. One technique involves artificially darkening the olive to make it appear black."

This was news to her. "Are table olives different from olives used to make olive oil?"

"Yes. Some olives are grown to cure and eat, while others are prized for their use in making extra virgin olive oil. Olive mills press the oil, and the sooner you get the product to consumers, the better the quality of the oil. Demand has increased since the health benefits of olive oil have been recognized. In the U.S., we currently import about ninety-eight percent of the millions of gallons we consume per year. You're not always getting the product you think you are with these imports. Fraud has become a multi-million dollar enterprise."

"Have you met Tony Winters from Amalfi Consolidated?" Dalton asked, getting back to the point of their visit.

"I know Zach buys products from his import firm, but I've never had the pleasure of meeting him. We have no need for imported goods here. Our products are all naturally grown and processed at the grove."

"Has Zach ever expressed concerns about the veracity of their ingredients?"

"Not to my knowledge. Those items are imported from Italy. Did you know that as much as eighty percent of extra virgin olive oil may be falsely labeled? Some of it contains lower grades of olive oil or seed oils that can cause allergic reactions."

"I read about a case where Italian police officers arrested a bunch of people in Operation Golden Oil," Dalton mentioned. "The crooks were bringing in cheap oil from elsewhere in the Mediterranean and relabeling it as Italian."

Ben bobbed his head in agreement. "In recent years, major shippers as well as producers have been caught passing off inferior products as extra virgin. Another scheme involved twelve companies in Italy and a certification lab. That case was similar in faking the olive oil's origins. Lab tests showed the product came from the Middle East."

"So how do consumers know what to buy?" Marla asked.

"It's good if you can taste a sample. Buy small bottles since opened oil deteriorates quickly. And try to buy olive oil that's less than a year old according to the pressed or harvested date, if given on the label. Do you think this Amalfi company is involved in your case?" Ben asked Dalton.

"It's possible," he replied.

Marla's heart rate accelerated. Maybe that's why Tony's relatives from Italy were paying him a visit. They considered him a threat to their operation. Francine could have caught on to his end of things, and later Alyce. This could be the exposé the magazine publisher had planned to publish.

Ben took them to see the mill and the big vat room where the olives were cured. Then they ended up back in the gift shop. As

Marla eyed the olive wood items such as serving spoons, carved wooden bowls, and cutting boards, Dalton had a few more words with the owner.

Laden with packages, they trundled back to the car a half-hour later.

"So what's next?" Marla asked her husband as they headed to the bed-and-breakfast where they'd made a reservation for the night. The trek outdoors and the shopping frenzy had left her feeling wilted. She looked forward to relaxing and mulling over what they'd learned.

"I'll take a closer look into the Italian connection for Amalfi Consolidated, and then I need to revisit Zach Kinsdale."

"How about talking to his attorney as Ben suggested? If Zach is having title problems with the property, his lawyer must know about it."

"Yes, but there's client confidentiality. I'll see what Zach has to say first before approaching the attorney."

Had this detour been worthwhile? They'd learned a lot about the Florida olive industry, fraud in the olive oil business, and other fascinating lore, but was it worth Dalton's time away from his cases? Gazing at his stern profile, she realized a break might be good for him. He'd return to work with better clarity of thought and so would she. She'd certainly learned a lot about olives and remembered what she'd read about the health benefits of olive oil.

Come to think of it, she hadn't had a problem when tasting the olive oil varieties in Ben's store. Her stomach didn't roil the way it had when Tristan had given her a sample at The Royal Palate. Had that product been doctored with seed oils that could cause allergic reactions?

Regardless of the cause, she was happy her queasiness hadn't afflicted her on this trip. And speaking of trips, Dalton had not once mentioned his drugged experience on the spiritual plane since his return to work. If he'd had any repercussions, he wasn't mentioning them.

They had a pleasant and romantic interlude that evening, followed by the long drive home on Monday. Dalton immediately went to work while Marla unpacked and proceeded through her household chores.

She was refilling the dogs' water dishes when a loud thud sounded from the front of the house. Her pulse rate rocketed. What was that?

Hastening into the dining room, she peered outside. Nobody stood on their stoop, but she noted a white car zooming away down the street. The house's windows were intact, so whatever had hit them hadn't penetrated. Their hurricane impact windows were designed to resist high winds and were nearly impossible to break.

After peeking out the peephole in their front door, she opened it cautiously. A rock with a note tied to it rested on the front porch. Should she call Dalton or bring it into the house?

Prudence propelled her to obtain an evidence bag. She put on her kitchen gloves and gingerly placed the rock into the bag. Dying to know what the note said, she brought the package inside and was about to shut the door when she spied Brianna walking home from the school bus.

"Hey, Marla, what's going on?" the teen asked, submitting to Marla's brief hug.

"Come in. I found this on our front stoop. Somebody drove by and threw it there."

"No kidding." The girl's dark eyes regarded her with worry. "Could it be related to your trip north? How did that go?"

"We learned a lot about the olive growing process and about fraud in the industry. I'd like to see what that note says."

"Have you notified Dad?"

"Not yet. He said he'll be home for dinner."

"You should call him. I'm going to change into something more comfortable." She slung her backpack onto the floor and turned toward her room.

Marla texted Dalton to phone her. As soon as he did, she related what happened.

"Take a photo of it from different angles, then use those gloves I'd brought home and untie the string. Read me what's inside."

Chills ran up Marla's spine as she scanned the message.

Mind your own business or you'll be next.

CHAPTER SEVENTEEN

"It looks as though the message was printed on a sheet of white computer paper." Marla snapped a photo and messaged it to Dalton. Then she refolded the paper and stuck it into the evidence bag along with the rock and piece of string. "Do you think this is a result of our trip north? Could our inquiries there have riled someone?"

"Possibly, but who else knew about it besides Ben? Guess I'll be late coming home after all. I want to pay another visit to Zach Kinsdale without further delay. He's the only other person who would know about our visit to the olive farm. Ben must have notified him after our visit."

"I'd love to hear what he has to say," Marla remarked.

"Hey, me too." Brianna sashayed into the room, clad in jeans and a sweater. She dragged her backpack along and plunked it onto the kitchen table. "Why don't we come along?" she said, loud enough for her dad to hear. "It might be safer than staying here, since the person who threw that rock knows where we live."

"Your daughter has a point," Marla told her husband. "We can always sit in the car if you prefer."

"All right," Dalton conceded with a sigh. "You've already shown up with me at their house, so it won't be so unusual. This isn't normally how I conduct police business, though. Don't tell the chief I'm letting you go along when I interview persons of interest in a case."

Oh, like Captain Williams doesn't know already? Marla thought with an amused smile.

Forty minutes later, Zach ushered them into his living room after they exchanged pleasantries. He wore dark blue pants and a plaid shirt. His hair was damp as though he'd just come from the shower. Cooking aromas emanated from the kitchen, where his wife must be preparing dinner. Marla hoped this visit wouldn't take long.

"What brings you back that's so dire, Detective?" he asked, settling onto an armchair while the three of them sat on a sofa.

"We got a rock thrown at our window with

a note attached to warn my wife off the case. It came right after we visited your cousin Ben. He seems to know something about your property, Mr. Kinsdale, and I'm tired of beating around the bush on the subject. Will you come clean, or do I have to get a subpoena for your lawyer?"

Zach's shoulders slumped, and a haunted look entered his eyes. "Very well. My brothers and I had always believed we owned the farm. But after Pop died, I couldn't find a deed. What I did find was a fifty year lease with an option to buy at fair market value. I tried to contact the landholder, but he had passed away without any apparent heirs. I hired a real estate attorney to see how we could go about making a claim."

"So you don't own the farm?"

"That's correct. We've been paying property taxes, which should count for something. It's kind of a legal tangle, but our attorney has filed an adverse possession claim. We're hoping this will work in our favor."

"What's that?" Brianna asked. She'd been quiet up until now but couldn't suppress her curiosity. Her eyes shone with zeal as she listened in to their conversation.

Zach regarded her with a frown. "Adverse possession means we're occupying property belonging to someone else with the specific intent of taking ownership. Several conditions must be met to qualify. There are two types of adverse possession filing. With color of title, we have to be in possession for at least seven years. In addition, we must be cultivating or improving the land and protecting it with enclosures. Without color of title means we've been paying property taxes and any liens on the property, as well as meeting the other conditions. Besides occupying the property for a minimum of seven years, we have to be in open use of the property, essentially acting as the sole owner."

"You've certainly met those conditions," Marla said.

"Yes, and once our claim is accepted, we can file a Return of Real Property in Attempt to Establish Possession Without Color of Title. Whew, that's a mouthful. Then the courts will rule as to whether we are now the legal owner and occupant of the property."

Dalton lifted his eyebrows. "It sounds as though your attorney has a handle on things."

"I'm hoping so. My brothers don't know about this problem, Detective. I haven't wanted to worry them. We've put so much sweat and energy into this land that it should be ours."

"Did Francine find out?" Marla asked. "She'd planned to write an exposé. Was your farm the subject?"

Zach gave a rueful chuckle. "Oh, she knew about it all right. That woman was smart, but her interests lay elsewhere."

"Did she also know about the accidents on the farm, like the silo incident?"

His lips compressed. "That's merely a rumor. Farm accidents are a hazard of our industry. Things happen all the time around machinery. But that silo fatality couldn't have happened at Kinsdale Farms since we don't store grain."

Brianna nudged Marla. "Ask him about the other woman," she told Marla in an undertone.

"How about Alyce Greene?" Marla asked. "The food blogger supported your sustainable methods. Did she discover you didn't own the place?"

"I have no idea, unless Francine told her. The two of them had more in common than people realized. They shared similar views on the food industry and often ended up at the same functions. They greeted each other with an easy familiarity."

Marla had gotten the impression they were casually acquainted from the bake-off contest. It made her wonder how long the two women had known each other. Did they share a closer connection than she'd thought?

"Look, I'm afraid of losing the farm if someone else comes forward to claim the title," Zach said, wringing his hands. "Maybe the former owner had a will and named an heir other than a relative. If word gets out, the town might seek another site for the spring harvest festival. That event brings in a lot of business."

"Is that why you invested in the olive grove?" Dalton asked. "As security in case you lost this property?"

Zach cast a glance toward the kitchen as though wondering at the sudden silence. Likely his wife was listening in to their conversation. Did Grace know about his secret? If not before, she did now, Marla concluded.

"That's only one reason," Zach admitted. "The Florida olive oil industry is just beginning to thrive. It could become a lucrative business, and I wanted to get in at the start. We can't grow the crop here, so we needed a property up north. My cousin loved the idea when I proposed it to him."

He leaned forward and regarded each of them with an earnest look. "I'd appreciate it if you'd keep a lid on things until I straighten out these issues of ownership. I'm still hoping we can make a claim if no one else stands in the way."

Marla gave him an assessing glance. Was he telling the truth about Francine and Alyce? Or had they gotten in the way of his plans?

"What if you lose out?" she asked him. "If you don't get the deed to the land, would you move your farm elsewhere? Are there any fields left further to the west?"

"Not really. You'd run into the Everglades. I could buy out someone else to the north. There's lots of property up that way. But we'd lose our customer base here as well as our crops."

"I understand you buy imported products for your marketplace from Amalfi Consolidated," Dalton said.

"We have a contract with them, yes. They haven't missed a shipment yet."

"So you're pleased with how Tony Winters handles the account?"

"That's right." Zach gave him a puzzled glance. "Are you implying there's something wrong in that direction?"

"His Italian partners are paying him a visit. Have you ever met them?"

"They came by with him once. Can't say

I took a liking to that bunch. I could tell Tony was uncomfortable with them. They seemed to be haranguing him."

"You're pleased with their products, then?" Dalton persisted.

"Sure, why wouldn't I be? Do you know something I don't? Oh wait, I get it. You've been talking to my cousin about olive oil scams. He's into that kind of thing. It's also a way to convince you to buy locally produced goods."

"True, but he may have a valid point. I'd consider getting a bottle of Amalfi's extra virgin olive oil tested if I were you."

Zach stood with an air of dismissal. "Is that all, Detective? Because I think our dinner is ready." Sounds had resumed from the kitchen, dishes clanking and sink water splashing.

Dalton rose, as did Marla and Brianna. "I appreciate your candor, Mr. Kinsdale. Please let me know how your legal issue resolves. I hope things work out in your favor."

Grace bustled from the kitchen to say farewell. She shot her husband a questioning glance. Marla could imagine the conversation that would follow their departure.

"So do you think Zach can be eliminated as a suspect?" she asked Dalton during the drive home. Her stomach growled. The food aromas in Zach's house had made her hungry. That was a good sign. Perhaps her sensitivity had gone.

"The Kinsdales have a lot at stake here, but Zach may be right in that Francine's interests lay elsewhere."

"Maybe she meant to drag Amalfi Consolidated's dirty dealings into the light. Tony Winters might have gotten wind of it and silenced her. Or Janet could have done it to protect her standard of living. And then Alyce discovered their secret while researching food sources for restaurants."

"We can't overlook other possibilities," Dalton told her. "Francine didn't have any close relatives to inherit her estate. But someone must be listed as her beneficiary. My team is looking into it to see if she had a will. Otherwise, that distant aunt is her only living kin."

"Alyce's death has to be related," Marla added. "It must be something they'd both discovered, which would have nothing to do with an heir. I get the feeling we're missing something important."

"How about the fellow who drugged you?" Brianna asked her dad from the backseat.

"Colin's alibi checks out for Francine's

death," he replied. "And I can't think of a motive for him to go after Alyce."

"Have you considered Alyce's acquaintances?" Brianna suggested. "Are there people she might have offended in her blog, like that newspaper critic you'd mentioned? And what about her family?"

Marla addressed her husband. "Did you ever interview Alyce's husband, Jon Greene? I remember you'd sent Sergeant Langley to see him after the hit-and-run accident."

Dalton nodded, his grip firm on the wheel. "He was proud of his wife's blog and her efforts to educate people about the food industry."

"Did he have a burial service for her yet? I didn't even think about it. I would have attended."

"It was on Sunday. Langley went, since we were out of town."

"What about the brother? He gave Alyce's husband a starter loan for his food truck operation. Alyce hoped to win the bake-off prize to pay him back. She told me Steve's firm manages Tony Winter's accounts and there might be something fishy about Amalfi Consolidated."

"Such as?" Dalton shot her a quick glance, his brows raised.

"Alyce wouldn't tell me more, because she

wanted to get evidence. Remember?"

"Guess I'll have to pay the brother another visit."

"Maybe Steve has met Tony's colleagues from Italy. If his firm does the books for this end of their operation, they may include him on their must-see list while in the country. Let me know if you want me to sound him out on my own."

"Nix that idea, sweetcakes. You'd better focus on taking care of yourself."

"Don't worry. I'll be safe." Was that what he'd meant, or did her husband refer to her stomach problems? Did he share the same suspicions regarding the true source of her ailment?

"How's your fundraiser coming along?" he asked, effectively diverting her attention.

Her face had heated under his scrutiny. Glad for the change in topic, she replied in a chattier tone than intended. "We've been concentrating on publicizing the event. Robyn has made up flyers for customers, and she's collecting emails to send a newsletter. Janet is handling the outside publicity. Hey, maybe we can get Raquel involved. A mention on her TV show would give us a boost. I'll give her a call myself."

Marla touched base with her team on

Tuesday at work. Robyn and Janet both thought it was a great idea to contact the food show host. Yet Marla hesitated to make the call. Had Dalton spoken to Raquel since the hit-and-run incident? Did she have an alibi for that afternoon?

She checked in with Becky instead via cell phone and proposed her idea. The museum curator replied in a gushing tone.

"It's a wonderful proposal. I'm sure Raquel will be glad to help us. Do you want me to ask her?"

"No, I'll get in touch with her. Is everything good at your end for the event?"

"Sure is. I've got a supply of flyers from your receptionist, and we've been handing them out. I can't wait, Marla. You're such a peach for pitching in."

"We've gotten food donations from Arnie at Bagel Busters and from Teri at the chocolate factory. And I spoke to the person at *Eat Well Now* magazine who's taken over Francine's position. She's willing to send a reporter to cover our event regarding the food tie-in angle and how we'd all met at the harvest festival. It's too bad Alyce can't be here, too. She would have promoted our cause to her blog readership."

Becky's tone cooled. "I can't say I'm sorry. She'd have put a negative spin on

295

things. If you're going to talk to Raquel, you'd better not mention that woman's name."

"Thank you for the advice. I'll let you know what she says. Oh, we've put a poster in our front window, too."

"That's great. I'm sure we'll have a terrific turnout. By the way, you and Tally have to come by the museum again. We just put up a new exhibit on wartime in Palm Haven. It goes through the major conflicts and how our town fared."

"My husband would love that one. Thanks for letting me know."

Before she could put her plan into action and call Raquel, Marla's next client arrived. The rest of the day flew by, although Nicole found a moment to corner her and get the latest news. Marla related their trip to the olive grove. The slim stylist soaked it up, her eyes alight with awe.

"I love it, Marla. You get to do the coolest things. But if you don't think that local farmer is involved in the murders, who's your main suspect?"

"That's what I'd like to know." Marla cleaned her station while they spoke in low tones. "Becky and Raquel seem to have a mutual admiration society. Francine's successor at work isn't ruled out. We have

Alyce's family and the people she'd offended, like Carlton Paige. Tristan the pastry chef seems innocent, but his executive chef or the restaurant owner at The Royal Palate might be involved in an olive oil scam with Tony Winters. I'd say he's the main guy in my mind."

Nicole tapped a painted fingernail to her chin. A set of bracelets jangled on her arm. "Your husband has his work cut out for him."

"Oh, I didn't tell you about the rock thrown at our door. It had a note attached." She repeated the message as Nicole's eyes widened.

"You must have upset someone with your inquiries."

"I know, and it came directly after our trip north. Nobody else knew about that excursion other than Ben Kinsdale. He must have notified his cousin Zach right after we left."

In a thoughtful mood, Marla squirted her counter with cleaning solution and wiped it down. The shampoo girl came by to sweep cut hairs off the floor.

"Our job sure would be easier if we had one of those modern vacuum systems," Nicole remarked. "You brush the hairs into a vent in the wall, and they get sucked into a trash bin by the rear exit."

"Yes, but you know how much that would cost to install? Our method works just fine."

"So what's your next move in the case?" Nicole asked, glancing toward the front to see if her next client had arrived.

"I need to call Raquel about our fund-raiser, and then I can ask her what she was doing the day Alyce died. How did your weekend with Kevin go?"

Nicole's complexion deepened. "I really like him, Marla. He might be The One."

Marla crossed her fingers and held them up. "Here's hoping he feels the same."

"He wants me to meet his family. I'm nervous about it. That's a big step. Even Eddie and I didn't get that far." Eddie had been her previous boyfriend.

"Does he have a specific date in mind?"

"He says we're invited for Sunday dinner. His parents and siblings live in Miami, so they're not too far. He has a brother and sister," Nicole explained. Her own family lived up north, so she had no relatives close by.

"Good, things are moving along then. You'll be fine."

"How is Brianna doing? Anything new with her?"

"She keeps busy with all her activities. I can't believe she's sixteen and will be applying to colleges next year. She still has her heart set on going to Boston."

Nicole chuckled. "Give her a winter in the snow, and she might rush home."

"Or she might love it and get a job there afterwards. We'd miss her terribly."

"You've come a long way, girlfriend. From someone who never wanted kids, now you're doting over your stepdaughter."

"Oh look, your next customer just walked in," Marla said in a bright tone. She turned away before Nicole could ask about her family expansion plans.

Those plans might be coming to fruition if instinct told her right. On the way home from work, she finally bought a pregnancy test kit. When later at the house, the results turned positive, she gasped with mingled joy and fear. Could it be true? At nearly thirty-nine years old, was she actually pregnant? Moreover, should she share the news with Dalton and Brianna?

She knew her husband's reaction. He'd be thrilled, but he would also forbid her from any further snooping into his cases. His overprotective nature wouldn't allow her to place herself in danger. Worry about her condition might even distract him at a critical moment.

Biting her lower lip, she debated what to

do. She'd hold off on telling him for now. Better to wait until he'd put Francine's killer behind bars. Meanwhile, she should consider getting confirmation at the doctor's office.

She hid the material, sticking it inside a bag and then placing it into the larger trash receptacle in the garage. Then she put on her best actor's face when her family came home. Using her conversational skills, she got Brianna and Dalton each talking about their day and avoided any mention of her own activities aside from work chatter.

She couldn't hide her secret the next morning from Nicole, however. The other stylist zeroed in on her as she was readying her station.

"What's up, Marla? Why do you have that weird expression on your face?"

Unable to keep the news from her friend, Marla gripped Nicole's arm. "Can you keep a secret?" she said in a low voice. "You know how my stomach has been sensitive lately? I bought a pregnancy test kit at the pharmacy. It came out positive."

"No way!" Nicole shouted. She stepped away and regarded Marla with keen pleasure.

"Hey, keep it down. I haven't told Dalton yet."

"What are you waiting for? We have to celebrate."

"He's too involved in his case. If I mention my condition, he'll worry about me. I could prove to be a distraction at the wrong time."

"Heck, he may already suspect. That guy is sharp."

"I know, but I'd rather not say anything until he wraps the case."

"That's your choice. I'll keep silent if you wish, but I'm so excited for you!"

Marla's personal concerns fled her mind when Tristan called to say he would be declining her offer to participate in the fundraiser. He'd rather not make waves with his boss. When he heard Marla had already found someone in his place, he seemed relieved.

She'd just hung up on him when Raquel Hayes walked in the door.

It must be providence, Marla thought, *since I'd meant to contact her.* The TV chef wore her bleached blond hair piled high atop her head. An emerald top matched her eyes and the earrings dangling from her ears.

"Marla, do you have a minute?" she asked in her honeyed Southern accent. "Becky told me about your fundraiser, and I said I'd be delighted to mention y'all on my next

show. I came by for a sneak peek beforehand."

"Welcome to our salon. I'm glad you're
willing to support us." Marla introduced
her to their receptionist. "Robyn came up
with the idea of giving goody bags to people
booking a service that day, so if you have
any promo items, we can include them."

"Sure, I have mini-spatulas with the
show's logo. I'll send you over a batch. So
have you done an event like this one before?" Her gaze darted about the salon, taking in the stylists at their stations, the
customers in the waiting area, and the
receptionist typing on the computer keyboard.

"It's our first bad hair day clinic, and I'm
already anticipating a success. We have Janet
Winters working on publicity. Robyn has
been handing out flyers, and we'll be sending an email newsletter soon. We've been
fielding a lot of calls about the event, so I'm
predicting a big turnout."

"That's great. What's in the back beyond
the hair and manicure stations?" Raquel
strode forward without waiting for an invita-
tion.

"Our pedicure stations have an alcove of
their own. Then we have the laundry facilities, a storage room where we mix our solu-

tions, and two restrooms. The day spa next door is ours, also. You can go there for full-service spa treatments."

Raquel halted, peering at Marla. "You're looking a bit piqued. Are you feeling all right?"

"I've got a lot on my mind. I suppose you heard the news about Alyce."

"Yes, such a tragedy. I can't imagine who would hit the poor woman and leave the scene without helping her."

"Where were you that day?" Marla asked in a casual tone.

"I was at home studying the script for my next show."

"May I ask what kind of car you drive?"

Raquel's face reddened. "Why all the questions? I might have had a disagreement or two with that nasty blogger, but I wouldn't cause her any harm."

"Does that mean you believe someone tried to run her down?"

"Of course not. It was a tragic accident."

"Dalton is working the case. He believes the incident might be related to Francine's murder. Maybe they both knew something that got them killed."

"Oh, dear. I'd hate to think any of us are next." Raquel put a hand on the nearest counter as though to steady herself.

"I'm sure we'll be fine. Did you travel far to get here?"

"Not really. I live in Pembroke Pines."

"That's a bit of a commute from your TV studio. Have you always lived there? Or did you move after culinary school?"

"I used to live in the Kendall area in Miami. That seems like ages ago. I worked under several chefs before striking out on my own."

Her credentials had been easy for Dalton to verify. So how come he couldn't find anything on her earlier background?

CHAPTER EIGHTEEN

"I've called the culinary arts school. Raquel graduated with her class," Dalton said when Marla spoke to him later on her cell phone. "She didn't take out any student loans."

"What does that mean?" Marla sat on a stool in the storeroom where she'd gone to get a bottle of water.

"She had cash available to pay the tuition. Yet I can't find any details of her past beyond the cooking jobs she'd held."

"Doesn't the school application give her relevant information?"

"Yes, and that stuff checks out, but it isn't what I'm looking for. There's a gap between her early years and the odd jobs she did before applying to the culinary arts academy. My gut feeling tells me something is off. But it could be irrelevant to this case. I learned other news today that's more important."

"Like what?" She heard voices in the

background on his end of the line.

"Sorry, I have to go. I'll text you later. I won't be home for dinner."

"Okay, but what is it —" A click sounded. He'd rung off.

"Drat." She frowned at the phone. Maybe Robyn knew how to access those databases where you could research people. She could help Dalton dig deeper into the TV show host's earlier years. Then again, he might not appreciate her interference in that regard.

While working on her next client, Marla kept her phone visible in case Dalton sent her a text message. Nothing came through during the entire afternoon.

It wasn't until she went home, let the dogs out, greeted Brianna, and started dinner preparations that she finally heard her phone buzz. She'd kept it on vibrate earlier and had forgotten to switch the ringer back on.

Marla stood by the kitchen sink as she peered at the text message from Dalton.

Francine's beneficiary is Alyce Greene.

What? Her heart thumped in her chest. Why in the world would Francine list Alyce as her heir? Those two must have had a much closer relationship than anyone thought. Or did Francine favor the food blogger because she and Alyce had shared the same beliefs?

Brianna breezed into the kitchen and halted when she saw Marla's face. "What's wrong?"

"You won't believe what your father just texted me. He discovered Francine Dodger left her estate to Alyce Greene, the food blogger. I realized they'd known each other before the bake-off but not the extent of it."

The teen's dark eyes gleamed with interest. "And now both of them are dead. Who inherits Francine's money now that Alyce is gone?"

"Good question. I imagine her husband Jon would be the one." She gasped as the implications hit. "You don't think he's responsible for their deaths, do you?"

"Maybe he knocked Francine off so his wife would gain her money, and then he bumped Alyce off next."

"That would only make sense if Francine had a sizable estate."

"Here's another theory," Brianna offered. "The women had a thing going, and Alyce's husband got jealous."

Marla wagged her finger. "You're not implying their relationship was more intimate than friendship, are you?"

Brianna spread her hands. "Why not?

Maybe Alyce was planning to leave her husband for Francine. He got rid of the rival and then later his wife."

"But Alyce seemed so supportive of him. She wanted the prize money to pay off his loan so he could expand his food truck operation."

"That could have been her bargaining chip for a divorce."

Marla put her hands on her hips. "I don't see those women as having that kind of relationship. Besides, Francine had a boyfriend."

"That's true." Brianna added dog food to the pets' bowls and refilled their water dishes. She let them back inside and they bounded to their meals. Slurping noises filled the air.

"What about the other suspects?" Brianna asked. "Is Dad close to nailing anyone?"

"We've been focusing on Tony Winters and his olive oil imports. He's still our best lead. There's something shady about his Italian connection, and The Royal Palate is involved. I got sick after tasting a spoonful of their extra virgin olive oil."

"Didn't you ask their pastry chef to participate in your fundraiser?"

"He declined. Anyway, we got Teri from the chocolate factory instead, and Arnie has agreed to provide appetizers. Robyn and Janet are doing a great job with publicity, by the way. It's going to be a fun event. I should give you some flyers to pass out to your friends for their moms."

Marla rattled on about the proposed bad hair day clinic while dipping chicken tenderloins in a white horseradish and mayonnaise mixture before coating them with bread crumbs and chopped parsley. She placed the prepared pieces on a greased baking pan then set the dish in the oven to bake for a half-hour.

While Brianna wandered off to finish her homework, Marla contemplated the possibilities on the case. Would Alyce's husband be able to shed more light on her relationship to Francine? Had Dalton contacted him about the will's provisions?

Another thought struck her. Alyce's estate likely went to her husband. But if he died, what then? Most likely, her kids would inherit, unless her brother Steve entered the picture somehow.

The links twirled round and round in her head. Each person seemed connected to another by a tenuous thread. And don't forget Carlton Paige, the food critic, she reminded herself. He'd sent his wife to Francine for the purpose of discrediting

Alyce at the festival. Did he realize the two women had a close connection? And why had Sally refused to comply? Because Francine knew about her affair with the personal trainer? Maybe Alyce had also discovered this indiscretion. If so, Sally may have been the one who eliminated them both.

As another option, Sally had said her information on Alyce related more to the brother. Once again, Steve Madison appeared to be implicated.

Marla scrubbed a hand over her face. These thoughts made her dizzy. Any one of her recent acquaintances might be guilty. She leaned against the counter and waited for the moment of instability to pass.

The garage door rumbled. Dalton must be coming home earlier than expected. She unlocked the inner door, eager to greet him and discuss the case despite her fatigue.

As her mother had trained her, Marla served dinner first before mentioning anything important. After they'd cleared the dishes, she faced her husband across the table while Brianna ran off to text her friends.

"Did you speak to Alyce's husband about her inheritance from Francine?" she asked, bringing up the subject foremost on her mind.

Dalton looked as tired as she felt. "I plan to stop by his house tomorrow. My team is checking into the possibility of life insurance policies as well."

"I hope Alyce had one. Jon will have to hire a housekeeper to help with the kids and to clean the place. Things work out nicely for him otherwise. He'll be able to pay off his loan with whatever money he gets. How well off was Francine? Did you access her accounts?"

"Yes, but her nest egg was modest. I could see why she'd hoped to win the contest prize. The only way she could guarantee everyone's jobs at the magazine was to take control. That way, she could also choose what to publish without having to get approval." Dalton swirled his glass of Chardonnay that she'd served him along with the chicken dish. He'd poured himself seconds and took another swig while Marla mulled over his words.

"It's too bad Francine didn't win," she concluded. "I should pay her staff another visit to sound them out regarding Alyce. The food blogger may have stopped by their offices, or perhaps Francine had mentioned her."

"Tomorrow is Thursday. You have the morning free," Dalton pointed out. "Why don't you come with me to see Jon Greene? We can go as a couple and express our condolences."

"Okay, I'd like to meet him. Did Sergeant Langley learn anything new at Alyce's funeral?"

"A lot of the folks from the food industry were present to pay their respects. He saw some people from the bake-off contest, but nothing noteworthy occurred. Alyce Greene's blog had a large following."

Marla wrinkled her nose. "Did Carlton Paige show up? He resented her popularity and accused her of stealing his readership."

"No, but his wife came. I believe the ladies knew each other from their gym."

"How about the TV chef? Alyce told me Raquel cheats viewers by using shortcuts behind the scenes, and that she only got her show from sleeping with the producer."

"Her name was on Langley's list. He spied her cozying up to Alyce's husband. Maybe Raquel was trying to find out what Alyce had told him."

"That's assuming there's any truth to what Alyce said. Maybe she was envious of Raquel's popularity and meant to bring her ratings down, although she did seem dedicated to the principles of sustainable farming and green resources. Still, why aim darts at Raquel's off-stage practices? She could have kept quiet about them. I liked Raquel's show and thought she did a good job of engaging the audience."

"You never know about people's motives. We'll ask Jon about these things tomorrow."

Jon Greene looked as slim as his wife when they met him at his doorstep. Either he didn't do much tasting of his food truck's fare, or he followed Alyce's precepts regarding healthy eating. His blue eyes wore a sad expression under sandy brows that matched his hair. A day's growth of stubble shadowed his chin.

He gestured for them to enter his salmon-colored single-story house. Luckily for them, he hadn't left yet to meet with his produce suppliers for the day. Or else, he was taking time off to mourn his wife.

Marla stepped past kids' toys strewn across the carpet and trailed him into the kitchen. His children must be in school, she surmised. Her practiced glance noted dirty dishes in the sink and overflowing trash cans. What a difference from when Marla had been here previously. She'd watched Alyce stir her vegetable gumbo, and all had seemed so normal. Now look at the place.

"Has anyone come to help out since your

wife's passing?" Marla asked in a sympathetic tone. They entered the family room, where a coffee table at least had been cleared. The TV blared in the background, and Jon shut it off. He bade them to take seats on the sofa and followed suit on a recliner chair.

Jon gave a helpless shrug. His sport shirt hung loose over a pair of faded jeans. "My brother-in-law has been over to see what he can do, but I'm managing well enough. It's harder on our kids. The school suggested a grief counselor, so I've made an appointment."

"That's a good idea," she said with a nod. The smell of burnt toast entered her nose. She put a hand to her stomach. *Oh please, not now.*

"Steve's wife isn't much good for anything," Jon went on. He noticed Marla's startled glance at his bitter tone. "Irina is his second wife. She's considerably younger than him. Stevie boy ditched Patty when she wanted kids. Children weren't on his agenda. They'd curb his lifestyle too much."

"I didn't realize he was married," Marla stated. "We haven't met yet."

"Steve's firm gave you a loan to get your business started, correct?" Dalton leaned forward, clasping his hands together. A stubborn lock of hair fell onto his forehead.

"Yes, Alyce and I were grateful to him. I'd gotten laid off from my IT job, you see. But I had always loved to cook. We tended to support food truck vendors, knowing how hard it is to be successful. So when Alyce suggested I go into the business, I leapt at the chance. My specialty is gourmet tacos. But there were legal fees to set up an LLC and get my license and such, not to mention the truck and equipment. We put our savings into it as well as the loan."

"So it's a big deal if you fail," Marla guessed. "Have you been able to save for your kids' college educations?"

"Yes, we've been squirreling away a small amount each month toward their college funds." His voice choked. "They miss their mother dearly."

"I'm so sorry for your loss." Marla's eyes misted. This poor guy seemed to be genuinely grieving. "Did you have any insurance on Alyce? I don't mean to pry, but it could help you hire a steady housekeeper," she said in a gentle tone, while Dalton let her take the lead. She came across as less intimidating than a police detective. "If you work late hours, who will stay here with the kids after school?"

"I've hired a high school student from the

neighborhood as babysitter. We'd used her before. The children like her, and she can fix their dinner." The man's shoulders slumped. "We thought Alyce would outlive me, so we never considered getting a life insurance policy in her name. With her healthy eating habits and jogging every day, you'd think she would be around for a while. Who knew something like this would take her from us?" He swiped at his eyes, while Marla and Dalton maintained a compassionate silence.

Too many women didn't value their lives enough to get insurance, Marla thought. With their household management, child-rearing, cooking and cleaning duties, all women with families needed coverage during their earning years.

"If you'd like me to help you find someone else, let me know. I have references," Marla said. She'd hired a housekeeper for Tally after she came home from rehab. Tally needed to build her strength while caring for baby Luke and dealing with her late husband's estate. She had been grateful to have assistance for mundane chores.

"How's the business going these days?" Dalton asked in an idle tone, while his stiff posture indicated his keen attention.

Jon's face brightened. "We've been zooming like rockets ever since I started. Alyce entered the bake-off contest, hoping she'd win so I could pay off my startup loan and expand the enterprise into a fleet. I'd have customers for more trucks if only I had the money to invest."

"We're still calling your wife's death an accident, but it happened so soon after Francine's death that it might be more than coincidence. Can you think of anyone who might have wanted to harm your wife?"

Jon gaped at them. "You think somebody hit her on purpose?"

"It's crossed my mind. But so far, we don't have any evidence otherwise."

"No, not unless —" Jon stopped abruptly.

"What?" Marla prompted.

"She was worried about her brother's association with Tony Winters. Alyce said he'd get Steve in trouble. She warned him that his firm should break off their relationship with Amalfi Consolidated."

"Did she say why?" Dalton asked.

Jon shook his head. "Alyce wanted to get proof before going public. She wouldn't even tell me what was bothering her. I know she liked to delve into thorny food issues for her blog. She'd uncovered more than one unethical practice in the industry."

"So she might have offended someone?"

"I suppose that's possible."

"Did she ever mention Carlton Paige, the food critic? He considered her a rival of sort," Dalton said with a glance in Marla's direction.

Jon gave a mirthless chuckle. "Oh, the fellow disliked her for sure. She dissed his reviews and hinted he took favors in exchange for a high rating. Paige accused my wife of eroding his readership, but have you eaten at those places he recommends? They're not all he's cracked them up to be. If his column is losing readers, it's because the man has lost his edge."

"Could he have wanted to get her out of the way?" Dalton studied the other man's face.

"Are you kidding? Man, that guy couldn't hurt a fly. He doesn't have it in him."

"And yet, somebody killed Francine Dodger, who'd been wearing your wife's jacket. The two of them looked alike from the rear."

Jon's face paled. "Wait, you don't think Alyce was the intended target, do you? And when the murderer failed to get her the first time, he tried again? Who would do such a thing?"

"That's what we're trying to learn." Dalton's gaze narrowed. "The guilty party had to be present at Kinsdale Farms on the day of the bake-off. I understand your wife didn't approve of TV chef, Raquel Hayes. Did you ever catch them arguing?"

"Not to my knowledge. Is she a suspect?"

"Everyone is a suspect at this stage, Mr. Greene. Even you. It appears you've come into some money. I was quite surprised to hear your wife was Francine's beneficiary. And now I suppose you'll inherit her estate."

"What? Good God. I had no idea." Shock distorted the man's features.

"Didn't Alyce know about this? What exactly was the nature of the relationship between your wife and Francine?"

Jon shot to his feet. "It wasn't what you seem to be implying. My wife was faithful to me, and I loved her very much. She was devoted to our marriage and our kids."

"Then please enlighten me," Dalton said in a patient tone. He rose to face the other man.

Marla remained seated, feeling tired for no reason. Maybe she needed another cup of coffee for an energy boost.

"Alyce got interested in genealogy research," Jon explained, staring at the carpet. "She looked up her family at one of those online sites and submitted her DNA into a gene bank that matches people. After a long

319

wait, Francine's name popped up."

Now it was Dalton's turn to stare. "You mean they were related?"

"There was a ninety-six percent probability. They'd met as acquaintances before at food industry events. When Alyce got the hit on the genealogy site, she contacted Francine. The magazine publisher admitted she'd been adopted and had become interested in learning her heritage. She'd tried to contact the adoption agency, but the place had closed and their records were gone. So she submitted her DNA to the gene pool in an attempt to discover any living relations."

"I had no idea Francine had been adopted, did you?" Marla asked her husband. She'd be miffed if he had withheld this information from her.

"No, this is news to me," he replied.

"Was Alyce's mother deceased by this time?" Marla asked. "If not, the girls could have asked her how they might be connected."

"Sadly, she had passed. But Alyce looked through her mom's documents and discovered adoption papers among them. She'd had a daughter at age seventeen and had given her up to an agency. A heartbreaking letter asking for forgiveness was included in the envelope."

"So she must have married later and had two kids with her husband."

"Yes, so we gathered. When Alyce called Francine with the news, the magazine editor was elated. She insisted they keep their relationship private, however. Nonetheless, I was excited for my wife. Unfortunately, her brother didn't have such a happy reaction."

"Oh no? You'd think he would be thrilled to discover a potential sibling."

"When Alyce told Steve about her discovery, he yelled at her and said their mom would never deceive them that way. So she decided to get proof. The women both submitted to further lab tests. The results left no doubts that Alyce and Francine were sisters."

CHAPTER NINETEEN

"Actually, my wife and Francine were half-sisters through their mom," Jon Greene told his guests. "Francine was happy to discover she had a family but also resentful. After all, their mother had abandoned her, while Alyce and her brother had a normal childhood."

"This means Steve was also Francine's brother," Marla pointed out.

"That's correct. He couldn't accept the evidence and got angry at Alyce. She wanted to get to know Francine better. The women proceeded at a slow pace. It was happenstance that they both entered the bake-off contest."

Dalton resumed his seat next to Marla. "Tell us about your brother-in-law's connection to Tony Winters' import company. Is he Tony's personal financial advisor, or does he handle the company's accounts?"

"I don't rightly know the answer, Detective. Steve has been hit hard by his sister's death. It's a little over a week now. I still can't believe she won't walk through the door anymore."

"It may have been an accident or not, Mr. Greene. A neighbor came outside after she heard a shriek. A white car was speeding down the road, but she didn't catch the plate number. She saw your wife lying in the street."

"We've been over this before." Jon slumped back into his chair and hung his head.

"I'm just saying . . . if this wasn't an accident, it means somebody knew your wife's routine. Have you noticed any strangers hanging around the area?"

"Heck, no. That's something we'd look out for with the kids and all."

This wasn't a gated community, Marla noted. Too bad, or there might have been a video showing visitors coming and going. So had the guilty party, if one existed, determined that Alyce jogged the same route every morning? Or had she been followed that day alone? What had she done to bring the killer down upon her?

Or it could have been an accident, some fool of a driver who hadn't been paying attention and then got spooked and ran.

Dalton had already put out a notice to all the car repair shops and rental agencies to be on the lookout for a white vehicle with damage.

The only real way to determine if this had been a deliberate act was to find a motive.

"What will you do now?" she asked Jon.

"I suppose I should hire a housekeeper as you'd suggested. I hate to be crass, but what does Francine's estate include, Detective?"

"I can put you in touch with her lawyer for a more definitive answer."

"Good, I'd like to pay off my loan so I won't have that debt hanging over my head. That's assuming I'm the beneficiary with Alyce gone."

"Will you expand the food truck business like you'd planned?" Marla put forth. Dalton stirred restlessly beside her. They should leave soon. She picked up her purse and slung the strap over her shoulder.

"With the loan paid off, I could approach investors. I'd rather use the rest of the money to finish funding the kids' pre-paid college programs."

"Maybe Steve will chip in. He's their uncle after all."

"I wouldn't impose on him that way. He's done enough for us."

After reaffirming their condolences, Marla

and Dalton left shortly thereafter. She gave a sigh of relief once outside in the fresh air. The house had seemed heavy with sorrow. Jon would have his hands full raising two young children on his own.

"Maybe we're looking at things the wrong way," she said to Dalton during the drive home. She needed to get her car before heading to work. "Alyce, as a blogger, must have dug into people's backgrounds for her articles. She could have quite a list of personal indiscretions hidden away. Have you checked her bank accounts to see if she had any unusual deposits?"

Dalton gazed at her askance. "You mean, she might have been blackmailing folks?"

"It's worth a shot to check out. I would doubt it based on my instincts, but you never know. Are you going to see Steve Madison later today? I wish I could come but my schedule is fully booked."

"Huh, like that's ever stopped you before. Actually, it might be useful for you to see him under the guise of needing an investment advisor. Let's see what I can learn this afternoon. If I'm not satisfied, you can give it a try."

"Okay, that sounds like a plan." Pleased by his faith in her, she ran into the house when he dropped her off. A half hour later, she left again after taking care of the dogs and changing into more comfortable shoes.

During a break in her work schedule, Nicole cornered her. The other stylist's eyes sparkled as she regarded Marla at the next station.

"I'm so excited. Kevin wants to take me to Atlantis in the Bahamas. That resort costs a fortune."

Marla's mouth curved in a grin. "Good for you. I love the food in Nassau." She'd been to the island while on another case. That visit hadn't turned out very well. "Do you want to use your vacation time for this getaway?"

"We'll see. Kevin says he'll make reservations after I meet his parents on Sunday."

"Oh, my. Do you think he's preparing to pop the question? Are you ready for that step?"

Nicole's face burst into a radiant smile. "I hope so. We'll never forget how you and Dalton introduced us."

"Yeah, well after he rescued Spooks from that hole in the neighbor's backyard, I had hero worship. And when I learned he was single, that cinched it."

"You'll be in our wedding party, won't you? Both you and Dalton."

"Let's not count your chickens until

they're hatched," she said, repeating one of her mother's favorite clichés. "I didn't tell you where I went this morning. Dalton discovered that Francine's heir was Alyce Greene. Would you believe they are half-sisters?"

Nicole's jaw gaped. "Do tell, girlfriend."

Marla rattled off the gist of their conversation with Jon Greene. She could confide in Nicole who would keep things under wraps.

"No kidding? That's an unexpected connection. You should visit the magazine offices again. Francine may have said something to her staff about this newfound family."

Marla's pulse accelerated as a memory surfaced. "Lynette Wilde from their office told me Francine had a sister who died when they were young. An aunt claimed Francine's body. Were these people from her adoptive family?"

"They'd have to be, if Alyce and her brother were her biological siblings," Nicole pointed out.

"You'd think Alyce would have stepped forward to take charge of Francine's final arrangements."

"She'd have to bear the burden of cost then. Maybe her husband didn't want her to get involved, especially since someone else had staked a claim."

"True, neither woman had admitted their connection in public. Perhaps they wanted to get used to the idea first." Marla tapped her chin. "I should revisit Francine's office as you said. Maybe Francine had let something slip about Alyce's relationship to her. Let me check my schedule to see when I can take a break."

She didn't have time to follow up until next Monday, however. The rest of the work week was fully booked. And Sunday was family day.

When the weekend rolled around, she picked up her mother on Sunday morning and drove to Delray along with Brianna to meet the teen's grandparents for brunch. Dalton was stuck working on his cases and couldn't take time off. Thus Marla and Brianna devoted their time to the elder family members.

Unusually tired when they got home, Marla flopped in front of the TV. She had to drag herself to prepare dinner. She'd better make an appointment with her gynecologist to follow up on her pregnancy test. He might want to do blood work to confirm the results.

"Are you planning to visit Francine's workplace tomorrow?" Dalton asked her later when they were both in bed. "If you do go, please tell them where to send Ms. Dodger's personal belongings. It would save me a trip. Note their reaction when you mention Jon Greene's name as the heir apparent. But be careful. Someone doesn't like your snooping."

Marla remembered the rock thrown at their door. "I will. Did you learn anything new today?"

"Alyce didn't have any unusual deposits in her bank accounts."

"Then likely she wasn't blackmailing anyone with the dirt she had on them. How did your interview go with her brother?"

"Steve was reluctant to talk about Francine. He didn't know her that well and didn't care for how Alyce seemed riveted by her discovery. Maybe he was afraid Francine would usurp his role as older sibling."

"You'd think he would be glad to find a long-lost sister. What did he say regarding Tony Winters and his firm?"

"He does Tony's personal accounts. Someone with more seniority there acts as advisor to Tony for Amalfi Consolidated and manages their funds along with an accountant, who does their books."

"How did Alyce's brother come to suspect something was wrong?"

"He came across a memo that struck him as strange. When he asked about it, he got an evasive response. Alyce's death hit him hard. I think he blames himself for telling her his suspicions. She went off on a tangent, saying she knew something was weird about that import company. His remarks strengthened her conviction that she was on the right track. All she needed was proof."

"Does Steve believe her hit-and-run accident was deliberate?"

"He's running scared. The guy doesn't know what to think and would prefer to avoid the subject. My showing up at his place couldn't have helped. I may talk to the judge about taking a look at the company records, but only if we have more to go on."

"Why don't you let Sergeant Langley take the lead in these cases? You're supposed to be doing more administrative tasks."

"I prefer a hands-on approach, especially since you're involved." His gaze darkened, and his fingers crept south to demonstrate his interest.

Marla's feminine parts stirred in response. "I guess we'll have to allow you to explore all the angles then." And that discussion ended as his mouth zeroed in on hers.

Monday morning, Marla called the gynecologist's office. When she stated the purpose of her visit, the receptionist told her to come in and they'd fit her into their schedule.

She sat in the office waiting room along with two other patients. In her mind, she reviewed her symptoms while trying to shut out the noise from a TV blaring in the corner. She didn't care to listen to advice regarding different diseases. Why couldn't the office staff put on the news instead? Maybe because it would raise people's blood pressure, she thought with a cynical twist to her lips. She considered playing solitaire on her cell phone but couldn't concentrate.

When it was her turn to be called, she followed the nurse with trepidation. She disrobed as instructed and put on the flimsy paper top and bottom that always left her feeling half-naked.

Dr. Gary Bernstein breezed into the treatment room a few minutes later.

"Marla, how are you? You're looking good."

So are you, she thought, regarding his lean, handsome face. "I've been busy with

331

work and other things, which is why I haven't been in sooner."

"What brings you here today?"

"I think I'm pregnant. I've had weird symptoms that started several weeks ago. I tasted some olive oil at a local restaurant, and it didn't sit well in my stomach. I haven't felt right ever since then."

"Meaning what?"

"I'm queasy a lot. Sometimes I go through the motions of throwing up but nothing comes out. And foods that I used to like now turn me off."

"And do you get this queasy feeling after every meal, or is it intermittent?"

She waved a hand. "It comes and goes. Oh, I have been feeling very tired lately. And once or twice, I've had a dizzy spell."

"Have you missed any periods?"

"Yes, I didn't get it this month. That's unusual for me. Normally, I'm pretty regular. At first, I thought I might have food poisoning or an allergy, but then I did one of those pregnancy test kits from the pharmacy. The results were positive."

"Any other problems, like diarrhea or abdominal pain? Fever or chills? Urinary changes?"

"No." She rubbed her belly. "It's hard for me to believe I might be pregnant after all this time."

His warm brown eyes regarded her. "We'll do some lab work to rule out other causes along with a more definitive pregnancy test."

He gave her a brief exam and then stood to toss his disposable gloves into the trash. "I think you're right, judging from the changes to your body that I'm seeing, but let's wait for confirmation before you celebrate."

"How long will I have to wait for the lab results?" Marla asked, sitting upright on the table.

"It should only take a few days. I'll call you after the reports come in. Meanwhile, I'd advise you to start taking a multivitamin and avoid alcohol."

Outside, Marla pulled down her long sleeves to cover the needle mark on her arm. She'd given both blood and urine samples at the doctor's office. Should she call Dalton and tell him about her visit? No, she didn't care to bother him at work. It could wait until later.

She focused on his case instead and headed north toward the offices of *Eat Well Now* magazine. The sooner he resolved his work issues, the sooner they could focus on growing their family. He had a better chance if they functioned as a team.

Lynette was surprised to see her again but politely guided her inside. "The receptionist said you have news for us?" the editorial director inquired.

"Yes, I'm wondering if you still have Francine's personal items."

"Sure, we've boxed up her stuff. We haven't had any direction from the police on where to send the package. They'd taken some of her possessions but left the rest."

Marla and Lynette stood in the general area segregated into cubicles. Clacking keyboards competed with the low hum of voices as Marla glanced around. One girl met her eyes and hastily looked away. Did she have something to say? Marla would like the chance to talk to other staffers. How could she get Lynette out of her hair?

"Francine's estate goes to Alyce Greene's husband," she said, watching the other woman's face.

"What? I figured she'd leave things to her distant aunt or to her boyfriend, if anyone. Or to one of her charitable causes."

"Actually, she'd named Alyce in her will, but with the blogger gone, it goes to her husband, Jon."

Lynette shook her head. "Wow, I didn't see that one coming. Why her? I didn't realize they were so well acquainted."

"They shared an unexpected connection," Marla admitted.

"Really? How so?"

"I'm not at liberty to say just yet. Do you mind if I look through Francine's stuff? I might find a clue that the police over-looked."

"I don't see the harm in it," Lynette said with a shrug. "Come this way."

Marla followed her to an alcove that held copy machines and storage shelves. Lynette plucked a large labeled carton off a shelf and dumped it on top of one of the machines.

"Here you go. Unless you need me, I have a deadline to meet and have to get back to work. Nice seeing you again, Marla. Oh, we received your press release about the salon fundraiser. We've added it to our online site, and it'll be going into this month's print issue."

"Thanks so much. I really appreciate it. I'm excited about the event, and so is the history museum's curator. We're anticipating a good turnout."

Marla waited until Lynette left before opening the box. A lump rose in her throat as she rummaged through the contents. How sad that a woman's life boiled down to these few items. A souvenir pen from the Library of Congress. A cute cell phone holder shaped like a shoe, and a pair of drugstore reading glasses in a case. A decorative desk clock, framed pictures of food from the walls in Francine's office, and an empty vase. The mouse pad had a picture of high heels. Francine must have liked her shoes, Marla thought as she explored the contents.

Her gaze stopped on an album. She yanked it out, hoping it contained photos that might be relevant. But as she thumbed through the pages, she noted articles about children dying in hot cars. How interesting. She hadn't realized Francine cared about this cause. Had the woman also volunteered for the Safety First Alliance?

Marla took part in the group's educational activities that aimed at preventing these tragedies. They'd had a booth at the harvest festival and benefited from a portion of the bake-off ticket sales. Maybe that's why Francine had researched the topic. Yet some of the pieces pasted in the album appeared to go back decades.

Another staff member ambled by, and Marla shut the book. She'd ask permission to borrow it to show her husband. Maybe it meant something more important. The cops may have overlooked it, since there weren't any personal photos included.

The young woman reversed direction and poked her head inside the room. "Hi, I heard you found a place for us to send this stuff. I'm glad Francine left her things to someone. I hope they'll respect her belongings."

"Me, too, Miss . . . ?"

"I'm Judi Leeston." The twenty-something woman came closer and lowered her voice. "We miss Francine. She was super organized and always had a kind word for everyone. Her idea for us to expand our scope would have worked if we'd had the chance to implement it."

Marla put down the album and faced the staff member. "Do you think it would have turned things around? I was led to believe the magazine's readership was in a decline."

Judi bobbed her head. "That's true. If you come across the article Francine meant to publish, can you tell us? Maybe her exposé would save our publication."

"And none of you has any idea what she'd been researching?"

"No, she wouldn't tell us. She probably wanted to verify her facts. Francine was a stickler for protocol and always insisted we confirm our sources."

"What's your role here, hon?" The smell of coffee drifted Marla's way. They must be near the staff's break room.

Judi fingered her floral patterned skirt. "I'm a photographer. The food pictures are my responsibility. We have to stage them so they look good."

"That must be fun. Is there a test kitchen for the recipes?" Marla hadn't noticed one on this floor.

"We outsource that part, but when they're ready, I go over to take the photos. I'll also cover special events for the magazine."

"Did you attend the harvest festival at Kinsdale Farms?"

"No, Francine said she'd get some pictures since she had to be there."

"Do you have those photos?"

"She never sent them."

Dalton hadn't mentioned finding a camera. Had Francine used her cell phone to take pictures? If so, she might have dropped it in the fields when assaulted. But then Dalton's team should have found it among the plants.

"Did Francine use an old-fashioned camera or her cell phone to take photos?" Marla asked the magazine photographer.

"I'd loaned her my Canon PowerShot. It's small enough to fit in a purse but has a good

338

telephoto lens. Your husband is the detective on the case, yes? I'd like my camera back once he's done with it. That device cost me a pretty penny."

"I'll tell him, but he hasn't mentioned finding a camera. Could Francine have emailed the photos to herself first? Did your camera have wifi?"

"Yes, but she'd need to send them through her cell phone unless she was in a hot spot."

Had Dalton found any photos among Francine's recent emails? Surely he would have mentioned them if taken at the farm.

"Are you familiar with this album?" Marla asked the other woman. "I'd hoped it might contain photos, but all I see are articles about children dying in hot cars. Could this be the article Francine was planning?"

Judi wrinkled her nose. "It has nothing to do with food, so I doubt it. Maybe that was a personal concern of hers."

"Do you think I could get permission to show this to my husband? It might be relevant in some way."

"I can ask Lynette for you. One moment." She bustled away, returning a few minutes later with a smile on her face. "Lynette said you can take the whole box if you want. She'd appreciate it if you could deliver it to the next of kin."

"Sure, I can take it. Did Francine ever mention Alyce Greene, the food blogger?"

"Are you kidding? She was a big fan of Alyce's site."

"How did they get along? I presume they met at industry functions."

"I wouldn't know, but Francine liked the depth of Alyce's articles. Maybe that's where she got the idea to expand our focus."

"Has Lynette spoken to her superiors about Francine's plans? Maybe they'd grant permission for her to broaden the scope of the magazine."

"The owners said they'd consider it if we had a lead piece. I can't believe Francine didn't keep notes somewhere in the office."

"Who actually owns the publication?"

Judi grimaced, her displeasure evident. "It's an investment firm called Viadome. We're merely one of their numerous holdings. I don't think it would faze them to close our doors."

"Viadome? Never heard of it."

"If you like, I can get you the name of our contact there." She pulled her cell phone from a pocket and texted a message. "Lynette says it's a man named Steve Madison."

Marla's heart skipped a beat. "No way. That man is Alyce Greene's brother."

CHAPTER TWENTY

Marla shoved the box along with the album into the backseat of her Camry and then started the engine. What could it mean that Steve Madison's firm owned Francine's publication? Had she meant for her exposé to lead directly to the company that controlled her magazine? If so, perhaps she'd discovered something about them that had gotten her killed.

Maybe Francine had learned Amalfi Consolidated was selling fraudulently labeled extra virgin olive oil. Dalton's team should get the product tested. No doubt the people involved in a fraud scheme of this magnitude would know how to hide their ill-gotten gains. Then again, the income would be legitimate, wouldn't it? It was the source product that was the problem.

She pulled onto Glades Road and turned west toward the turnpike. More likely, the scam originated in Italy with Tony Winters' relatives. They would be the ones producing the mislabeled product. Sales would merely reflect normal earnings. The Italian authorities would have to be notified if Dalton suspected fraud at that end.

If this was true, then Steve's firm might not have anything to hide unless the import company didn't report all their revenue. Drat, she felt like they were going around in circles without discovering anything of substance.

Dalton had already interviewed Steve twice. He'd even suggested Marla pay him a visit. However, she'd use the excuse of needing an investor for her salon café rather than seeking an investment advisor for her personal needs. She already knew his company invested in small businesses like Jon Greene's food truck operation.

She pulled over to notify her husband about her plans before diverting her route.

"Watch your back," he cautioned on the phone. "There's a viper under one of these rocks."

"Speaking of rocks, have you gotten any prints off that missile thrown at our doorstep or the message attached to it?"

"Yes, we did. I've sent them out for analysis."

"Good, let me know if you get a match."

This could be the break in the case we've needed, but don't get excited over it yet. Wait until the results have proven fruitful. "I went to the magazine office and met their food photographer," she said. "Judi Leeston loaned Francine a digital camera to take photos at the festival. Did you find one in Francine's purse or in the fields at Kinsdale Farms?"

"We have the victim's cell phone, but no, I didn't realize Francine had brought another camera to the event. The photos on her phone didn't show anything significant."

"If she dropped the camera, one of the farm hands might have turned it in to their lost-and-found. Check at the marketplace." She gave a description of the model.

"Thanks, I will."

"Oh, here's another thought. Hundreds of people were present that day. Did you look online to see if anybody posted photos or video footage?"

"You are super sharp today. I'll put my boys to work on it."

"Also, I took an album from Francine's box of belongings, which they gave me to deliver to her next of kin. It has old newspaper articles about hot car deaths of children. It's interesting that Francine shared this concern of mine."

"It couldn't have been the topic she'd been investigating. Her article would have had to include a food angle."

"I know. Anyway, I'll show it to you later." The news about her doctor visit bubbled on her tongue, but she suppressed it. She'd tell him another time, when he wasn't distracted by the case. "Love you," she said before ringing off and setting her mind to the next task.

Viadome had its own building in downtown Fort Lauderdale. Nestled between two bank towers at the west end of Las Olas Boulevard, the place shared a parking garage with its neighbors. Marla found a space and paid for a couple of hours at the meter machine.

She'd be wasting her effort if Steve wasn't in, but then maybe she could do some shopping. She didn't get downtown very often since the mall in Palm Haven had most of what she needed.

Fortunately, the receptionist nodded at Marla's request to see Steve Madison without having an appointment. She accepted her rushed explanation about being in the area and claiming a friendship with his sister.

"I'm sorry for your loss," Marla told Steve, taking a seat across from his desk.

He had an expansive corner office with wide window views. Marla, not thrilled about being on the eighteenth floor, studied the man instead of the scene below.

"Thanks. I can't believe it's been two weeks already. I'm still expecting Alyce to phone me and sound excited about her next article." He scraped stiff fingers through his dark brown hair. His matching eyes regarded her from behind wire-rimmed glasses.

"Alyce suggested I see you about my proposed business plan. We'd both entered the bake-off contest, and neither of us won. She told me how she meant to pay off her husband's loan so he could expand his food truck operation."

"That's true," Steve admitted, his pained expression plucking at her heartstrings.

"So your company provided Jon with the money to start his food truck business? Or was it a personal loan?"

"I didn't have the funds myself. That's what our company does. We not only provide brokerage services, but we invest in small businesses that have the potential to grow." He studied the card Marla had handed him. "You own a salon and day spa?"

"Right, and I've been thinking of adding a

345

café to our spa premises so clients don't have to go off-site for lunch. We have a lounge that could be converted. But I don't have the capital necessary for renovations, plus we'd have to hire a chef."

"Or a caterer could prepare the meals offsite for you instead. You're thinking in terms of grab-and-go items, yes? The main outlay would be for permits and remodeling."

Marla could see he had a grasp of the situation. "Actually, there's a deli next-door. I could ask them to supply the food," Marla said as though she hadn't thought of it before.

"There you go. Do you have blueprints for your planned counter space?"

"Yes, I do. I can email them to you along with my business proposal."

"That would be helpful. It's obvious you're already successful. I don't think you'll have any obstacles, Ms. Vail." He frowned suddenly, his face flushing. "Why does that name sound familiar?"

"Perhaps because I'm married to the homicide detective investigating your sister's case," Marla replied in a wry tone.

He stared at her, the atmosphere chilling a few degrees. "Is that really why you're here? To question me on his behalf? He's already interviewed me twice."

"As I said, Alyce gave me the idea to see you about my business expansion. But I am curious since my husband learned about Alyce's connection to Francine Dodger."

His mouth compressed. "Your husband thinks the same person may have targeted them both."

"Francine was hit on the head from behind. She'd been researching a topic that she boasted would be an exposé. Maybe Alyce came across the same material. Nobody at Francine's magazine office can find her notes. My husband's team has even searched her computers to no avail. Either she kept the data well hidden, or someone swiped it. Who would go to such means to cover up their trail?"

He tilted his head. "Has your husband spoken to Francine's boyfriend? I forgot to ask him. Alyce said the guy was leading Francine down the wrong path."

"He's into spiritual mysticism and Egyptology. Dalton doesn't seem to think he's a suspect."

"No? Then who is on his list?"

"You tell me. Who might have wanted to harm your sister?"

"Alyce only meant to educate people about healthy eating," Steve said, his voice choked. "She shouldn't have died. If your husband finds the culprit, I hope he's put away for a long time, even if it was an accident."

He shoved his chair back and rose to pace the room. Marla glanced at the clouds outside in a clear blue sky. Why was she here instead of enjoying the day? Hadn't she learned to mind her own business yet? Was there any hope for her to lead a normal life of tending hearth and home?

"Alyce didn't like how this boyfriend influenced Francine," Steve added. "My wife paid for those databases where you can check on people, you know? They've proven helpful for her work. So she looked up this guy."

"What did she learn?" Marla leaned forward to better hear his response.

"Several of his colleagues have expressed concerns about plagiarism issues. They say he included plagiarized material in published research claimed as his own. He's under investigation by the university's Integrity Office. I suppose he could be fired if the accusations are proven true, or at the very least, he'll be demoted in rank."

"I wonder if Francine knew this about him. Did your sister ever meet Colin in person?"

Steve shrugged. "Not to my knowledge. Nor has Jon said anything on the subject, but Alyce often wouldn't tell him about her research. He wanted to be the main bread-winner and insisted she keep her income for personal needs."

"Did you tell my husband any of this?"

He shook his head. "I get flustered when he comes by. You know how it is with investigations, especially being in the finan-cial sector."

That's why Marla often found out stuff on her own. People were more willing to talk to a woman who didn't appear threaten-ing.

"Would Colin have acted against Alyce for any reason?" she asked.

Steve sank back into his seat and rubbed a hand over his face. "It wouldn't make sense, unless my sister informed Francine about his misconduct, and she told Colin their relationship was over. He could have run down my wife out of revenge if he blamed her for their breakup."

"I'll mention these thoughts to my hus-band. He can check to see what kind of car Colin drives and where he was when the accident happened." She paused. "If Fran-cine's inheritance had been more substan-tial, Dalton might have suspected Jon

349

Greene of doing in both women to gain the money. Will he be able to pay off his loan with the amount coming to him?"

"He's already paid off most of the interest, so hopefully he can cover the remaining principal. Jon has been very reliable in his payments. He's a hard worker and a great cook. The man should have gone to culinary school."

"It's rare that someone gets to work at what they love. I hope he achieves his dreams."

Steve gave a surreptitious glance at his smartwatch. "Is there anything else, Ms. Vail? I have another appointment in ten minutes."

She gripped her purse in her lap. "I've one more question, and then I'll leave. I was surprised to learn Viadome owns *Eat Well Now* magazine. Francine hoped to buy out their investment if she'd won the bake-off competition. Would the prize have been enough money? Do you think your firm would have accepted an offer from her?"

His brow wrinkled. "Their magazine has been steadily losing readership. It isn't a new trend. Look at what's happened to newspapers. As for an offer, I'm not at the level to make those decisions."

"Francine wanted to do more investigative pieces. She felt a broadened scope would arouse more interest."

"Alyce was ahead of her in that regard. She and Francine had more in common than they realized."

"How did you feel when your sister told you about Francine's match at the DNA site?"

"I didn't want to believe it. Our mother deceived us. As far as I knew, I had one sister. That was enough for me."

"So your mom never hinted at having another child before her marriage to your father?"

The corners of his mouth turned down. "Nope. Alyce got into genealogy as a lark. She thought it would be fun to trace our roots. I was just as surprised as she was when a hit came through. Even more surprising, she and Francine were already acquainted through their business circles."

"Did you expect Francine to leave her estate to your sister?"

"Certainly not. It's sad that we were her only living blood relatives. It must have hurt to learn our mother had cast her aside even if Mom thought it was the best choice at the time." He shook his head. "I still can't believe she never told us."

"Could someone other than you or Jon

have an interest in your family?"

"What do you mean?"

"I'm still trying to gain a sense of motive in both women's deaths."

He stood, placing his palms flat on his desk. "I'd say, let your husband do his job. This interview is over."

Marla collected her purse and rose. "I meant what I said about my business proposal. May I still send you the plans?"

"Sure, we can take a look at them." He gestured toward the door, his meaning clear.

She took a few steps and then halted. "Oh, wait. We didn't talk about Amalfi Consolidated. Jon said your sister was afraid their company would get you in trouble."

"I'm not the one in charge of their accounts."

"I know. Someone else at your firm works with Tony Winters in that regard. It's possible Alyce might have been investigating their company for a piece on her blog."

"Those guys aren't people you want to mess with. The ones from Italy, I mean. They're coming here for a visit. Maybe my sister would still be here if I'd kept my mouth shut."

"I've read about olive oil scams. Is that the problem? Or does it have to do with tax evasion?"

He cast a fearful glance at the door. "I've told your husband what I know, which isn't much. It's bad enough that my remarks might have gotten my sister killed."

Sensing his reluctance to talk further, Marla thanked him for his cooperation. "I'll email you my business proposal," she said loudly as he escorted her to the exit. "I'm really hoping your firm decides the investment will be worthwhile."

Outside in the autumn-scented air, Marla walked to her car while mulling over their conversation. It appeared Colin Abubakar wasn't as innocent as he'd seemed. The college professor was engaged in alleged misconduct and might have gotten angry if Francine broke up with him. Assuming he'd learned about Alyce's role, he could have gone after her in revenge.

Yet if this were true, who had followed Francine into the fields and bashed her on the head? Dalton had verified Colin's presence at the conference he'd attended.

She unlocked the door to her Camry and slid inside. The air-conditioning, when she turned the engine on, gave a welcome blast.

Tony Winters was still a major player as far as she was concerned. Did he take orders from the head honchos in Italy, or did he work autonomously on his company's behalf in the States? Either way, had he killed the women because they'd been about to blow the lid on his firm's fraud scheme? Then why were his relatives coming to town?

Perhaps they planned to deal with the loose ends, like Tony himself. If so, no wonder the man was nervous about their visit.

Marla called Dalton before pulling away from the parking lot. She reported on her conversation with the financial advisor.

"He didn't tell me about Abubakar," Dalton said with a note of surprise. "I'll look into those accusations against him, and I can see what model vehicle he drives. Are you on your way home, or could you stop by the station? I've just learned something else that's interesting."

Pleased he valued her input, Marla agreed to meet him. A short time later, she was seated in his office. His colleagues had called out friendly greetings on her way in. These people were his second family, she realized. While she'd encountered them on social occasions, she should make more of an effort to get to know each person individually.

At first, it had been hard to view the members of the police force as having real lives. But as they got better acquainted, she'd noticed how they had the same problems as everyone else. More so, actually, due to the dangerous and often distressing nature of their work.

She kissed Dalton before taking a seat opposite his desk. "What's up?"

He shuffled through some papers and placed a folder on top. "Remember how you said Grace Kinsdale seemed out of tune with the role of farmer's wife? I did a background check on her. Her maiden name was Laker."

"So what does that mean?"

"The name on the property deed for the farm is Wilson Laker."

Marla drew in a sharp intake of breath. "She's related to the owner on record?"

"It appears that way. The question is, does Zach know?"

"He didn't see the lease until after his father died. That's when he realized the farm might not belong to them."

"By then, he and Grace were married," Dalton said. "It wasn't her first time at the rodeo. She might have gone by her married name when she met him."

"How did they meet each other?"

"I don't know, but I'd like to find out. Grace has agreed to meet me at the deli in

Davie. I'd like you to come along to soften her up."

CHAPTER TWENTY-ONE

Grace didn't look happy to see them when they arrived at the deli, where she'd already gotten a table. At three o'clock in the afternoon, the crowd had diminished and they almost had the place to themselves. Marla and Dalton took seats opposite the blonde and waited while the waitress filled their water glasses.

"What is it that's so urgent, Detective?" Grace glanced from Dalton to Marla and bit her lower lip as she regarded them with anxious blue eyes.

"We'd like to know how you met your husband, Mrs. Kinsdale."

"Zach?" She gave a nervous laugh. "That's easy. He'd lost his first wife, Lucy." She noticed their startled glances. "Oh, you didn't realize he'd been married before? So was I, to a good-for-nothing jerk. Anyway, I'd been divorced and Zach had been widowed. He was left with an infant son.

Yes, Rory isn't mine. You've seen his red hair? He got that from his mother. The other kids are mine and Zach's."

"Does Rory know this?" Marla inquired.

"Zach hasn't told him yet. I've loved and raised him as my own son. Anyway, I had my friends scouting for prospects after my divorce, and Zach's name came up. Being a single father is never easy. He'd be looking for a new wife."

"Tell me," Dalton said in a casual tone, "did you go by your maiden name when you met, or were you using your married one?"

"What difference does it make?"

"I guess it wouldn't have mattered since Zach had no idea his family didn't own the farm. But yours did, isn't that so?"

The waitress chose that moment to interrupt. The three of them ordered coffee, while Dalton asked for a slice of homemade peach pie.

"So you've discovered my secret," Grace stated after they'd been left alone. "When my father passed, I didn't know anything about the farm or the lease agreement. Payments must have stopped earlier when Hank Kinsdale died, but my father was sick by then. Probably he lacked the energy to track down Hank's next of kin. We owned a number of properties and made substantial income from the rentals. When Dad got ill, this lease must have slipped through the cracks."

"How did you find out about it?" Dalton asked.

"I was sorting through my father's business papers. This happened before my divorce, and I was going through a bad time. I couldn't deal with any more problems."

"So you let it go?" Dalton's face brightened when the server brought their orders. He dug into his slice of pie with alacrity.

"I reviewed the lease terms. Hank had an option to buy, and I thought maybe he'd purchased the land and the bill of sale was missing from my father's records. If not, Hank owed my father's estate quite a bit of money. I'm an only child, my mother is deceased, and I'm the sole heir," she explained. "I didn't follow up until I was single again."

"How much time had passed?" Marla said.

"A few years. I found out that Hank Kinsdale had died. His sons ran the farm. I had two choices at that point. I could engage a lawyer and pursue the money they owed us, or I could assess the situation for myself. I decided to meet Zach without telling him about our connection. Did he intend to make a squatter's claim, or did he have proof that his dad had bought the property?"

"That's when you learned he had no clue his family didn't own the place?"

"Yes, the poor guy was totally ignorant. He was also a hunk. I liked his forthright manner, and his redheaded kid was a doll. It didn't take much for me to fall for him. So I chose to remain silent, because after all, the land would sort of belong to him through marriage."

"Why didn't you reveal your identity when he was searching for proof of ownership?"

Grace bent her head. "He'd accuse me of deceit or worse. I should have confessed earlier. Then he wouldn't worry about the farm's title. It's my fault I kept quiet until now."

"What about the legal process he's begun? Are you going to let him proceed without telling him it's unnecessary? You could sell his family the property for a dollar, or whatever the law allows in that regard," Marla suggested.

Grace met Marla's gaze. "What do you think I should do?"

"It's always best to come clean," Dalton advised. "A marriage shouldn't be based on lies. Why don't you consult a real estate attorney and see if you can transfer the deed or add your husband as co-owner?"

Grace straightened in her chair, an expression of hope in her eyes. "Why, that's a wonderful idea, Detective. I could use the same lawyer he's hired. That guy is sharp, and he'll know what to do if I see him privately. By rights, Zach's siblings should be included, too."

Marla smiled at her. "There you go. A solution that works for everyone."

Arnie would be pleased. Once these machinations took place, Rory and his family would feel secure. Maybe down the road, when his kids left the nest, he'd consider that bed-and-breakfast idea she'd suggested.

Outside, Marla gave a weary grunt as she leveraged into the car. Everything seemed to be such an effort these days. Maybe the multivitamins the doctor had suggested would give her more energy.

"It doesn't seem as though we're any closer to nailing the bad guy," she said in a discouraged tone.

Dalton had a thoughtful frown on his face as he put the sedan in gear. "I still think Tony Winters is involved. He has the most to lose if his company is busted."

Marla waited until he'd pulled out of their parking space. He always backed in, so he could leave quickly if necessary. It seemed to be a cop habit, like sitting against the wall in a restaurant, facing the entrance. "According to Tristan, the former executive chef at The Royal Palate left rather abruptly. Maybe you should talk to him."

"You're right. I also want to check to see if Winters is under investigation by another agency. If his company is engaged in consumer fraud, he's their representative here. That would make him responsible, whether he's aware or not of what's going on."

"Oh, he's aware. Maybe he wants out, and his relatives are coming to deal with him."

"Then he should admit what he knows before they get here. I still mean to look for that missing camera. It's not in our evidence stash. I'll check with the farm as you suggested, but it's a long shot. Your idea to look online for pictures from the festival is a good one. We can do that from home."

"What's next on your agenda?" Marla settled restlessly in her seat as they entered the main highway heading east. It would take them home faster than the back roads.

"I need to have another talk with Mr. Abubakar. He wasn't being entirely truthful with us. How about you?"

"I'll be busy at the salon for the next few days." Anxious for the doctor's report, she wouldn't be able to focus on crime-solving until her test results came in.

Dalton's phone call the next day provided a distraction.

"I found out where the former executive chef works," he said, having caught her at work in between clients. "He has a position at The Green Lizard. I've made us a reservation for seven-thirty tonight."

"What about Brianna?"

"I've texted her, and she wants to go."

"Okay, great. Shall I pick her up and meet you there, or will you come home first?"

"I'll swing by our place, so be ready at seven. By the way, I ran over to the university and spoke to Colin. He drives a black Lexus SUV. He's not our man for the hit-and-run unless he borrowed a vehicle. And he was teaching class then so his alibi checks out."

"What did he say about the plagiarism? Did Francine know about it?"

"Yes, Alyce had told her. Francine wanted nothing more to do with him. He wasn't upset about it. She hadn't really shared his beliefs, and those are more important to him."

"That means he wouldn't have been mad enough at Alyce to do her in."

"I agree. I'm eliminating him from my list."

"Who does that leave? Wait, never mind. We'll talk about it later."

She didn't broach the subject again until the three of them were seated in the restaurant that night and had placed their orders. Chitchat centered on Brianna's school day and Marla's activities at the salon.

The Green Lizard had a Caribbean ambiance with tropical plants adding splotches of greenery, bamboo partitions, and colorful paintings depicting jungle scenes on the walls. Steel drum music in the background added to the atmosphere. Marla and Brianna each ordered raspberry lemonade, while Dalton got a craft ale.

"Did you contact the farm and determine if they have a lost-and-found department?" Marla asked in a hushed voice after they'd given their food orders. As usual, they were seated by a wall where Dalton could face the entry to observe the new arrivals.

"Yes, and they don't have the camera you described. The lady there said she'd look in a few other places and get back to me if she finds it."

"I meant to search YouTube for videos but haven't had the time."

"What's this about YouTube?" Brianna

asked. She wore her dark brown hair curled at the ends and a light application of makeup that made her appear more grown up.

Marla felt a pang of loss at the thought of her leaving for college. She hadn't even begun dating yet, at least not in the sense that Marla knew. Come to think of it, Brianna hadn't mentioned Jason's name beyond that one time when she was meeting friends at a jazz club. Was the young man merely an acquaintance from school or something more? Would Brianna even tell them if she liked a boy?

Probably not. She'd be leery of her dad's reaction, and rightly so.

"We had the idea to check for videos or photos posted online from the harvest festival," Marla said, keeping her thoughts to herself. Nonetheless, she resolved to be more aware of cues from the girl when she talked about her friends. "Someone might have uploaded a picture that pertains to the case."

"I could help," Brianna offered.

"That would be great. It's more up your alley, and it would free your dad for other things."

"Awesome. This will be fun. Who are your lead suspects? Bring me up to date."

"Francine's boyfriend has alibis for both Alyce's and Francine's deaths," Dalton replied, helping himself to the platter of conch fritters they'd ordered as an appetizer. "She didn't have any other relatives except for a distant aunt who claimed her remains. Or so we thought."

He got busy chewing, so Marla picked up the thread. "Then we learned Francine had been adopted, and she had siblings. Her half-sister was none other than Alyce Greene. This meant she was also related to Alyce's brother, Steve, and by marriage to the husband, Jon Greene. Moreover, Francine left her estate to Alyce."

"Are those men still persons of interest?"

Dalton exchanged a glance with Marla. "Not so much Mr. Greene. Francine's estate wasn't large enough to kill someone over. He seems to be genuinely mourning his wife, plus I've verified he was consulting with food suppliers during the window of her death."

"The brother has more to hide," Marla inserted, anxious to sort out the suspects in her mind. "His firm, Viadome, handles the accounts for Amalfi Consolidated. They also own *Eat Well Now* magazine."

"That's where Francine was publisher, right?" Brianna responded, her brows raised.

"Yes, and it's where I met the magazine photographer. This woman said she'd loaned Francine her camera to take photos for their publication. The camera wasn't in Francine's purse and hasn't been turned in by anyone."

"Do you believe the killer took it?"

"It's possible. The pictures Francine took could be useful to the case."

"I'll check online for other photos later."

Marla laid a hand on her arm. "You'll be going to sleep to get a good night's rest. Tomorrow after school will be time enough."

Brianna compressed her lips but didn't protest. "Did anyone at the magazine seem to hold a grudge against Francine?"

Marla shook her head. "They miss her being there. If anyone had a reason to resent both Alyce and Francine, I'd put my finger on Carlton Paige. The food critic wasn't happy with either one of them. His wife, Sally, could be considered in the running as well. She has her own secrets to keep. Or she could wish to preserve her lifestyle by boosting her husband's ratings."

Dalton agreed. "I'm not finished with either one of them. But back to Steve Madison. He knows something fishy is going down with Amalfi Consolidated. That puts

Tony Winters, VP of the firm, in our crosshairs. Whether or not he's complicit, he still has the most to lose."

"Do you suppose both victims got wind of his company's wrongdoings?" Brianna asked.

"It's my working theory at the moment. Alyce told her husband she meant to get proof, and she wound up dead. Francine had been planning to publish an exposé, and the same thing happened to her. It's the strongest motive."

"But not the only one," Marla reminded him. She bit into a crunchy fritter, savoring the warm texture and the mustardy sauce.

"What about the farm family? Have you eliminated them?" Brianna said.

"Zach had been worried about losing the farm," Marla replied, "and Francine could have learned about his questionable ownership. But he seems to have things under control. I don't believe that's the topic she meant to address in her article, although she may have asked him about it."

"Here come our meals." Dalton pointed to the waitress headed their way. "Let's put a hold on this discussion until after dinner."

"Our thanks to the kitchen staff," Marla said once they'd finished their entrées. Her grilled grouper with a mango-coconut sauce had been divine. "May we speak to your executive chef? We have a message for him from someone he worked with at The Royal Palate."

"Sure, ma'am, I'll go see if he's available," the woman replied.

Ten minutes later, a stocky fellow in chef whites with a toque on his head, approached their table. "I'm Jeffrey Tobias. You wanted to see me?"

Dalton rose to shake his hand. "Our compliments on an excellent meal. Tristan Marsh sends his greetings from The Royal Palate and wishes you were still there."

The ruddy-faced fellow swept his arm in an expansive gesture. "I'm happier here. I've partnered with an old school friend of mine who owns the place, and we're doing great. It's a much better environment." At Dalton's insistence, he took the empty chair at their table for four.

"Tristan was upset when you left suddenly. He said you'd told him things that may have gotten you in trouble."

The chef's face reddened. "Tristan talks too much. Why do you care?"

Dalton showed his badge. "We're investigating two potential murders. The first one occurred at Kinsdale Farms during the fall harvest festival. You may have seen it on the news. Chef Marsh was there as judge for the bake-off contest, which my wife participated in. She found one of the contestants dead in the strawberry field. The woman had been hit on the head from behind."

The chef sucked at his lower lip. "I'm sorry for the lady, but what does it have to do with me?"

"The dead woman was publisher for *Eat Well Now* magazine. You are familiar with this periodical?"

"Sure, it's a respected publication in the industry. Do you mean Francine Dodger? We'd met before."

"I saw her speaking to the farm's owner that day," Marla cut in. "Are you aware Amalfi Consolidated sells their imported products at the marketplace?"

The chef frowned. "What of it?"

"Tristan gave me a taste of the extra virgin olive oil in his restaurant kitchen. It made me sick. Could the oil have been tainted? Or perhaps mislabeled, in that it contains seed oils that people with allergies should avoid?"

A sudden thought struck her. What if Francine hadn't been talking to Zach about his farm's ownership problems that day but about the import firm instead?

What had Zach said when they'd interviewed him last? Marla had told him about Francine's proposed article and asked if his farm was the subject. *Oh, she knew about it all right, but her interests lay elsewhere,* he'd replied. Maybe Francine had been confronting him with her findings about the import company.

Chef Tobias leaned forward. "I knew there was something wrong at The Royal Palate. The oil tasted bland to me, and I am an expert. At first, I didn't say anything to the owner, Mr. Romano. But when I did, he shrugged it off. I had a bottle tested. My instincts were correct. The oil originated from the Middle East, not from Italy as claimed, and it contained a blend of plain oils with a trace of EVOO. That's extra virgin olive oil."

"What did you do?" Marla asked.

"I confided in Tristan, since he also had doubts. Then I asked our boss where he bought these supplies. When I questioned his source, he got angry and dismissed me. Later, I learned that Damon — Mr. Romano — is friends with Tony Winters."

"It's no surprise he fired you," Dalton commented in his wry tone. "The two of them must have been colluding together. Perhaps your boss gets a kickback for ordering supplies from Tony's company."

"That's what Tristan thinks. I told him to keep his mouth shut. Damon, and hence this Mr. Winters, already suspect he knows."

"Is Tony just following orders from his higher-ups in Italy, do you suppose, or is he complicit in the fraud scheme?" Dalton queried.

Chef Tobias shrugged. "I washed my hands of their business when I left the restaurant. Here we order from suppliers whom we know personally and whose products we have vetted."

"I see. Well, thanks for the information. Is there anything else you can add that might be relevant?"

"I heard those boys from Italy are coming for a visit. I'd steer clear of them if I were you. Last time they came, Damon acted petrified that they might stop by. He'd heard bad things happened to people who didn't play their game."

CHAPTER TWENTY-TWO

"Excuse me, I have to get back to work," Chef Tobias said as he stood to take his departure. He waved to a guy who signaled him from the rear. Clearly he was needed in the kitchen.

"Wait, one more thing. Do you know Raquel Hayes, the TV chef?" Marla asked. "She was another judge at the bake-off contest."

To her surprise, he laughed. "Her audience loves her, but what she does is mostly showmanship. Sure, she offers useful cooking tips and keeps her audience entertained. But she isn't someone I'd want in my kitchen."

"Why is that?"

"Sorry, I've said enough."

He turned to go but stopped when Marla said, "Has Carlton Paige reviewed your new place yet?"

Chef Tobias rounded on her with a snarl.

"That snake had better keep his head outta here."

"Oh, my. I gather you've had problems with him?"

"I'm unwilling to provide perks for a good review, so I don't expect much from his quarter. Readers know his reviews have gone downhill. It won't be long before his column is shut down."

"Mr. Paige must have achieved his reputation somehow."

"In the early days, you could rely upon his integrity. But then his head got stuffed with his own importance. Nowadays he expects special treatment."

"How was his relationship to Francine Dodger?" Dalton asked as he rose.

"They knew each other. I saw them talking at industry events," Chef Tobias said.

"And Alyce Greene, the food blogger?"

A sorrowful look came over the chef's face. "I was saddened by her loss. Alyce Greene did the world a service. She promoted healthy eating and sustainable food sources. We need more folks like her on our planet. If we don't monitor our agricultural methods and fishing techniques, our food supply won't keep up with the population's demands."

Dalton, as though sensing a lecture coming on, offered a nugget of news. "What if I told you we suspect Alyce's accident may have been deliberate? That both she and Francine might have been onto something that got both of them killed?"

The chef's face paled. "That would be horrible. Look, I'd appreciate it if you wouldn't mention to anyone that we've had this little chat. Thanks for dining at my restaurant. Spread a good word about the food if you will."

Marla watched him vanish into the kitchen. Dalton resumed his seat with a thoughtful expression. Brianna slurped her drink, her cell phone face up on the table.

"Did we learn anything?" Marla asked.

"He's scared," Dalton replied in his stern tone. "He respected Alyce Greene, didn't have much to say about Francine, and came down on Raquel Hayes. As for The Royal Palate, I might have a talk with the owner. Meanwhile, I should contact the FDA to see if they have anything on Amalfi Consolidated."

"I'll look online for photos or video from the harvest festival," Brianna said, reiterating her plan.

Both Dalton and Brianna glanced at Marla. She shrugged at their inquiring looks. "I have to work tomorrow. There isn't much I can do."

"How are the plans for the bad hair day clinic coming?" Brianna asked with a bright grin. "I love the idea. Some of my friends are coming with their mothers."

"That's great. I appreciate your help handing out flyers."

"It's a cool idea. Dad, we still have to go to the history museum to see their new exhibit."

He wore a chagrined expression. "That's right, I keep forgetting. I'd met the curator briefly when I interviewed her, but I didn't have time to tour the place."

"Did you ever ask Becky how long she's known Raquel? They seem to be tight together," Marla said.

"That's because Raquel greases Becky's wheel each time she has a new cookbook out," Dalton reminded her. He signaled to the waitress for their check. "There's still a gap in the TV chef's history, however. Maybe Becky knows what Raquel did in those early days."

"If she'd lied on her application to culinary school, Francine might have caught onto her." Something niggled in Marla's brain about Francine, but it wouldn't surface.

"Her work experience checked out, so I

can't imagine what it would be," Dalton replied.

"Did you speak to the producer of her show? I believe it was Alyce who implied Raquel had slept with the man to land her gig. It might be useful to talk to the guy. He may know more about Raquel's background."

"True, I can add him to my list."

The waitress headed their way and smiled at Dalton. "Chef Tobias thanks you for joining us tonight and says your meals are on the house."

"That's very generous of him." Dalton pulled out his wallet. "Can we at least pay for the drinks?"

"No sir, it's all covered. Have a lovely evening." She turned away toward another customer.

"Well, that was unexpected. I'll leave a good tip," Dalton said, calculating what they would owe and how much gratuity he should give.

Over the next couple of days, Marla wavered between wanting to tell Dalton about her personal news and holding off until she got confirmation from the doctor's office. When Thursday morning rolled around, she put in a call to the gynecologist asking about her results. Enough time had passed that they should be ready.

Waiting for the return call made her pace the house, so she went into the salon earlier than her usual one o'clock arrival. She greeted her staff, tossed her purse into a drawer, and plugged in the implements at her station.

"How did your dinner with Kevin's parents go?" she asked Nicole, when the other stylist had a moment free. They hadn't had a chance to chat since the work week began.

Nicole grinned. "They're nice people. I think they liked me. His mom is a good cook."

"That's great. Has he said anything else about a trip to the Bahamas?"

"We have to coordinate our calendars first."

"Take off any time that you need. Robyn can adjust your schedule." Her cell phone rang, and she snatched it so fast that her fingers almost dropped it. A glance at the caller ID told her it was the doctor's office.

Marla hastened toward the back storeroom, glad to find the place empty so she could have some privacy.

"Marla? It's Doctor Bernstein. I have good news. The tests have confirmed that you're pregnant. Congratulations."

"Omigod. It's true." She put a hand on the counter to steady herself. "What do I have to do next?"

"Make another appointment, and come in with your husband. We'll go over things together."

Marla hung up, stuck the phone in a pocket, and rubbed her belly. A tiny life was growing inside her. She had to share the news with Dalton, despite her reservations about his reaction. He'd be ecstatic and only concerned for her welfare.

"Marla, why do you have that look on your face?" Nicole said, accosting her when she reappeared by their stations. "Who was that on the phone?"

"My doctor's office. The gynecologist confirmed my pregnancy test."

"Fantastic! Have you told Dalton?"

"Not yet, but I'll spill the beans this evening. I promise."

The day passed slowly until she and Dalton were finally alone in bed that night. Marla rolled on her side to face him. "I have some news to share."

"Oh, yeah?" He turned in her direction, his piercing gaze making her heart flutter.

"You know how I haven't been feeling well lately? Now I know the reason. I've been to see the doctor, and he's done some tests.

They came out positive."

"What's the problem?" His expression didn't change, but his voice deepened. Not with concern, but with something else.

"I'm pregnant."

Instead of acting surprised, he gave a low chuckle. "I've known ever since my journey on the spiritual plane when I saw another aura inside you."

"You're kidding? Why didn't you tell me?"

"Would you have believed my vision? You had to come to the realization yourself."

"You might have spared me the anxiety that I was sick with a stomach ailment."

"Your symptoms fit perfectly with pregnancy. When did you figure it out?"

"Not that long ago. I did a drugstore pregnancy test and then I went to see my gynecologist. I wanted to be sure before I told you, but I don't want you to worry over me instead of paying attention to your work."

Dalton drew her close and kissed her. "We'll always have distractions. This is wonderful news. You're already a terrific mother to Brianna. She'll be thrilled to hear she's going to be a big sister."

Marla kissed him back, rejoicing in his easy acceptance. She should have had more faith in him. She'd be careful and would heed the doctor's advice. Otherwise, she wouldn't curtail her activities as long as she felt well enough to carry on.

Saturday came around before she could catch her breath. Her eleven o'clock wanted a trim that reminded her of Alyce's cute pixie style. While cleaning her station afterward, Marla stiffened. Hadn't Alyce mentioned at the farm festival that she and Francine went to the same hairdresser?

Excited by this idea, she hastened to the front desk. "Robyn, can you look up the location for a place called Salon Style?"

"Sure, Marla. Is it in Palm Haven?"

"I don't know. Francine Dodger and Alyce Greene went to the same stylist there."

"Give me a moment." Robyn's nimble fingers flew over the keyboard as she peered at the computer monitor. "It's in The Fountains shopping center."

"Really? We eat at the restaurants there all the time, but I don't recall a salon by that name. Then again, who can keep track of them all?" She took the slip of paper Robyn handed her with the address. "I'm going to run out. Hopefully I can be back before my two o'clock arrives."

It took her less than fifteen minutes to zip over to the shops off University Drive. She located Salon Style in the corner where a salad buffet restaurant had gone out of business. It was a less populated section, but the place had a crowd when she entered. Approaching the reception desk, she sniffed the familiar scents of holding spray and chemical solutions.

"Hi, I'm looking for Karen. Is she here today?"

"Yes, ma'am," said the receptionist with a stud in her lower lip and a blue streak in her blond hair. "I'm afraid she's fully booked. Would you like to make an appointment for another day? Or we can have you see someone else. What is it you want done?"

"Actually, I'm not here for my hair. I need to speak to Karen for a few minutes. It's about your former clients, Francine Dodger and Alyce Greene."

The woman's eyes rounded. "Let me see if she's available."

A few minutes later, the woman returned accompanied by a brunette with curiosity in her hazel eyes. "Hi, I'm Karen. What can I do for you?"

Marla handed over a business card. "I'm Marla Vail, and I own the Cut 'N Dye Salon and Day Spa. We're located west of here. My husband is Detective Dalton Vail. He's investigating the deaths of Francine and Alyce. I understand you were their stylist?"

"Yes, I was. My next customer isn't here yet. Let's go somewhere private." Karen grabbed Marla's elbow and escorted her toward an empty facial room in the back. The treatment table lay empty, a clean towel awaiting the next client.

"Had they been coming here for a long time?" Marla began. Karen had left the door ajar, but no one should be able to overhear them.

"Francine started here first, and later Alyce. Poor dears. I can't believe they're both gone, especially since they discovered their relationship as sisters only recently."

"You knew about it?"

She bobbed her head, her hair in a high ponytail. "Francine told me everything. I think it brought her comfort to have someone to confide in, you know? She didn't have any relatives nearby, at least until Alyce contacted her about a hit on the genealogy site."

"Francine must have been excited to discover her new family."

Karen smiled wistfully. "You should have seen her eyes sparkle. She thought she'd lost her only sibling. Now she'd found a whole new family."

"This other child was a younger girl who died?"

"Yes, she'd been a toddler who attended a local day care center. The owner inadvertently left her in a van one summer afternoon, and she died of heat stroke. It was a horrible tragedy that affected their entire family. It turned out the place was unlicensed and run in a shoddy manner."

Marla's heart jolted. Some of those news articles in the album Francine had kept went back years ago. Did they relate to her adoptive sister's death?

"Was this other girl adopted like Francine, or was she a biological daughter to the mother?" Marla asked.

Karen shrugged. "I've no idea. But that incident scarred Francine. It made her not want to get close to people for fear she might lose them."

"Did she ever talk about her boyfriend, the college professor who specialized in Egyptology?"

"Yes, she'd mentioned him. Francine liked his brains and his looks but said he was a bit of a kook. I didn't get the impression they were in a serious relationship. It was more a lark for Francine to go out with him. He was married to his mythology, she used to say."

Karen's eyes misted, and she swiped at a tear. "Sorry, but I miss Francine. The magazine where she worked was her passion. She truly believed in bringing a message to her readers."

Marla leaned against the treatment table. "Did anyone there hold a grudge against her or challenge her position as publisher?"

"Not to my knowledge. She spoke fondly of her staff as though she got along well with them."

"Did she tell you about the bake-off contest and what she'd planned to do with the prize if she won?"

"Francine said she was entering, but that's all. She and Alyce would be competitors but it didn't faze them."

"When did Alyce start coming to you?"

"After she met Francine and liked her haircut. Alyce had a forthright manner. I followed her food blog but didn't agree with all her advice."

"Did she mention any enemies?"

"Alyce didn't talk much about herself. She kept the topics less personal and focused more on the news."

"Did she and Francine come in separately or arrange to make their appointments back-to-back?"

"Sometimes they met up here and then

went to lunch together, but not often." Karen glanced at her watch. "Sorry, my next client should be walking in at any moment. I need to get ready."

"I have to get back to my salon, too. Is there anything you remember about either one of the women that could be significant?"

"I don't see why it matters. Wasn't Alyce killed in an accident?"

"My husband believes their cases are related and that someone may have purposefully run Alyce down."

"No way. Well, in that case, I have nothing more to report on Alyce. Her blog posts will be missed by her fans. As for Francine, it came as a shock to her when she recognized the person responsible for her sister's death so many years ago."

CHAPTER TWENTY-THREE

"Didn't you say the owner of a day care center left the child in a van?" Marla said to Karen. "When did this incident happen?"

The hairdresser from Salon Style counted on her fingers. "Francine was thirty-five when she died, and she'd been five years old when the tragedy occurred. So it would be thirty years ago."

"And she recently recognized the person responsible? Who is it?"

Karen cast a glance at the door. "I don't want to get in trouble for spreading rumors, Marla. It's not for me to say. I hope you understand."

Marla narrowed her eyes. "Would you rather my husband make you an official visit? That way, you won't have to feel guilty about sharing confidences from a deceased client. One who was *murdered.*" She emphasized the last word to encourage the woman to speak.

Guilt and fear wrestled on the stylist's expression. "Oh, very well. I'll tell you, if it'll help get justice for Francine." She leaned inward and whispered in Marla's ear.

When Marla heard the name, she gave an exclamation. If true, this would explain a lot. It should be easy to verify if the articles in Francine's album confirmed a connection.

She thanked the other woman and left. She'd have to examine the scrapbook later since the rest of her day was filled with clients.

The afternoon passed quickly until finally she left the salon at five o'clock.

"Dad called," Brianna said after Marla greeted her inside their house. The teen was doing her eye makeup in the master bathroom. "He's staying late tonight to follow a lead. I'm going out."

"With whom?"

"A friend who's picking me up. I'll be back by curfew."

Marla glanced at her wedge heels, short skirt, and low-cut top. If Brianna were just hanging out with the gang, wouldn't the girl say so? How much should she pry?

"All right," she said, trusting her step-daughter to make the right choices. "We won't put on the alarm. If you come in later and see your father's car in the garage, you can arm it."

"Hey, I almost forgot to tell you." Brianna paused, mascara wand in hand. She'd curled her hair and it hung in soft waves past her shoulders. "I found a video online from the festival."

"That's great. Can you show me?"

Brianna's cell phone, sitting on the counter, buzzed with a text message. "I've got to go. My friend is outside. I'll show you the video in the morning when Dad can see it, too."

Brianna ran to grab her purse and dash out the front door. Marla hurried after her, dismayed to see a boy at the wheel of a Dodge that looked a few years old.

Her heart rushed to her throat. Could this be the elusive Jason? Was Brianna going out with him alone?

It was a good thing Dalton wasn't home, or he'd have a fit.

Marla shut the door and headed for their home office. If Brianna had used their desk computer, maybe the browser history would tell her what her stepdaughter had been researching regarding the harvest festival. But she didn't find anything relevant, meaning Brianna must have used her laptop. Tempted to look there instead, Marla resisted. She might end up peeking at the teen's email, and that would be an invasion of privacy. If she'd thought Brianna was in any danger, she wouldn't hesitate, but not otherwise.

She got occupied checking her own emails and then lost an hour to social media. Eventually, fatigue overruled her and she went to bed. She was reading a trade magazine when Dalton walked in, his face weary.

Marla got up to kiss him hello before he disappeared into the bathroom.

"Where's Brianna?" he said, tossing his tie onto the bed along with his sport coat.

"She went out with a friend. How was your day?" Marla asked, the news she'd learned from Karen hovering on her tongue.

"Productive. I spoke to the TV producer of Raquel's show as you'd suggested." His molten gray eyes regarded her thoughtfully. "He admitted they'd had a thing."

She raised her brows as he unbuttoned his shirt and took off his belt. He locked his weapons in their closet safe and then carefully placed his other police items on the shelf by his side of the bed.

"You mean they slept together? Are they still an item, or was it merely a means for Raquel to get her show?"

"He knew why she was doing it, so he had

his fun and let her go. His station keeps renewing her contracts since her ratings are good."

"What does he say about Alyce's accusations that Raquel uses shortcuts off-camera?"

"Ted Hastings — that's the fellow's name — said he doesn't care what she does off the air. As long as the live audience is happy with her performance, and she goes through the proper motions while being filmed, he's okay with it."

Marla sat on the bed facing him. "Did you ever fill in the gap in her background?"

He gave a brusque nod. "Raquel Hayes is her married name. She'd been divorced a number of years ago and has been raising a daughter on her own."

"Yes, she told me. Did she use this same name for all the cooking jobs she'd had before culinary school?"

"I believe so."

"It might be important to find out her maiden name," Marla suggested. "I paid a visit to Francine's hairstylist today. The woman said Francine had recognized Raquel as the owner of the day care center where Francine's adoptive sister had died. This incident happened thirty years ago. I meant to check the album I borrowed from

Francine's office, but I left it in the car."

"Good work. Let's follow through on this stuff tomorrow. I'm so tired that I can't think straight anymore." He added his pants and shirt to the pile on the bed.

"Okay, although I can't sleep until Brianna gets home."

"Spoken like a true mother hen. Where did she go?"

"I've no idea. Brianna is an independent woman now. She'll be back by curfew."

"She's not independent as long as she lives here and needs my money," Dalton stated before heading into the shower.

Dalton fell asleep soon after, while Marla thumbed through her magazine until she heard a commotion from the front end of the house. A door opened and closed, and then the alarm beeped into the armed position. Brianna must be home.

She got up and padded into the kitchen where the girl was getting a drink of water. "How was your evening?" she asked.

"We had a good time."

"You two do anything interesting?"

Brianna plopped her water glass down on the counter. "Marla, you don't need to question me. I don't have to share my entire life with you or my dad."

Marla held up her hands. "Sorry, we're

just concerned about you."

"Fine, but can you be concerned without being nosy?"

"If you wish." She turned away, aware she wasn't wanted. And remembering how she'd acted this way with her own mother.

It's only a phase. She'll mellow out in a few years.

Meanwhile, it promised to be a bumpy ride. Dalton likely wouldn't approve of any guy she brought home for them to meet until he'd done a thorough background check and conducted a personal interview. She couldn't blame the girl for being guarded about her love life and had to trust her to make the right decisions.

On Sunday morning, Marla served breakfast consisting of blueberry pancakes while the three of them dodged personal questions from each other.

She defused the tension in the air by focusing on Dalton's cases. As soon as the killer was behind bars, she and Dalton could broadcast their momentous news. Meanwhile, she needed to help him wrap things up.

"Will you be looking into Raquel's maiden name?" she asked to divert his attention.

"I'll have my team get on it. Despite what

you told me about Francine's younger sister, I'm not convinced Raquel plays a role in her murder. Tony Winters interests me more. His company is under investigation by another agency. Either the guy knows what's going on and is a willing participant, or he wants out and that's why the head honchos are coming to town. But did he murder the two women who caught onto their scam? I don't have enough answers yet."

"Let me get my laptop so I can show you what I found," Brianna said. She scurried out, looking young in her pajamas and with her hair in a ponytail.

Dalton shook his head. "I can't get used to the idea of her growing up. She's still my baby."

"You won't be able to track her movements once she's in college."

His gaze skewered her. "I know. I'll have to focus on you instead. Feeling better this morning?"

Marla's cheeks warmed. "Yes, thanks."

"Here's a video from the harvest festival," Brianna said, breezing into the kitchen with her open laptop. "Watch this."

Marla studied the recording made by a random person attending the fair. "Look, there's Francine. She appears to be arguing with Raquel. Francine isn't wearing Alyce's jacket, so this must have happened before the bake-off contest."

"Is that Ms. Wilde in the background?" Dalton pointed out.

"Yes, I recognize Lynette. Too bad the magazine photographer didn't hear what the other women were saying. Remember when Raquel said Francine wouldn't win despite her threats? This could be where Francine confronted the TV chef."

"About what?" Brianna asked. "Deceiving viewers by using cake mixes and such? I thought Alyce was the one who made those accusations."

"According to Francine's hairstylist, Francine recognized Raquel as the owner of the day care center where her adoptive sister died nearly thirty years ago," Marla said. "But even if true, what could Francine do about it all these years later?"

"Whoa, Marla, what if Francine's exposé was targeted at Raquel?" Brianna suggested.

Marla straightened in her chair. "I doubt Raquel would have been pleased. If news about this early scandal got out, it could have ruined her reputation. But we don't have any proof to connect the two of them back then." She turned to Dalton. "You said the shovel that killed Francine didn't have any prints. What about that set from the rock thrown at our front door?"

Dalton stuffed the last bite of pancake into his mouth and pushed his plate away. "They don't match anyone familiar to us."

"So you did get a hit?"

"Yes, for a woman named Theresa Mendez."

"Did you look her up?"

"She's a ghost who vanished. We can't find a trace of her anywhere."

Marla tilted her head. "You said the same thing about Raquel's early background. We should get a set of her prints for you to run through the database."

Brianna poked her. "I have an idea. Call Raquel and tell her I have a school project and would like to interview her. Plus, I've always wanted to see a TV studio behind the scenes. Can she meet us for a quick tour and chat?"

"I can give her a call, but I don't think you should come," Marla said.

"You're not leaving me behind. Besides, I'm your excuse for the visit. I can distract Raquel with my questions while you grab an item from her set kitchen that might have her prints."

"We'd have to take your car," Dalton said to Marla without actually accepting Brianna's proposal. "My driver's side window is sticking. I need to take it in to the dealer."

"Okay, but Raquel may refuse to see us since today is Sunday."

However, the celebrity chef surprised her. "I'd planned to go into the studio anyway to do my prep work for tomorrow's show. Wouldn't you rather get VIP tickets to sit in the audience during a live demonstration?"

"Brianna will be in school then," Marla told her on the phone.

"What's the subject of her report again?"

"Successful women and how they achieved their dreams."

"How lovely. I'm doing a practice run of my recipes for the show. I'll give you a taste. See you soon."

Dalton wagged his finger at Brianna. "You won't get near her, understand? Once you meet the woman and ask her a few sample questions, find a reason to go outside and wait for us there."

"I know the drill, Dad. I'll be safe."

"If you think this isn't a good idea, we'll stay home," Marla said. "You can call your team for backup and look around the set yourself."

"Then I'd have to get a warrant, and I don't have probable cause. Raquel may have hidden her past, but that doesn't mean she's

guilty of murder. Lots of people have secrets. In my opinion, Tony Winters has more
at stake."

"You might think so, but the person who
threw that rock at our house was a woman."

Marla let the dogs out again before she
and her family tumbled into the car for the
morning's excursion.

"Hey, what's this?" Brianna called from
the backseat once they were underway.

Marla glanced over her shoulder. "Oh,
that's the album I took from Francine's office. I meant to look through it and forgot I
had it there. We can examine it together
once we're home. By the way, did you finish
your report for physics class? I should have
asked before we left the house."

"It's done. I still have to read through my
history chapter. That's the most boring subject."

Dalton's brow creased. "You should pay
more attention to what you learn. The lessons of the past influence our present and
affect the future." A fan of world history, he
began a lecture of his own that ended when
they arrived at their destination.

Raquel was already at work on the kitchen
set, an apron tied around her khakis and
blouse. Her assistant, Carlos, stood by the
sink. The thin-faced fellow had a besotted

expression on his face as he observed the chef. Marla was surprised to see him there on a weekend, but maybe his relationship to Raquel went beyond a professional one.

Raquel grimaced at the sight of Dalton accompanying them. "I didn't expect to see you here, Detective," she said while dicing peeled shallots on a wooden cutting board.

"I'd hoped to get a glimpse of what you do behind the scenes. What are you preparing?" He spoke in an amiable tone and sauntered forward, seemingly at ease in his jeans and sport shirt. He didn't show a visible gun but Marla knew he kept one at his ankle.

"Tomorrow's menu is a tasty mushroom pie for the starter, followed by chicken *en papillote* with parmesan potatoes and buttered asparagus, and apple ginger tarts for dessert."

"Do you give out recipes to the audience members?" Brianna asked, taking out the notebook she'd brought along to play her part.

"You must be Brianna. I'm honored you've chosen me as the subject of your report. To answer your question, our recipes are available online at the network's website."

"So your entire kitchen is usable? It isn't

just a set for the TV show?"

"All of our appliances are real, child." She nodded a greeting to Marla. "Nice to see you again. Becky told me about your fundraiser. It's generous of you to offer your salon to help raise money for the history museum."

"I'm happy to support them." Marla stood to the side where she had a good view of Raquel's preparations.

"When did you realize you wanted to become a chef?" Brianna asked, pen poised above her notebook. She looked very studious with a serious expression on her young face.

Raquel scooped the chopped shallots into a small bowl. "I'd always liked cooking. It seemed a good path to take. And I'd get college credit for attending culinary school."

"Did you get your training right after high school?"

"No, I did various jobs to earn the money for tuition."

Brianna coughed. "I'm sorry; could I get a glass of water, please?"

"Of course." Raquel wiped her hands on a dishtowel and turned to the sink. She filled a glass and handed it to Brianna.

"Thanks," the teen said, appearing to take a sip as she turned away. Her father stood in the shadows, out of reach from the studio lights.

Marla, gathering Brianna's intent to pawn off the glass to her dad to bag as evidence, jumped into the conversational foray.

"What did those earlier jobs entail, Raquel?" She watched as the chef withdrew a set of packaged deep dish pie crusts from the fridge. So what Alyce had said was true. Raquel wasn't making her own pie crusts from scratch. These were store-bought items. A couple of containers of pre-sliced mushrooms followed.

"Oh dear, I forgot to replace the egg substitute, and we're all out of fresh eggs." She sidled over to Carlos and patted his arm. "Darling, would you mind running to the store for me and getting a carton of egg whites? I forgot to give Ted a list of items to buy. We could also use some regular eggs as well as vanilla yogurt for the dessert."

Carlos frowned as she mentioned the producer's name, but he gave a sullen nod and disappeared.

"I worked in a number of kitchens to gain experience," Raquel said in response to Marla's question. She shaped one of the defrosted pie crusts into a glass dish.

Marla watched her technique as she sautéed the mushrooms along with the diced shallots. A delicious aroma entered her nose. When the vegetables were wilted, Raquel removed the skillet from the burner, turned off the heat, and mixed in two different grated cheeses. Then she spooned the mixture into the pie crust and folded the other crust on top.

"Where's your stepdaughter? She's missing the demo. I'm done with the starter course until Carlos brings me the egg whites to brush over the top."

"Here I am," Brianna replied in a bright tone. "I want to see how you fix the chicken."

"Before I start putting a dish together, I get all the ingredients ready." Raquel bustled around the set as she gathered items for the main entrée. Her face flushed, and Marla couldn't tell if she was pleased or annoyed by having visitors.

Marla drew Brianna aside. "What are you doing here? You're supposed to be waiting outdoors. Did your dad get any prints off that glass?" He'd remembered to bring along a fingerprint kit. They could leave once they'd accomplished their purpose.

"I don't know. He's busy right now. Look, I brought you something you'll want to see." Brianna led her to the darkened audience section. She pointed to the album from the

402

car, which she'd placed on an empty seat.

"Where's your father? What is keeping him so busy that he can't join us?"

Brianna made an impatient gesture. "He saw a white car parked nearby and wanted to run the plate. Then he noticed Raquel's assistant heading that way. Dad went over to talk to him. He told me to go back inside. Take a look at that book, will you?"

Marla lifted the heavy album and opened the pages. As she'd noted earlier, they contained a collection of articles relating to the death of a toddler at an unlicensed day care center in South Miami.

"Do you see the resemblance?" Brianna said, indicating the photos. "The owner looks like a younger version of Raquel."

A jolt of recognition hit Marla as she studied the faded pictures. The story Karen at Salon Style had told her was true except for one fact. According to these articles, the proprietor's name was Theresa Mendez. Did that mean Raquel and Theresa were one and the same person?

"Go outside and tell your father to get in here," she said to Brianna. "This confirms my theory about why Raquel might have wanted Francine out of the way." She waited until the teen had vanished into the shadows before approaching the kitchen set.

"Did any of your early positions involve running a day care center?" Marla asked the chef in a casual tone.

Raquel, back at the work counter, gave her a startled glance. "Why do you say that?"

"Francine had a younger sister who died at one of those places. It turns out the owner had taken some of the children home but had forgotten the last kid. She left her in the van in the middle of summer. The poor toddler died. When the police investigated, they found the place's business license had lapsed. The proprietor vanished before she could be held accountable."

Raquel's complexion turned the color of pastry crust. "Where did you get this information?"

"Francine kept an album filled with articles about that incident. The proprietor looks like a younger version of yourself. However, her name was Theresa Mendez. You got married after this tragedy happened, didn't you? And you took on your husband's last name of Hayes."

Raquel sneered at her. "I thought you might figure things out. That's why I threw the rock at your front door. I'd meant to warn you off, you stupid snoop."

"Francine caught onto you, didn't she?"

"The magazine publisher saw me on TV and thought I looked familiar. She confronted me at the farm festival and threatened to expose my past. If I wanted her to keep silent, I'd have to make sure she won the competition."

"Is that what you meant when you said she wouldn't win despite her threats?"

"I didn't trust her. She might still publish her story and ruin the reputation it took me years to build. You won't get the chance to tell what you know, either."

Raquel opened a drawer and withdrew a butcher knife. She turned toward Marla, the blade in her hand and a murderous look in her eyes.

CHAPTER TWENTY-FOUR

"What happened to the child in the van?" Marla asked in an attempt to distract the chef. "It must have been an accident. You'd forgotten about her, hadn't you?"

A sad expression washed over Raquel's face. "I took kids into my home to earn money for culinary school. It's not as though I didn't care about them. I gave each child my personal attention. And yet, that day I was distraught. My boyfriend had just dumped me. The little girl was in the back of the van, and I thought I'd unloaded everyone. I went inside my house and was doing laundry when I suddenly wondered if I'd dropped her off. I ran outdoors but it was too late. Temperatures were in the mid-nineties. The kid couldn't breathe."

"So you called for help?"

"I dialed nine-one-one, but nothing could save the child by then."

"The toddler's family must have been

devastated." Marla backed away, noting the mad gleam in her opponent's eyes as Raquel advanced, knife in hand.

"It didn't matter that she'd been adopted like her older sister. I'd gathered the parents couldn't have children of their own. They threatened to sue me for wrongful death, harmful neglect, not having a valid license to operate a business, or anything else they could throw my way. I closed the center and disappeared before they could serve papers."

"You were scared. It's understandable," Marla said in a soothing tone. What was keeping Dalton from joining her? Brianna wasn't anywhere in sight, either.

"If I were lucky, I might have gotten off with a fine and probation. Or I could have faced a jail sentence. Either way, it would ruin my chances to get into cooking school. The best choice was to go off the grid and figure out how to change my identity."

"You should have accepted responsibility. That would have made it easier for you to move forward. I experienced my own tragedy when I was a teenager. A toddler in my care as a babysitter drowned in a backyard pool. It took me years to get over my guilt and sorrow."

"But you weren't threatened with jail, were you?"

"It was deemed an accident, but the parents tried to sue me. I did some unsavory things to earn money to pay a lawyer. Over time, I regained my confidence enough to go to beauty school and move on. My efforts failed to keep my past under wraps. Secrets like ours will surface to haunt you no matter how hard you try to hide them. It's best to come clean when you can."

Raquel took a few steps closer. "I prefer to bury my past. I worked as a housekeeper for a while and took cash only as payment. Nobody does a background check on their maid. You're just happy to have someone to clean your house. It wasn't easy. I couldn't use my credit cards for fear the authorities would track me. I sublet an apartment and paid my rent in cash. I felt like a fugitive."

You were then, and you are now, Marla thought. "Who's Theresa Mendez?" she asked.

"That's my maiden name. Theresa Raquel Mendez. When I got married, I took on my husband's name and became Raquel, and that was the beginning of my new career. I worked my way up through various restaurant kitchens until I had the money and credentials for culinary school."

"You must have been upset when Francine recognized you. Had you ever met in

408

person before?"

Raquel ran her finger along the knife's edge as though caressing the blade. "I'd seen her when the parents dropped off their younger daughter at my place. Francine was in kindergarten that year."

"Why don't you put the knife down, Raquel? The child's death happened years ago. You don't want to hurt me over it now."

Raquel cackled. "Like it's going to matter. I have too much blood on my hands already."

"Is that why you followed Francine into the field that day? You were afraid she'd expose your true identity?"

"I couldn't let it happen. I'd worked hard to train as a chef and earned my rewards through sweat and grime. I wasn't about to let Francine destroy all I'd accomplished. That's what ruined my marriage. Barney discovered my secret and couldn't live a life based on lies. And now Francine threatened to destroy everything else I held dear."

"So you sneaked after her to the fields where she went to hide for the Find Franny game?"

"No, I asked her to meet me there to discuss our options. In addition to persuading the other judges to vote for her entry at the bake-off, I'd give her a tidy sum that would allow her to buy her magazine. You see, she'd told me why she wanted the prize money. The stupid woman was waiting for me when I smacked her on the head from behind."

"Where did you get the shovel?"

"I found it in one of the sheds. No one will ruin the life I've made for myself and my daughter. If my ex got the chance, he'd sue for custody. I won't let you destroy our family."

She raised her hand holding the knife. Marla wanted to search the shadows to see if Dalton was listening and biding his time. He'd have his weapon out by now.

"What about Alyce?" she asked for his benefit, if indeed he was waiting in the wings to make his move. Too bad she hadn't thought to record this conversation on her cell phone.

"Alyce was an annoying pest who kept buzzing me like a hornet. She had the nerve to accuse me of sleeping with the producer to get my TV spot. So what if I did? My shows get high ratings. I make sure they're entertaining as well as educational. I've finally discovered my calling."

Marla pointed to the discarded pie crust package. "Alyce also said you took shortcuts off-stage, and that you tricked the audience

410

into believing you made everything from scratch."

"Sure, I might use a cake mix or a can of beef broth instead of homemade stock, but that's merely for expediency. We have to make a large amount of food so everyone can have a taste. On the air, I make the dishes properly to show how it's done."

"Did Alyce discover your past as well?" Marla asked, wanting to know if Raquel had been responsible for the hit-and-run.

"She dug too deep, the nasty little worm. So I asked Carlos to get rid of her for me. He'll do anything I ask, the sweet man. But he's not here now. I'll have to take care of you myself."

Marla heard a gasp from the shadows. No, that couldn't be Brianna, could it? She should have stayed outside.

Raquel lifted the knife and lunged forward. Marla sidestepped her and ran toward the kitchen, meaning to draw her away from the wings. Her gaze swung to a bowl of vegetables on the counter. Before Raquel could reach her, Marla grabbed an onion and tossed it at the chef. Raquel dodged the missile and plunged after her.

"Don't make a mistake you'll regret," Marla cried. "My husband called for backup. He might be able to make a deal for a lesser prison sentence if you put the knife down."

Raquel moved forward, her mouth thinned and her eyes determined. From the corner of her eye, Marla noted Brianna dashing around the woman and onto the kitchen set.

As Raquel lunged at Marla again, Brianna whacked her on the head from behind with a heavy frypan. Raquel's limp hand dropped the knife as she slid to the floor.

Dalton rushed at them, his weapon aimed. "I've got this. Sorry it took me so long. Her boyfriend Carlos is responsible for the hit-and-run accident that killed Alyce. I recognized his car in the parking lot and ran the plate. He gave me trouble when I went to talk to him."

Sirens sounded in the distance as he took in the chef's limp form and his daughter holding a heavy cast iron frypan in both hands. "It looks as though you two handled things on your own quite nicely."

"Your daughter deserves the credit," Marla said. "It was smart thinking to bash Raquel on the head, and deserving as well considering that's how she killed Francine. We heard her whole confession." Marla's body trembled as she thought of a different outcome that might have happened. If not for Brianna's timely intervention, Marla

412

might be the one lying there with a bleeding wound on the floor.

Dalton holstered his weapon and pulled out a set of restraints from his pocket. He used them to bind Raquel. "You hit her pretty hard," he said, feeling for her pulse. "She'll live, unlike the victim she struck with a shovel. My boys are arriving. They can take her and Carlos in together."

"When Francine recognized Raquel as the owner of the day care center where her sister had died, she must have been stunned," Marla said once they were home and had eaten Chinese takeout for Sunday dinner. "Francine confronted Raquel, who did what she had to do to maintain her status and protect her daughter." The comfort food had worked its magic. She felt calmer and able to talk about what had happened, now that they were safe.

Brianna seemed unfazed by her role in the drama. She'd dashed off to her room as soon as she'd finished eating. Marla didn't have the heart to chastise her for sticking around the TV studio instead of remaining outside. Brianna had witnessed her entire conversation with the celebrity chef and had saved Marla's life at the end. It only troubled her that Brianna could be so blasé

413

about the whole thing.

Brianna hadn't been blasé about Marla's news when they'd told her the morning after her confession to Dalton.

"Awesome," Brianna had cried, getting up from the breakfast table to hug Marla. "I can't wait to be a big sister. She'll be lucky to have you for a mother, as I am. I love you."

Marla's breath hitched, and her heart sung with joy. It was the first time Brianna had uttered those words. They'd come a long way as a family.

"I love you, too," she said in a choked tone, hugging her back.

Her attention returned to the present as she faced her husband across the kitchen table. "I can understand Raquel wanting to safeguard her daughter. She was afraid her ex would sue for custody if her reputation was smeared."

"She compounded her problems by killing those two women. Carlos might have done the deed with the hit-and-run, but he was following her orders."

"It's a shame she chose that route. A scandal might have ended her career on television, but she could have moved elsewhere and opened a small restaurant. People wouldn't know her there."

His smoky gaze seared hers. "She ran an unlicensed day care center and let a child die, whether accidentally or not. You've confirmed what Alyce said about her taking shortcuts off-stage. Those indicate to me a broken individual who finds a way to justify her mistakes."

Marla lowered her head, saddened by the loss of two members from their community. Francine's staff would miss her, and Alyce's husband had to raise their children alone.

"What about Amalfi Consolidated and their olive oil scam? Is that out the window now that your murder investigations have concluded?"

"It's an open case that's being pursued by another agency. I'm still not sure if Tony Winters is a collaborator or a victim of his greedy relatives. You can be sure they'll be watched when they set foot on U.S. soil. The Italian authorities may need to get involved as well."

"At least that's out of your hands. The food critic must be happy Alyce won't steal any more of his readers." Marla rose to clear their empty dishes.

"Carlton's drop in readership may have had nothing to do with the quality of his reviews or Alyce's blog. Journalism everywhere is suffering from the same problems.

People are going online for their news." Dalton stood to put away the leftovers.

"That's why Alyce's site was so popular. Carlton should think about going freelance and syndicating his column. Or maybe he should stop accepting bribes in return for good ratings. His wife needs attention, too. Her personal trainer at the gym is a bit too familiar with her."

"Their problems aren't ours, not anymore," Dalton said.

"No, but we've gotten to know these people. Hey, maybe Tristan will relocate after this fiasco. I should warn him to quit The Royal Palate before Tony's Italian contingent arrives."

"Oh yeah, that reminds me. I spoke to his boss. Mr. Romano admits to being nervous about a visit from Tony's relatives. When threatened to be named as an accomplice in a potential fraud scheme, he willingly confessed to buying their company's olive oil despite lower bids from other suppliers. He gets a kickback from the sales and referral fees if he recommends their company to other restaurateurs."

"I'm amazed by how much people in the food industry lie to customers."

"It's too bad the world lost Alyce Greene. She was a voice of light among the darkness." Dalton approached and put his hands on Marla's shoulders, turning her toward him.

She sighed. "So many people will be affected by Raquel's arrest. I suppose her ex-husband will get custody of their child. And Becky can no longer look forward to the publicity from being on the TV show for her new cookbook releases."

"She can always contact the producer. Likely he'll cancel Raquel's show, but he may find another chef and retool the production."

"That's true." Marla ignored the warmth seeping into her from Dalton's proximity. "This news will come as a pleasant surprise to the Kinsdales. The blotch on their farm's reputation will be expunged. Hopefully, Zach's bid for ownership will come through."

"Or perhaps his wife will confess her role. That's not a story for us to tell." His face split into a grin. "We have our own stories ahead."

Marla's face heated as he rubbed her belly. "Yes, we do."

Marla glanced at her watch during the bad hair day clinic at her salon on Thursday. The pace had been frenetic ever since they opened at nine o'clock. Besides dealing with regular customers, they'd had a crush of walk-ins who wanted free consultations about hair problems, and members of the press who requested interviews.

True to their promises, Teri had delivered desserts and Arnie had contributed platters of cheese and crackers, mini-potato pancakes, and smoked salmon pinwheels. She'd let them both display business cards on the counter next to the soft drinks and paper plates. Customers lounged by the food display, eating and chatting. Marla's stylists juggled their appointments for the day along with the ten-minute consults.

Marla was watching for new arrivals, aware her mother and Dalton's parents had promised to stop by. She and Dalton had delayed sharing their private news until their families were together.

"Hi, I hope you can help me," said a middle-aged ash blonde. "I had my hair bleached about four weeks ago, and I hate it. I want to dye it a light auburn to cover my whole head and keep it one color. Will this work on me? My hairdresser said I couldn't use anything with red in it because my hair would turn pink."

Marla ruffled the woman's locks. "We could tone it with a neutral color like brown to close the cuticle, and then put in the auburn color. Otherwise, your light hair will soak up the red, and it may turn pink. Would you like to make an appointment? You'll get twenty percent off any services booked today, and the museum gets thirty percent of proceeds from all bookings."

After sending the woman to Robyn at the reception desk for scheduling, Marla turned to the next lady in line.

"Yes, ma'am, what can I do for you?"

"You're the owner, right? First, let me tell you how generous you are to hold this event and to support the history museum. My husband and I love that place."

"We're happy to help. It's an important part of our city."

The woman touched her brassy red hair. "My natural color used to be almost black, but now it's mostly gray. I wanted a new style and consulted a colorist who specializes in curly hair like mine. I take meds and informed her up front. Needless to say, the cut and color I chose were not what she did. My previous color had been a medium brown with taupe highlights. Look at this hideous red she gave me this last time. Plus, she cut off a year's growth. Now my hair curls so tightly it's impossible to smooth out. The colorist tried to sell me more salon products to correct the mistakes she'd made. Can you do anything to fix it?"

Marla tapped her chin. "It's possible your meds are affecting your hair. We could use a chemical relaxer to soften the curls and make them more manageable. Then we can think about toning down that red shade."

The next lady had a common problem. She'd been doing her own hair and now needed a correction from a professional.

"I've been bleaching my hair for years," said the woman, "and it feels so dry and makes crunching noises when I squeeze it. What can I do to make my hair healthy again?"

"When you bleach your hair, it's important to apply the solution only to your roots and not the ends. We can give you a thorough conditioning treatment. Then I'd suggest a single process instead of bleaching it."

Her next regular appointment arrived, and she got busy until noon. She gave a reporter a brief interview and then trudged to the back storeroom for a break. Dying of thirst, she grabbed a Coke from the fridge and popped the lid. She took several gulps before feeling satisfied.

Nicole sailed into the room. "Finally, we have a minute or two to breathe. This morning has been incredible. Listen, I caught Dalton's statement on TV last night. Can you talk about what happened this past weekend?"

Marla had refused to discuss the case until Dalton gave the go-ahead. Now that the killer's identity had been revealed in public, she could share her news. She brought Nicole up to date.

"How's Becky doing after Raquel's arrest?" Nicole asked.

Marla glanced toward the front, where the museum curator had set up a table to hand out brochures. "She seems cheerful, unless she's faking it. Whoever takes Raquel's place might still have her on the show, unless the producer cancels the entire production. Hey, maybe I should suggest Tristan to him? A pastry chef would be different. He's quit The Royal Palate."

"Good for him. He can do better elsewhere."

"I heard Carlton Paige has resigned his position, too. That's a smart move on his part. Then there's Grace Kinsdale. She told her husband the truth about her background. They've spoken to their real estate lawyer, and a new deed will be issued to the Kinsdale family."

"Arnie should be happy for his friend, Rory."

"Yes, he's glad Francine's exposé had nothing to do with the farm."

"Speaking of the farm, did the camera belonging to the magazine photographer ever turn up?"

"Raquel had taken it when she saw it lying in the grass. From the photos, it looked as though Francine had been stalking the bake-off judge that day."

"What will happen to the publication now?"

"I found Francine's notes in the back of her album. Her article would have outed Raquel's true identity while discussing the dangers of unlicensed day care centers. Lynette Wilde said they'll finish her article and publish it. Although it was more of a personal vendetta, the research on day care centers will be useful. In order to fit the requirements of her magazine, Francine had addressed the feeding angle. Like, what do these places serve to their young clientele who are past the infant formula stage?"

"That's an interesting thought. Peanut butter and jelly sandwiches?"

"Tally might know. I'll ask her about it." Marla finished her drink and tossed the can into the trash. "We'd better head back out there. How are you and Kevin doing?" she asked as they strode into the main room.

Nicole gave her a bright smile. "He made reservations for us to go to Atlantis in two weeks. It should be good weather in the Bahamas before Thanksgiving."

"I'm excited for you."

"How are Brianna and Dalton doing since you told them your news?"

"Dalton is being so sweet. He's concerned but not restrictive like I'd feared. And Brianna can't wait to tell her friends. I told her we'd make a public announcement today when our parents arrive. Oh, there's Tally. Please excuse me."

Marla hurried past the throng crowding her salon. Tally stood by Becky's table and was speaking to the cookbook author. Marla had suggested Becky bring some of her recipe books for sale, but the curator had declined, not wanting to distract from her museum display.

"Hey, Tally," Marla called, waving to her friend. "I'm glad you could stop by."

"Of course, I wouldn't miss it with two of my friends at the center of attention. Looks like you have a great turnout."

They embraced each other and exchanged a few words until she noticed her next client in the parking lot. That wasn't all she noticed. Marla's mother and Dalton's parents headed her way. She greeted them with hugs.

"Your fundraiser appears to be a success," said Anita in her singsong voice.

"Have you had many consultations for your bad hair day clinic?" Kate asked, her hazel eyes shining with pride as she regarded the milling crowd.

"Yes, business has been nonstop ever since we opened this morning." Their refreshments needed replenishing, Marla noted. She signaled to Robyn at the reception desk to take care of it. "Oh look, here come Brianna and Dalton. He picked her up from school."

After another round of greetings, Marla gave Dalton a meaningful glance. They stood in the center of the reception area and faced the crowd.

"Hey, listen up, everyone," Marla shouted. Numerous pairs of eyes turned in their direction, and a hush fell over the assemblage. She signaled for Brianna to join their family circle. "We have some news to announce. We're going to have a baby."

"Mazel tov," Anita cried. "It's about time! I knew you looked different. You have a glow about you."

"I can't believe it," Dalton's mom said

with a shriek of joy. "We'll be grandparents again. This calls for a celebration."

"That's my cue," said Arnie, rolling inside a cart with a load of Champagne bottles and plastic glassware. "Dalton notified me ahead of time," he told Marla with a sheepish grin.

Marla turned to her husband. "You're a sweetheart," she said with a quick kiss.

"And you're mine." He gave her a more passionate kiss in return.

Everyone clapped and cheered as they faced their new future together.

BONUS RECIPES

MUSHROOM PIE

2 Tbsp. olive oil
16 oz. sliced mushrooms
8 oz. sliced Portobello mushrooms
2 large shallots, peeled and diced
1 cup grated Parmesan cheese
1/2 cup shredded Swiss cheese
2 deep dish pie crusts
Egg Substitute

Sauté mushrooms and shallots in olive oil in large skillet. Remove skillet from heat. Mix in Parmesan and Swiss cheeses. Put the mixture into one pie crust. Fold other pie crust over top. Brush with egg substitute. Bake at 350 degrees for 30-45 minutes or until browned.

CHICKEN CACCIATORE

1 package Perdue Italian seasoned 5 bone-less, skinless chicken breasts

2 Tbsp. olive oil

1 onion, chopped

1 green bell pepper, seeded and chopped

16 oz. fresh mushrooms, sliced

1 Tbsp. minced garlic

1 tsp. dried basil

1 tsp. dried oregano

1 cup dry red wine

28 oz. can diced tomatoes

In a large skillet, sauté the chicken breasts in olive oil until browned on both sides. Remove to a plate and set aside. Add onion and bell pepper to pan and cook until soft, about 5 minutes. Add mushrooms and garlic and stir occasionally until mushrooms are tender. Sprinkle on basil and oregano. Pour in the red wine and raise heat to a boil. Cook until wine is reduced, about 5 minutes. Stir in the tomatoes and add the chicken to the mixture. Cover and reduce heat to a simmer. Cook for 30 minutes or until the chicken is cooked all the way through. Serve over cooked noodles or rice.

CHICKEN TENDERLOINS

1 pound chicken tenderloins
2 Tbsp. mayonnaise
2 Tbsp. white horseradish
1/2 cup seasoned bread crumbs
2 Tbsp. chopped fresh parsley

Sauce
1/4 cup mayonnaise
1/4 cup fat-free plain yogurt
1 Tbsp. white horseradish
1 Tbsp. Dijon mustard
1/4 tsp. paprika

Preheat oven to 400 degrees. Combine 2 Tbsp. mayonnaise and 2 Tbsp. horseradish in small bowl. Dip chicken in mixture and then roll in bread crumbs mixed with parsley. Place chicken tenders in greased baking dish and bake for 30 minutes or until done. Meanwhile, combine the next five ingredients for the sauce and put aside. Serve baked chicken with sauce.

EGGPLANT ROLLATINI

1 large eggplant, peeled and cut lengthwise
  into half-inch slices
2 cups tomato basil sauce
1/2 cup part-skim ricotta cheese
1/2 cup grated Parmesan cheese

1 large egg
1 tsp. minced garlic
4 oz. shredded mozzarella cheese

In a microwave-safe dish, lay out eggplant. Microwave on high for 6 to 8 minutes until pliable. Transfer to plate and drain liquid from baking dish. Pat eggplant slices dry. In a separate bowl, combine ricotta and Parmesan cheeses, egg, and minced garlic. Mix together.

Starting at the wide end of each eggplant slice, spread a teaspoon or so of the cheese mixture. Roll up each piece and lay seam-side down in greased microwave-safe baking dish. Pour sauce over all. Cover and microwave on high for 15 minutes or until eggplant is tender. Sprinkle mozzarella cheese on top. Microwave until cheese melts, about 2 more minutes. Optional: sprinkle on oregano or chopped basil leaves before cooking. Serves 4.

VEGETABLE GUMBO

3 Tbsp. olive oil
8 oz. container chopped celery, onions, green peppers
1 Tbsp. minced garlic
1 large bay leaf
1/4 tsp. dried thyme

36 oz. vegetable broth
1 lb. sliced zucchini
1 can crushed tomatoes
1 can baby corn, drained
1 can red kidney beans, drained and rinsed
1 lb. peeled, cubed butternut squash
1-1/2 cups Arborio rice
2 Tbsp. fresh parsley, chopped

Heat oil in a large soup pan over medium heat. Add celery, onion, and green pepper mixture along with garlic. Cook for 7 minutes. Add bay leaf and thyme and cook for 2 more minutes. Add vegetable broth, stir and bring to a boil. Add zucchini, tomatoes, baby corn, and squash. Reduce heat and simmer for 5 minutes. Stir in rice.

Simmer covered for another 20 minutes, stirring occasionally so rice doesn't stick to bottom. Mix in beans and parsley and cook for 5 minutes more. When rice is done, serve hot.

APPLE RUM CAKE
18-1/4 oz. spice cake mix
21 oz. can apple pie filling
3 eggs
3/4 cup light sour cream
1/4 cup rum
2 Tbsp. canola oil

1 tsp. almond extract
2 Tbsp. dark brown sugar
1-1/2 tsp. ground cinnamon
2/3 cup powdered sugar
2 tsp. reduced fat milk

Set aside 1 Tbsp. cake mix and 1-1/2 cup pie filling. In a large bowl, combine eggs, sour cream, rum, canola oil, almond extract, remaining cake mix and pie filling. Beat on medium speed for 2 minutes. Pour half the batter into a greased fluted baking pan coated with nonstick spray. In a separate small bowl, mix together the brown sugar, cinnamon, reserved cake mix, and remaining pie filling. Spoon over batter. Top with remaining batter. Bake at 350 degrees for 45 minutes. Cool on rack before turning over onto plate. In a small bowl, mix powdered sugar and milk. Dribble glaze over cake and serve. Serves 10-12.

CHOCOLATE KAHLUA CAKE
1 box yellow cake mix
1 oz. instant chocolate pudding mix
4 large eggs
1/2 cup vegetable oil
3/4 cup brewed coffee
2/3 cup Kahlua
1 cup mini chocolate chip morsels

432

9 oz. semisweet chocolate morsels
1 cup heavy whipping cream
2 Tbsp. Kahlua

Preheat oven to 350 degrees with rack in lower middle position. In a large bowl, add the cake mix and pudding mix and stir to blend. In another bowl, stir together the eggs, oil, coffee, and Kahlua until smooth. Gently fold wet ingredients into dry ingredients. Add the mini chocolate chips. Transfer to a greased Bundt pan. Bake for 45 minutes or until a toothpick inserted in the center comes out clean. Cool the pan on a wire rack.

Meanwhile, pour the heavy whipping cream into a pot and bring to a boil. Remove from heat. Stir in the chocolate chips and Kahlua until smooth. Cool slightly and then drizzle over cake.

COCONUT FUDGE PIE
3 oz. unsweetened chocolate
1/2 cup butter
3 eggs, slightly beaten
3/4 cup sugar
1/2 cup all-purpose flour
1 tsp. vanilla
2/3 cup sweetened condensed milk
2-2/3 cups flaked coconut

Melt chocolate and butter in a saucepan over low heat. Stir in beaten eggs, sugar, flour and vanilla. Pour into greased 9-inch pie dish. In a separate bowl, combine sweetened condensed milk and coconut. Spoon over the chocolate mixture, leaving a 1/2 to 1 inch border. Bake at 350 degrees for 30 minutes. Cool and serve.

LEMON BREAD PUDDING

Pudding
2 cups dry bread cubes
4 cups scalded milk
1 Tbsp. butter
1/4 tsp. salt
3/4 cup sugar
4 eggs, slightly beaten
1 tsp. vanilla
1/2 cup golden raisins

Sauce
1/2 cup sugar
1 Tbsp. cornstarch
1/8 tsp. salt
1/8 tsp. nutmeg
1 cup boiling water
2 Tbsp. butter
1-1/2 Tbsp. fresh lemon juice

Preheat oven to 350 degrees. Soak bread in milk for 5 minutes. Add 1 Tbsp. butter, 1/4 tsp. salt, and 3/4 cup sugar. Pour slowly over eggs. Add vanilla, raisins, and stir. Pour into greased baking dish. Place the baking dish into a pan of shallow hot water. Bake until firm, about 50 minutes.

Sauce: Mix 1/2 cup sugar, cornstarch, salt and nutmeg in a medium saucepan. Gradually add water and cook over low heat until thick and clear. Add butter and lemon juice. Blend. Pour over pudding. Chill in refrigerator.

PEACH COBBLER
1/4 cup butter (1/2 stick)
1-1/2 cup prepared biscuit mix
1 cup sugar
2/3 cup reduced fat milk
1 can peach pie filling
Cinnamon

Preheat oven to 400 degrees. Spray a 9 × 12 baking pan with cooking spray. Melt the butter and spread in it evenly in the pan. In a separate bowl, whisk together the biscuit mix, sugar, and milk. Pour batter into pan. Drop the fruit evenly onto the top of batter. Sprinkle cinnamon on top. Bake for a half

hour or until browned and bubbly. Serve warm.

ACKNOWLEDGMENTS

It takes a team to launch a book, and so I'd like to acknowledge my gratitude to the following:

My critique group — Alyssa Maxwell, Zelda Benjamin, Tara L. Ames, Karen Kendall, Ellen Kushner, and Cynthia Thomason. I wouldn't be where I am in my career without you.

Deni Dietz, Editor from Stray Cat Productions and my former editor at Five Star.

Patty G. Henderson, Cover Design by Boulevard Photografica

Judi Fennell, Digital Layout by www .formatting4U.com

Kat Sheridan, Cover Copy by BlurbWriter .com

Sally Schmidt, my Beta Reader and online friend. Thank you for your insightful comments and suggestions that made this book stronger as well as more plausible. It's so important to get a reader's viewpoint, and I appreciate the time you spent to offer your remarks. They were invaluable in improving this story.

Stacey Miller, my manicurist, who listens to my plotting ideas while doing my nails. She suggested I visit Bedner's Farm in Boynton Beach when I mentioned the opening scene in my book. Stacey also gave me the idea for Pioneer Women's History Month. So thank you for the inspiration and most of all for listening.

AUTHOR'S NOTE

The Egyptian ritual I mentioned in the story actually takes place in the spring. I renamed it from rebirth to renewal and cast it in the fall to suit my story. Banyan and acacia trees do play a role in various mythologies. The park where Marla and Dalton went at night is modeled after Tree Tops Park in Davie, a favorite place of ours for a shady stroll. The banyan with a hollowed-out central core is one I saw on a Caribbean island where the tour guide said meetings used to take place.

As an olive fan, I enjoyed researching olive lore and olive oil scams. Olives can be healthful as long as they are eaten in moderation like anything else. It was interesting to learn the difference between green and black olives in terms of their production. The olive branch as a symbol of peace dates back to biblical times.

Marla has now come full circle in her

character arc that began with *Permed to Death.* She and Dalton face a promising future together with a new addition to their family.

If you enjoyed this story, please help spread the word. Customer reviews and recommendations are the best ways for new readers to find my work. Here are some suggestions:

Write an online customer review.
Post about this book on your social media sites and online forums.
Recommend my work to reader groups, mystery fans, and book clubs.
Gift a Bad Hair Day mystery to your hairstylist or nail technician.
Add my books to your holiday gift bags.

For updates on my new releases, giveaways, special offers and events, join my reader newsletter at https://nancyjcohen.com/news letter. I do not share your information with anyone else, and you can unsubscribe at any time. Free Book Sampler for new subscribers.

ABOUT THE AUTHOR

As a former registered nurse, **Nancy J. Cohen** helped people with their physical aches and pains, but she longed to soothe their troubles in a different way. The siren call of storytelling lured her from nursing into the exciting world of fiction. Wishing she could wield a curling iron with the same skill as crafting a story, she created hairdresser Marla Vail as a stylist with a nose for crime and a knack for exposing people's secrets.

Titles in the Bad Hair Day Mysteries have made the IMBA bestseller list, been selected by *Suspense Magazine* as best cozy mystery, won a Readers' Favorite gold medal, and earned third place in the Arizona Literary Awards. Nancy has also written the instructional guide, *Writing the Cozy Mystery*. Her imaginative romances have proven popular with fans as well. These books have won the HOLT Medallion Award and Best Book in Romantic SciFi/Fantasy at *The Romance*

Reviews.

A featured speaker at libraries, conferences, and community events, Nancy is listed in *Contemporary Authors, Poets & Writers,* and *Who's Who in U.S. Writers, Editors, & Poets.* When not busy writing, she enjoys fine dining, cruising, visiting Disney World, and shopping. Contact her at nancy@nancyjcohen.com

Follow Nancy Online

Website - https://nancyjcohen.com
Blog - https://nancyjcohen.wordpress.com
Twitter -
https://www.twitter.com/nancyjcohen
Facebook -
https://www.facebook.com/NancyJCohenAutho
Goodreads -
https://www.goodreads.com/nancyjcohen
Pinterest - https://pinterest.com/njcohen/
LinkedIn -
https://www.linkedin.com/in/nancyjcohen
Google Plus -
https://google.com/+NancyJCohen
Instagram -
https://instagram.com/nancyjcohen
Booklover's Bench -
https://bookloversbench.com